Textures of Life

Books by Hortense Calisher

IN THE ABSENCE OF ANGELS

FALSE ENTRY

TALE FOR THE MIRROR

TEXTURES OF LIFE

Textures of Life

A NOVEL BY Hortense Calisher

Secker & Warburg · London

FIRST PUBLISHED IN ENGLAND 1963 BY
MARTIN SECKER AND WARBURG LIMITED
14 CARLISLE STREET, SOHO SQUARE, W.1

Printed in England by
Latimer, Trend & Co. Ltd., Whitstable

For Bennet and Peter

Textures of Life

I

"To the happy couple!"

The toast was acknowledged with faintly disowning smiles from both family sides of the twenty-five people at table — as coming merely from a Chicago aunt-of-the-bride's second husband, whom nobody had ever seen before and was the only one of the party who was getting drunk.

The couple themselves did not appear to notice him at all. The bride was the thin girl with stork neck and messily naiad hair, her dress no more than the shift in which they all slouched about the streets these days as if proclaiming that to be nineteen was chic enough. Beside her, the stolid, blond boy, nice-looking enough behind thick lenses, wore his unmatched jacket and trousers with the same arrogance. Confronting the garb of the guests, theirs had the value of an affectation. The two of them stood ready to go now, outside the celebration as they had been from its beginning.

The girl's mother, a widow, had pleaded for it, carefully not for herself but for the boy's father who, alone like herself, but with only a year or two to spare now, was said to be dying. The father headed the table, that dark-eyed, still quick-moving man whose features, though tanned, were — even to the casual eye — of a certain saintly tightness, phosphorescence, whose deft fingers, if one knew their sentence as they played with a heart-shaped box in front of him, seemed already ringed with St. Elmo's fire. The widow was at his side, a sleek woman, still pretty, only fortyish, turned out in those subtle tonalities, stolen from modern art, which one could pick up now in the department stores. Through those there came nevertheless a certain Jenny Wren-ness, ingenuous plumpness of the girlhood one would still be able to see in her face if raised — but she too had her eyes lowered to her white, silver-stamped, frilled heart-box.

"Good champagne!" said the flushed uncle-by-marriage, then glanced apologetically at his wife, the widow's sister. A shrewd, good fellow, he hadn't meant to sound surprised, to press in any way what must be known to all here: that he was worth enough (when he let himself think of how near a half-million it was, his pulse nearly stopped in awe of what had happened to him, a half-*million*) to buy and sell everybody here, singly or together — certainly at least those on his wife's and the bride's side of the family, on the New York side. There was no telling for sure about Pagani, the groom's father and almost sole representative, for if there was any special way of rating Italians from California, it hadn't yet reached Winnetka, but fashionable photographers made a mint these days, and this one (like his own father, the Pagani before him, it was even said) was the best children's one in a town where even the toys were gold-plated. The boy's dead mother had been Jewish, just like Jacobson, the girl's dead father. Not that Jews or any other kind meant anything for sure one way or the other these days. The uncle himself was probably the only full Protestant in the room, not that he wished to make anything of that either, live and let live; his own wife was a Catholic — lapsed. All it meant was that the happy couple were about even on the racial mixture, just as well matched there as they seemed on everything else. It made him uncomfortable just to look at them, that girl who hadn't been to a hairdresser even on her wedding day, the boy neat enough, with a build that could even have been football, but with something indoors about him, not four-square — the thing, whatever it was, that let him stand there so coolly united with her, letting the way she looked speak for him, that had made him choose this girl.

Glancing aside, the uncle saw that his wife's glass, next to his, was still full. He drained it. No surprise that it should be good; though Margot Jacobson, the widow, and his wife were no longer close, he'd seen at once how like the sisters still were — thrifty, spendthrifty New York-bred women who knew how to cut a thousand corners — not too fine. The scene was good enough, too — private dining room of a small hotel on the Square (one he'd never heard of but might be no worse for that), with only as seedy-velvet a look to it as all such rooms, and on the embroidered tablecloth, at each place set with the silver that must be Margot's own, there was a natty roses-and-violets nosegay. The guests, the usual lot, were nice and chatty enough, or had begun so. Then why was this the chilliest damned wedding lunch they had any of them — he could see that — ever been to in their lives?

It had nothing to do with the recognizable chill of generation that came over the older guests even at the high jinks of the weddings he was used to — four hundred strong at the country club in a hot, yellow June — as they waved off the clear-eyed pairs, the Easter-in-Nassau tanned girls risen for a day like Venuses on their scallops, the boys with that short-lived glow to the flesh, like a stallion's nostril — waved them off, off, ruddy in their white, to fecundity. That sort of qualm came from knowing the score too absolutely ever to want to go through it again — and from being left behind, never to go through it again. The chill in this room came from the couple themselves, fragile with youth as they still were, that city-rat pair. From the lack of awkwardness between them, he suspected that they already knew the score in one way. But, leaning together, their attitude suggested that they knew it in all, by prevision if not experience — and it was the success of this that made older eyes in the room glide sideways, genial voices die. The vibrance that joined this pair, looked at him out of their eyes, was contempt — not for his half-million, which he could have understood — but for any such sentiments as he, the room, was prepared to offer them. The two didn't make him feel old, but rather: angrily, clumsily young. It was the girl Elizabeth, really; either she led, or the boy showed it less; he had left her for the moment, going down the line to say good-bye affectionately enough to his father. The girl remained where she was, her gaze lowered on one of the nosegays. One of her ears shone through hair, poodled at the front, that straggled down her back like a guttersnipe Alice's. The earlobe, pierced with a tiny earring, like an immigrant baby's, looked as young — but he would not dare pity it. He thought he had never seen anybody stare so venomously at a rose. Shocked, he drained the next nearest full glass, and heard himself say, with the same loose surprise, "Good champagne."

"Chateau D'ay, Ayala. Really remarkably good for the price. Sherry's stock it." This was from Margot, the girl's mother. Acquaintances cherished her as one of those animated little women who, not too obtrusively, always knew a "little" place to find anything from amethysts to eggs, but today the tip came automatically, like the cardboard ticket from the set smile of a glass-enclosed Princess Fatima at a fair. Only Ernest, her recently dead husband, would have known that she felt like crying, and why. In a dim way not quite apart from intelligences she had been given in the municipal college twenty-odd years ago, and had drunk in renewed, through the modern private school for which they had sacrificed to send their only child, she understood that her daughter's animosity toward her — against the way they'd brought her up, against this very occasion — was connected with her own very blamable dependence on nice things. "Things!" Elizabeth called them simply, and sullenly. For if, at nineteen, she could see any of her mother's needs with clarity, this lay in her awareness, scornful as it was, that "things" were not merely a taste or a boastfulness in her mother's life — or even a love — they were her gravitation.

"I can't help it," Margot had replied once, during the short week finally granted her for wedding fuss, "I was brought up that way," and her voice, wavering toward excuse, had resolved, as it so often did, on pride. Her family, first established here uptown in Yorkville by her grandfather, a young chiropodist trained in Vienna, had brought with them the finest merchant-fingered sense of their own small dynasty, as real to them as that of the monarchs of the empire from which they had come, and based like it on the clearest image of a certain standard of noblesse from which, even in a cellar, they must not fall. Naturally, they, not being monarchs, must try rather harder to keep out of cellars, and had — this was part of it. Theirs was that lower-middle-class noblesse which had had to build not on lineage, but on the living itself — on a cookery never below butter, linens fit enough for any Hapsburg injured on their doorstep, and on a fanatically embroidered cleanliness — below which combined surfaces lay always the dark turds of shame. Yes, there'd been that too, of course, in the stony tone of her grandmother's *"Schmutzig!"*, in her whisper to the five-year-old Margot's mother, when the little girl had wet herself publicly, "Meta, the child has shamed herself!", in her own mother's hiss to the short skirts of sixteen, "Knees together, you shame!" — below that moral surface, poverty, dirt and what went on between the legs were all somehow tangled together. Above it were the nice and their "things," objects which in time acquired their own minor heraldry, if as nothing more than as tokens of safety. Such

8

a family, never risen to *rentiers*, never dropped into poverty, had known only the middle-class terror. Even now, if Margot chanced on the catchword "security" in a newspaper, what she thought of at once, before thinking, was a large pseudo-Sèvres candy dish always reared on its ugly pedestal in the bay of her grandmother's parlor-floor-front, the dominant center — below a dado of beer steins and grotesques from the Tyrol — of a room in which even the shadows were scrubbed, and always (even on the day of her grandmother's funeral) filled.

Through three generations it had remained so, down the dark days of her father's failure in the wholesale bakery business, through all Ernest's ups and downs as a manufacturers' agent, when the household had often fattened on every sample of his trade except money — for Ernest, son of a German-Jewish auctioneer on University Place, had been even closer to her, in their mutual faith in things, than many a couple of the same religion. She would have brought the dish here today, to be set out for the family to recognize, if he had only been with her to dare Elizabeth's scorn.

"Candy!" Elizabeth had said, looking down on it — just refilled with the bright pastilles Mrs. Jacobson always kept there — on that day, not a week ago, when she had come in from life-class to report that she and David would be getting married next week, now that they had found the very loft to live in. "Candy! I'll smash that thing for you yet." As she turned to survey the whole overscrupulous room, the great swinging book-bag that was her reticule, purse and home had almost done so. Eyes hard on her own dreams, she had shrugged and gone out again — now she didn't need to. As it was, Margot, reminding herself that lofts could be chic now, grateful that celebration was to be allowed at all — even if an impending death had had to be invoked to alter her daughter's stark plans — had consoled herself with her own last-minute hunt, almost hysterical at the end, as real pre-bridal days should be, for the object she now held in her hand.

It had taken all her ingenuity to find it, and when it had been passed to her over the Armenian caterer's zinc counter, she had not known, in her grim-soft mood, whether to weep or laugh. It was exactly like the one at her own wedding, the one from her mother's for that matter — in her childhood always kept in a drawer of the sideboard, together with the 1910 caterer's bill for that wedding in the parlor-floor-front — a bill which she still had. *Louis Mazzetti, Cordon Bleu.* Then the menu, for forty guests, *complete service, 2 Candelabras, 2 Waiters, 1 assistant, 36 Camp Chairs, 6 Round Tables*, and down at the bottom, *Extra — 40 Wedding Cakes in boxes Heart Shape, "M.C." in Silver and Gold.* In her mother's saved one, sometimes opened for her to see, the cake had been black as lava; she had therefore not kept her own. Except for the initials, the box she now held was the same as the other two, but if Elizabeth had noticed its resemblance to the often described others, she had not said, and now that she was leaving without having done so, her mother was glad. She saw that her daughter, well-mannered enough in some things, was now making her adieux, coming toward her down the far line of relatives, inclining an ear, a cheek, with a reserve that Margot knew to be as hard as the dried-clay busts Elizabeth was leaving behind in her bedroom, but hoped that relatives would mistake for poise merely — on Elizabeth's lips the small smile that even they must see to be a mocking one.

"Rice!" said the uncle-by-marriage, from the other end. "Whassama no rice?"

Mrs. Jacobson sent him a smile. Parents and children, she told herself, were always strangers in the end of course, but staring now at the daughter who felt herself so original, she had an awful sense that it was the school that had made Elizabeth, the newspapers, all the Tini-books, Tini-records she had been fed with, to whom, along with her schoolmates, she had been ceded up. Whereas, whatever the dark plague-spots in Margot's own make-up, the influences that had molded her had at least *seemed* personal — a dark dowry which the college, where she had been a run-of-the-mill fine arts major, had subverted perhaps, but could not change. She could even see how her own parents, in their simple, Dutch-interior fanaticisms, had been that very middle class whose next or next generation would bring its scrupulosities to art. Hence Elizabeth, who was a sculptor — who was not "going to be" or "wanting to be," but with the confidence she had been molded toward, had studied it, had picked it; at not yet twenty, therefore *was*. Hence Elizabeth, to whom her in-between parents had given "everything" precisely because they could not afford to — including the right to call them unspiritual.

Mrs. Jacobson hid the hand holding the box in her lap. Now that she could see their lives as clearly as two heads seen enclosed in the lens of a raindrop, she could see too how stupid it was — that frilled, heart-shaped replica — for a child brought up on mobiles.

" 'Bye, Mums."

At least Elizabeth had not made use of her usual, detached "Mother." Mrs. Jacobson put her arms up to her daughter; the box fell. At her side, Mr. Pagani, leaning carefully, his leaky heart a chalice, picked up the box and set it on the table beside his own. Out of the corner of her eye, she saw that David, an affectionate boy, motherless since birth, had put both hands on his father's shoulders. Dropping her arms, she let one fall so that the nearer box was pushed directly under Elizabeth's gaze; there was no doubt that she saw it. Take it, her mother said silently. Instead, Elizabeth joined hands with her husband. "Good-bye, Mother."

At the door, the couple turned, odd pair in their unbridal clothes, hands still joined against the festive enemies behind them. Before turning away again, the boy waved with his free one. The avenue sun came through the open door, enveloping them in its aura as they paused. Behind them, the air in the room darkened to plum, as if particles of its own plush had gathered to take the place of the rice which had not been thrown. A lozenge of yellow fallen across the hotel carpet barred their way. They stepped over it, and were gone.

In the room behind, people leaned back, guests shortly to be on their way, but — now that the couple themselves were gone like a symptom — able to dream for a moment, hypochondriacs all fixed on the same ailment, of a world that was still in health. Each secretly wondered, also, how the night would be for this generation. The bride's mother was crying, but this too was now appropriate. "She'll see!" she said fiercely. She'll see what life is, Margot said to herself, through the tears which could not bear that she should.

Her neighbor leaned toward her, with the care of a man whose disease has already been confirmed. "Dine with me, Mrs. Jacobson — Margot," said Mr. Pagani.

Outside, the couple walked on past the Square without speaking, unlinking arms after the first curb. They could afford not to touch, having so much else in which they were joined. It was some blocks before either of them spoke.

"Brr-r-r," Elizabeth said. Their pace continued even. After half a block or so, David answered. "Brrrrr-r." This was their only comment on the wedding.

At the subway entrance, Elizabeth suddenly halted under the kiosk, tossed back her hair and smiled at him; swinging her book-bag for her, he smiled back. Serious again, they tripped down the stairs together, matching their steps in a rhythm of threes.

They got out at Spring Street.

Above them, a liverish warehouse, tall for these parts, converged to a sharp point at the street's corner. Modeled on the Flatiron Building, once offices perhaps and once stone, its cornices hung now on what seemed the softly compressed grime of the city itself. Its triangular shape made it a crossways, excited up from the pounded dust of the nearby machine shops, reared above other low, long-lying stretches housing nail oil, tanners, ink. In its shadow, the air was snuff, the passers-by eternally mulatto. Passengers from uptown rose out of the ground here, smelled the labor-sweat at once, and said to themselves, "This is the part where things are made; this is real." And now once again, as the couple looked at it, they joined hands. From far off, perhaps in the heart of the financial district, a carillon struck. Under its spreading bands of iron Victorian sound, they walked slower, faces illumined, as if down an aisle.

To get to their entrance, one had only to go round the side of the building past two stores not much more than counters set diagonally in its point, a cigar store huddled under its broad LA PRIMADORA, and a lunch stall from which came the familiar short-order smell of raw cookery bubbled in tallow — both 9 P.M. oases in a district where curfew came around five. This meant, as Elizabeth, who had found the place, had pointed out, the coziness of late packs of cigarettes, last-minute cartons of milk, and a telephone. All was quiet now to their turning key. Their entrance was private, after five.

The loft itself was four stories up, exactly in the center of the building. Light came through a small hole in its door, from which the tenant before them, a painter like David, must have removed the heavy Yale lock; they quite understood his taking it. A gaunt boy, evicted by the city marshal for nonpayment of the $47 rent, he had found an even cheaper place for which he would not pay either. With the collusion of the rent laws, this was the way he lived, posing as model at the League for artists whose work he would not even spit on, doing his own on brown paper or cardboard, with samples of deck paint, or a rare gallon of the casein for which he claimed to know the exact limits and nuances of water dilution. "Going to write a book on it, *Secrets of the Old Masters*," he had smiled, whistling through the gap left by four or five missing uppers — ceded to art, for their admiration — when he learned of David's part-time income from photography and allowance from his father. *His* father, a banker, gave him nothing. And now, with the same admiration, they quite understood about the lock; he meant to sell it. His valuables, like theirs, could not be stolen.

"See, there's still light." She spoke in awe, her hand still in his, before they pushed in the door.

The room, some forty-five feet at its far base, converged steadily toward them, narrowing to an apex, little wider than its door, whose point seemed to pass through their breasts, leaving these lightly pinked, and on to the other side. David gave her a pat forward, but she stayed as she was, her arm around his waist, fixing in her mind forever the room as it now was, before clutter. Windows lined the three walls, interspersed with spade-shaped outcroppings that shafted to the factory-high tin ceiling. Under a torn patina of plaster held up by remnant Sanitex, repatched paint, the dank wood floor looked almost as wise as earth. To their left, water dripped into a sink from a single tap, flanked by a toilet in a half-open stall and a laocoön of pipes tipped with a butterfly cock that might once have meant gas.

"Ten of them," she said, waving at the windows. "One, two three, four. Five six seven. Eight nine ten. Ten!" Some trick of the late afternoon, poised in that air, sent the light through the narrow factory windows as if they were clerestory. Here were all her things. In a pile at the far corner, their possessions announced themselves like the signature at the bottom of a canvas — an old camp bedroll of David's, his worn carry-all marked NORTH-WESTERN AIRLINES, her old cloth hatbox from college, with two of its rubberized initials gone. She intended never to make her possessions her only signature on life. Space lay in the sharp room like a weapon, barred with light. She leaned her breast on both. All her things were here.

David gave her a pat on the backside. Looking down at the threshold, she stepped over it, in the new way, into her new condition, and stood there bemused.

"My God. A home away from home." Peering into the book-bag, he set on the floor, one by one, a small Genoa salami, a plastic bag of the long rolls used for hero sandwiches, a round red-and-white tin of Dutch chocolate, and a Manila bag from which he drew a bunch of Malagas, slightly crushed. He held these high over his head, in the bacchante position, before he replaced them. "Don't see how the American woman does it! Between facials, too!"

She grinned at him. He had backed her up in her refusal to do anything bridal. But other times, they had shopped together, on their way to the borrowed places, strange rooms. She was embarrassed at having been caught so soon in the role of domestic forethought — and proud. "I wasn't sure — what we could get down here."

"And what's this, Madam X?" He held up a parcel which, from its shape and gurgle, could be a bottle only. He raised one eyebrow, sending his heavy glasses sliding down his nose. Many of his gestures were still the exaggerated ones of a high school boy at a party, under them the sweet awkwardness of the motherless one, and though she meant never to mother, she loved this circumstance. She could see he was really astonished, though. Beer was their drink, their crowd's drink. Whisky was for the arrived.

"Surprise. No — omen."

When it was unwrapped, his exploding laughter

touched off hers. Only last week, David's photographer friend and employer had taken them to a party where the guests, in their late twenties or early thirties, were already one or two rungs up — painters who had been shown in groups, the playwright and cast of a production in rehearsal in a downtown church, two boys whose non-objective film had been shown at Cannes. The hosts themselves, owners of a "studio" whose white fur rugs and Nubian concert grands already had an old-fashioned nineteen-fortyish solidity, were even older — two jazz pianists who earned, and were ignored. In the talk of their guests, reassuringly bull-session, art still predominated over money, but their heroes, no longer the great, dim figures of the past over whom David's crowd brooded, were those more touchable greats who were alive to be met and sometimes had been, and their judgments, no longer ranging with the imprecise passion of the unpublished or unshown, had the consanguinity of what the talkers felt themselves about to be — the important flying wedge of the almost present. They were what David and Elizabeth's crowd might be five years from now. And most of them had been drinking a cheap brand of domestic crème de menthe that must be this year's *syrop du jour* at the studios of those still blown by the absinthe-colored winds of youth, not yet rich or dull enough for whisky — the brand that was in the bottle here.

Above the bottle, their smiles met in the shrewdest sympathy, like two children so precocious that, trapped in a roomful of adult poses, they could catch themselves in the mutual act of adopting one. Above the smile, their eyes met in a vow more serious. They knew the

17

difference. On the *qui vive* brink of life, they would carry forward what was uniquely theirs. They knew the difference between the artificial and the real.

"Want some?" he said aloud.

"Mmmm-mm. Too full of champagne." Her lips made a puritan moue of the word, but that life was already behind her. She walked past the toilet stall. "Have to get a door on it. Salvation Army, maybe, when we get the furniture." She knelt, peering under the basin. Her voice came, muffled. "Oh, look. He's left us a present. Some t.p."

"Some *what?*" He held the half unwound bedroll in front of him.

Bending over had made her face pink. "Sorry. A Margot expression. Toilet paper, of course."

"Of course. Takes marriage to teach a man the real facts of life." He thought this such a subtle inversion that his glasses slid all the way down, but she had already turned away.

"And oh look — he's left us a painting."

"Canvas?" he said thriftily, his back to her. Into the room's one light-socket, which hung bulbless on a long wire from the ceiling over their bed-corner, he fitted a double socket into which he plugged the extension cord that led to the record player.

"No, glass. Guess it's just a palette, really."

He took it from her, a sheet of cheap windowpane, encrusted with swirls of color. "Yeah, I guess." He held it at arm's length, screwing up an eye, hamming it. "Ah-*hah*. Upside down, Miss J., that's the test." She giggled. Clearly the thing had no axis. "See," he said, encouraged, "how it holds, how it ve-ry def-initely holds. Influence, early —" He peered closer. "By God, no. You know what this is? Honey, this is the newest. This paint hasn't been dripped, or even thrown." He took his glasses off, knowing she knew he saw almost nothing that way. "It's been *fed* on. By one of those intravenous feeders." He put the glasses on again. "You got a valuable find here, Mrs. Pagani."

The expression on her face was obscure to him. Not the disapproving sharpness of a few hours ago, the sour, assured masque that he'd learned to recognize in their earliest dates, even surprising her to laughter by saying, once they were down in the street, "Still got your house-face on, Liz. Shift." Girls had their own brand of the rub between the generations, the latter something he knew less about than most anyway, because of always having been so close with his father, with a father so remarkably knowing and relaxed. He meant to make it up to Liz for that, not to be fatherly, but just for not having had that kind of thing at home.

He rubbed a finger softly over the place on her neck, just over where the Adam's apple would have been, where she had, unnoticeable except to a mouth, a little tuft of long, silky, almost invisible down, of which she could not be persuaded to be unashamed. A suggestion of his father's, once over lightly, about women, made him suspect what her look meant. "I know something about you."

"What. My moustache?" That was what he had called it. She caught at his finger.

"Nope. Should think you'd recall the day I found *that* out."

The corners of her mouth were still down, but once again their eyes exchanged glints, like two thieves in congratulation over what they had filched from the general. "What, then?"

"You don't like to be called Mrs. Pagani. So quick."

Her burst of laughter was honest, in relief louder than intended. "Silly. Why should I mind that. Half our crowd is." True enough. More than half the coterie they felt themselves to be forming, some verging toward the professions but most of them with their eyes hot on the arts, were already paired off, most of them legally. It was the other thing that was old-fashioned. Theirs was the van. "Listen," she said, still hearing her own echo. "Listen how quiet it is. You ever heard the city so quiet? What time is it?"

"Half-past seven."

In the late-summer evening, the light was still pure but as surely descending, as if it came to them mirrored from a great conflagration somewhere else. The silence up from the trafficless streets, seeping toward them from the deserted building, came to them that way also, not a calm but the uneasy, industrial silence of things that have stopped. Neither wished to be the first to speak. They felt themselves to be the only life beating inside that great shroud.

One of her hands stole into his, hollowing for warmth. She'd been on the point of saying it to him, hadn't known she was, until now: I don't like it when you kid about it — about painting. Not that she doubted his seriousness. If he wasn't as angry as she against what he came from, it was because he didn't have to be, and not only because of his father, who had once been a painter himself. Obscurely, she felt that his other circumstance — two men keeping house alone — had left him, made him already unordinary enough. He had his whole childhood to show, for difference. But with herself, under all the serene, teacherly reassurances of her gifts, only her anger, harbored like a gift, reassured her. Frightened now by her own thoughts, almost wishing to be back in school where nothing had begun yet, she looked up at him dumbly. Let's never kid it — ever. Otherwise we shall be the ones to slip — from the van.

"Talk — sounds queer here." His voice was strained. For no other reason than that, she was as comforted as if she had spoken and he had answered her, explaining what the "it" was that hung over them, showing her the path through the orb of their life to come.

Suddenly he was brisk. "Come on, whyn't we hang this acquisition of yours, huh? Christen the joint." Cradling the pane in his arms, he time-stepped the length of the room with it. "A-bmm. A-bmm. A-bmma, bmma, bmm. A-bmma, b-mma, B-MM, bmm —" He stopped, looking down. Somewhere along, he had taken his shoes off. "Hey, this is neat. Hey, listen. This floor *answers* you." He cocked his head. "Take yours off."

She did so, but now they no longer needed the soles of their feet to feel the rumble far below, a long anaconda of sound that drew a faint double-bass from the window frames, faded, and was gone.

"Oh. He said we'd only notice it at night. It's the subway." She looked at him doubtfully, but his slow headshake of admiration was honest, if a little absent.

"Neat." He had drawn close enough to squat on his haunches beside her, placing the palette at a safe distance; then, with one of those lax, elongated changes of posture which made him such an other being to her, he stretched himself at full length on one elbow to regard her, from which he raised himself to rake a palm along the outline of her breast, her hip. "A-bmmm. And a-bmmm. Very neat." He tugged at the hem of her dress, whose tight tube, catching her knees, prevented her from falling. With a sigh, pretending to walk up her body with his hands, he stood up. They remained so for some moments.

"Excuse me." He made as if to break away, toward the stall, but murmuring his name, she held onto him. "Mmm?"

"What's your house at home like?" she said. He had been rooming up here.

"Why bring that up now?" He held her away from him, squinting. "Oh, they warned me," he said to an audience seated just above her head. "They warned me. And after I'd given her everything. *Everything!*"

"I never thought of it until now."

He considered. Built for them when he was about twelve, by an architect crony of his father's, who had given it a cathedral ceiling, sectional walls that formed a few causeways, a bar-kitchen that swiveled between two of them, and no inside doors anywhere except on the can and on a combination darkroom-studio that was *not* in the basement, it had two Hollywood bathrooms and every known appliance, had never offended or surprised the conventions of its neighbors — or of anybody else, including himself (until recently) — and had cost, much like theirs, about forty-five thousand dollars. Nothing in it was irreplaceable; everything in it worked, and out of this it had achieved a sort of character — it was a house to be ignored. Women envied it, verbally. His father said that none of them would be able to leave it as it was for more than a week. Because he himself had lived in it so long, if he wasn't very careful now to leave its remembered corners unpoked by too exploratory a finger, he might find out that he was very fond of it. Under her round gaze, so faithfully expectant beneath that swamp-angel hair, he rejected it. "Oh — it's just — a package."

She nodded gravely.

"Excuse me," he said again, and made for the toilet-stall.

Behind him, she waited with interest for that basic sound, made by a man, which she happened never to have heard, certainly not in her parents' house. Even the borrowed flats had had bathrooms. But he was being very delicate, perhaps waiting for her to move off. She did so. Kneeling over their pile of goods, she wondered whether to plug in the record player, and giggled; they weren't going to be able to do that every time. Crouched in the growing shadow-play, watching, down the long marvel of the room, the gradual drama of any room that was bare, she wished it that way forever.

"Jesus, that guy had hidden depths." He was still in the stall. "Come look."

"Feelthy pictures?" She came to look over his shoulder. The two wallboard sides of the stall were unmarked, even clean. He moved aside. The toilet bowl was set directly under one of the windows looking out on a building opposite — there was no third side. Vaguely she recalled that. But now, shielding the window as far up as it could, a heavy white shower curtain hung there, its thick miracle fabric shining in regal folds. Obviously it was very expensive — the best. A chromium expansion rod held it, through rings of silvered glass which matched a broad border-design that glimmered luxuriously in the twilight — a silver Greek-key scroll.

"Something, isn't it!" he said. "Suppose he was a queer? And we thought he took the lock because he needed it."

"He did. Oh he did!" she cried, so passionately that he stared at her. She thought she would never get the words out. They came in a wail. "Why does *she* always have to do it? Why does she have to *follow* me!"

"Oh." Now he could see that there was still a ticket on the curtain, as if the giver were saying humbly: You can take it back, you know — I'm only suggesting. "She means well," he said.

"Oh, I know what she means," said the girl. "She means to start us off right. Her way." She reached for the curtain, to tear it down.

"Come on now," he said. "Come *on*." He held her wrists pinioned behind her. "After all — it serves a purpose."

She bent her head sullenly. "She must have done it yesterday. That's the only day I didn't come here." She kissed his breast with small kisses. "I came every day, you didn't know that, did you. Just to look."

Raising her head, she felt his answering warmth, wanting both to be and not to be a child for him. Why should he take *her* side. She'd be here right now, between us if she could, saying "Elizabeth! Keep your legs together!" But he was romantic about mothers, women in general, always discomfited by the shock-value lingo Liz herself had picked up in school. "Don't talk like that!" he would say in answer, "she did you a good turn, then. That's why I noticed you, the day I fell for you. Sitting there in life-class, hanging on to your pencil like a teaspoon." It had been her first life-class.

But you're the one who's shyest when we're naked, she thought — and said none of any of this.

He had dropped his arms, looking up. "You happen to notice any light bulbs then, around this place?"

She clapped a hand over her mouth, shaking her head. In the spectral instant before dark, she could just see him. "Maybe — there'll be a moon."

"My little housewife."

She could hear him smiling. All that silent dialogue, with him right in the room there — she had never done that before. And he had not heard her. She took his hand across a distance.

"Watch out for that glass." The dark made them whisper. In the far corner, the pile of goods, as they picked their way to it, looked like an oasis. They settled themselves in its circle like people at a picnic ranging themselves against the wild. He made a lap for her, crossing his legs almost in the lotus position, and she curled there, as was their custom. They sat for some minutes that way, regarding the view.

"Tell me what you saw," he said, "when you came and looked."

"Oh — ." She had seen that the room's shape had its drawbacks, and had shifted her glance — to the windows. She had shied from the list in her purse, feeling the sudden burden of a taste whose judgments were still mostly negative, and had fixed her gaze on the floor, in whose timeworn blend all possibilities had already drowned themselves. "This!" she said fiercely. "*This.*"

After a while, he reached over and plugged in the

record player. A disc already on it began to revolve, one of the old, fake records of the Forties they were collecting. Haitian drumbeat eddied through the room, enlarged by its empty sounding board. He rapped a heel-and-hand rhythm to it. She matched a body-rhythm to it, in the crook of his arm. "A — ten!" he sang. "And a tennah ten. Ten stone windows in de *mar*-ket AND. And a one, *one* door."

"And a *five*," she sang. "A five, and. And a five. And-a *five* stone chimneys in de market. And a ONE — *one* door." He turned up the player until it thundered, dragged her to her feet, and stamping and shuffling, bumping hilarity like a beanbag between them, they danced to the end. In the silence, formal as a couple at a ball going back to their chairs, they returned to their spot on the floor and rewound themselves. Whatever waited for them, past lovemaking, not even to be delayed by it, was still there.

"Not many in town who can afford to do that," he said conversationally.

"Not many with five chimneys, either."

"Considering the cost of firewood —" he said, "*we'll* have to burn rather brightly."

"You talk like a householder."

They were silent again.

"Why are we talking like that!" said the girl. "You know. Like in a drawing-room comedy. Repartee. We been doing it on and off since we got here."

"I understand it's the customary thing. For the first two weeks."

She had to laugh. "There, though. See?"

"After all . . ." she said. "Isn't as if we'd never — been together before."

"No," he said. "No."

Entwined together as they were, his hands at her breasts, his mouth on her ear, they sat stiffly as idols. No — his voice had just not added — but not here. They both had heard it. Certain intelligences were closing off forever, others rising — and it was the room that caused it. This room, that they themselves had chosen and in bright of day would choose again, held something inimical to them. Something anti-intelligent lay there. Smart as they were, knew themselves to be, the room was a lair of attitudes not yet encountered nor imagined — and they were already inside it. They themselves were what was couched in the lair.

"Let's — only whisper again," said the girl.

He was asleep when the moon rose in the third window. In the winters, where would it rise? At the thought of this, of his always falling asleep first, leaving her to wake alone to this islanded silence, she tried to weep, meaning to wake him with her wet face, call him back to endure with her all the noble frictions of this night. Sleep felled her, one soft blow from a woman's white boa, in which a final thought frivoled. They couldn't have drunk from the bottle. They had no corkscrew.

Sometime later he woke, very hungry. Rummaging as noiselessly as he could, he ate some of the sausage, half the bread, none of the chocolate, then, skirting her quiet form, he tiptoed to the stall, rinsing his face afterward under the drip from the faucet. There was no glass. Returning, fully awake, he saw that she lay wholly off the bedroll, spread-eagled in deep sleep, face upturned, on the bare floor. He resettled them, edging the bedroll deep in a corner, bracing the thicker end of it between his back and the brick wall, stretching his feet in front of him. She moved with him, unresisting as a good child still asleep, at the last moment falling dead-weight, her shoulders across his knees, her face again upturned. He wrapped an arm about her, doubled the covering over them both, searched with his other hand for the grapes, found them. One by one he ate them, quenching both his thirst and the night-anxiety he had learned to deal with very early from his father — always a night-prowler, even before his illness. "Insomnia?" his father had answered not long ago, when pressed by a solicitous neighbor. "Treat it like ten o'clock in the morning — tea, logic, work." Never really didactic, his father's talk had the compression of one who had reached his conclusions. But as a child, he had known only that if he woke alone, his father, if not elsewhere, would be in the darkroom, whose door, opening behind him, would draw no comment other than, "Hey, Davy, come look at this."

Well, logic told him now that this loft would barely run to studio space for one plus the living, much less a corner for the darkroom he was ashamed of missing most. He would cede the work-space to Liz, use his friend's darkroom and paint as he could, careful not to let her see how little this worried him. She was so sure of his painting, far surer than he, reared as he had been in a journeyman closeness to it, with an ability to draw that he'd had since the age of six. She was as sure of him, of what he'd just got past merely liking to do, as he was of her — intensity. Too young yet to have shown, even as far as he, what she might have, it was a dead cert that she would never let go of what she did have. Even in the arrangements of their life, this room, she was not to be deflected, with a purpose against which his agreement seemed merely mild. She meant their very life to be a significant arrangement — of the best. They both meant. Scrabbling in the bag, he found that he had finished the grapes. Neither of them was old enough to show what he had, for that matter. All of their crowd were in the same boat — this was what made them a crowd. They were sure about each *other's* talents. He and she. The crowd, too. That was the important thing. He found a last, shrunken grape. Some things were taken out of our hands, his father often said, not with any implication that he knew *which*. But Liz would never buy that. It troubled him, not to know whether he did himself.

He put his glasses on the better to see her, marveling at the distance he had roamed from her, even in thoughts that concerned her, even with her weight on his groin. His watch amazed him — not yet eleven. In the same moment that he bent to take her to him for the long hours which were not to be endured alone, he felt that the night's solstice had passed, just as it does for a season, leaving no course but to endure. Braced against his wall, mentally he paced off the loft, knelt with his carpenter's level, calculated inches between shelves. Running on nimbly through his maze of wire and wood to the finish, he opened the door — to the crowd — and laughed suddenly in his drowse. "Come in," he said to them. "Come into the Drawing Room!" In that pleasant lightness, he thought he slept, while the moon outsoared their roof, leaving them in the never-quite-dark that is the comfort of cities. Head sunk on his chest, he did not look like a boy who had dozed off laughing. Now and then the subway, coiling below, stirred their island like that one, in an old mythology, whose castaways woke to find themselves on the hump of some mammoth of the deep. Fallen so, with all his family goods around him, he looked like a man uneasily drowsing at his post but still sentinel against his Indians, his burden across his knees. He looked like a householder.

And this is the way the night was, for that generation.

2

Meanwhile, in the apartment that Elizabeth had left
forever, her mother and Mr. Pagani were just settling
back after the late, light supper she had served them, the
homely prospect of which he had gladly declared for
against a publicly continued evening — it being well
understood, when she had accepted his dinner offer, that
neither was hungry for food. Back there at the Square,
standing together more like joined parents than odd ones,
they had suffered the long partings from those distant
cousins who seemed always the last to leave any of the
formal rites of existence. Sympathy bred between them
as they stood there. She was so naturally warm with two
old Pagani ladies mired in suddenly regurgitative memo-
ries. He was so forcefully adroit, ill as he was said to be,
under the drunken arm of her brother-in-law, who,
against the warning toot of the airport limousine, delayed

to offer them the confidence, heavy as doubtful money, that many young people turned out better than they looked.

In the taxi, with the chest of her silver between them, they were almost merry over both these incidents. Up to now, she had thought his manners good, even too good for a man, rather like the taste of his gift to the bride (minutely carved pierced-ear gold retainer earrings of whose design even Elizabeth had approved) or, like the brusquerie of the card enclosed (*a retainer on your good opinion*), perhaps too observantly cold. Now, recalling his stance under her brother-in-law's buffets, she was able to imagine how a man unable to live with physical flourish might cultivate small flourishes of taste. She knew he had seen the byplay with Elizabeth and the box — of which he made no mention.

Until he had seen it, Mr. Pagani had thought of Mrs. Jacobson only in her role in the week's minuet they were all so traditionally engaged in, that is, scarcely at all. Now, as he directed the doorman to unload and carry up the silver chest that any normal man could have carried himself, he noticed that she spared him the affectation of not noticing — one of the more boring trials of his invalidism. By the time they were in the apartment they had passed a certain stage without a further word spoken. Neither's tact was any longer a surprise to the other.

Now they were at the cheese, after the plainest of omelets, served however in Basque ramekins which Mr. Pagani recognized from a bicycle trip of his youth, after endive — dressed with that lightest of oils which so few knew to be Spanish, and after their mutual refusal of the tortoni she always had on hand in the refrigerator, in favor of some mandarin oranges she liked to keep, for the sight of them, on the sideboard, in a remarkably footed, large bowl. Over the crisp, ancestral napery with which all this was set out, her guest remarked that fine linen, which he always found so soothing to the spirit, was however only so in houses where it was still taken for granted — as here.

And now, approaching the coffee, if any awkwardness, so likely between two strangers with only the one subject, had altogether failed to appear, couldn't she ascribe this to these very vanities of existence which were her pleasure and in her daughter's presence her guilt? — almost wishing Elizabeth home again, to witness how these might serve. By now, she herself had stopped wondering just why she had asked him here. Like most people's actions, Mrs. Jacobson's emerged through a flutter of reasons from which she usually felt it a duty to extract one, all the more so since her sex was said to be unable. Recently, under Elizabeth's eyes, she had been made to feel even more fluttered than most — the young were always at one to ascribe things singly.

Now, with the coffee, they had at last reached their real subject, in the comfortable knowlege that it was not their only one.

The young, she said, were so very demanding.

"And the middle-aged so very grateful." His smile warmed the immobility with which he sat in his straight chair. He closed his eyes for a moment in which his ease, potent gratitude, spread like a force, and she recalled how ill he was said to be.

He reopened them quickly. "Oh, the young. Nobody's

really fitted to living with them. Not past their cradle."
He left her to make what she could of this, knowing that
statements he always meant literally, and were to him
only those crystals fused by ten years of trying to stay
alive, others invariably handled like coals still warm from
a very peculiar furnace. He could never express to her, of
course, the full nature of his ease, about equal to that of
an addict safe for a few hours in the humming blood-rise
of his drug. For, out of the self-control demanded of his
daily habits, one vice had been left to him, or had come.
He would do almost anything to secure the company —
of almost anybody — down the long hours of his insom-
niac night. Since he must spend those hours in a chair
very much as now, this was not simple, though at home
he had quite a roster willing to chat with him until he
could tolerate himself again — until about four. They
came, not out of pity, which never went far or long, but
for the charm of his company, a fact he was able to take
literally only after some years of it. The need born of living a muscle-wall away from death had never seemed to
him as foreign as this resource which had answered it.
Surprises, a whole lagniappe of them, it was said, gathered at once round the head of him who lived with one
sparse goal — in his case, his fight, now won, to see David
to manhood. Some men might hopefully adopt that line
as doctrine; he knew it to be so from experience. Still, it
was clearly not possible to tell this rueful, kindhearted
woman, rather charming in her aura of muddles and pre-
cisions — and so patently eager to exchange with him
the bruises of parenthood — that her company was
exactly as necessary to him as that of the off-duty hotel
clerk who had drunk his liquor and played gin with

him last night, or that of the out-of-town buyer whose ripe ego, God bless the garment trade, he had plucked until almost dawn of the evening before. He wondered if Mrs. Jacobson played gin.

"I wish you could have seen the place," she was saying. "I had to go way downtown to a — to a caterer's, not too far from there. So I — dropped by. I wasn't expecting too much of any loft. But that one!" She described it.

Up to now, his only reaction to this place — one of the 1910 vintage not yet reached by the wreckers, its dark-bayed exterior resembling the brownstones it had succeeded — had been relief at its having an elevator. Inside also, he saw now, its thick-walled ambling waste of space and doddery pediment belonged to that era when both builder and tenant harked back to the villa lost in the panic of 1907. He'd almost forgotten interiors like these, and how they refreshed him, the strewn superfluities that left the overtutored eye unguided, the evasive personality — mixed, or not up to the mark, if you will — which came of not having applied for one. The homes he'd grown used to, in a town where the 1920 section was the old one, were most of them staged, either to a period or to those broad manipulations which dramatized the functional, although there was evidence now of a super-subtle effort to mix things, break them up with a few canny irrelevancies — in fact to engage for what he saw here. The flow of man's history, as seen through what he massed behind his hedge, how he cluttered his hearthstone, was eternally manipulatory too — in time even those houses would get what they wanted. But there was no denying the brittle, centrally produced look of any room furnished by only one generation.

Not that this room lacked signs of conscious effort, pretty tricks from the stores, lucky bits of chinoiserie with which its present owner, evidently priestess to the lucky find, would have added her impress. But under these he thought he could see at least two layers, one composed of certain lumpily art nouveau objects, of a kind often used as photographers' props, that had come perhaps from "Ernest's father's gallery," beneath these a second layer of some provincial flavor perhaps European, no longer definable, tenacious enough to have detached itself from objects altogether. No, this room had not engaged for just one generation, and it did not refresh, it *reminded*, each to his own — in his case, to the Massachusetts house where he had been born of an Italian father, New England mother, vaguely Portygee great-grandfather, the house whose sitting room, floated free of its objects also, had nevertheless been transported to the cottage in Monterey where his mother had sat in it like its concierge, staring at the Pacific as she had once stared at the Atlantic, until she had died in it — of his own ailment. How could he have forgotten them? — these eternal rooms that were never "done" because where living was the goal there was nothing one could do, whose surface, cannily resistant, suffered only the decorator-touch of life? No one under thirty could stand them. No one of twenty would ever want anything of them but out.

"You won't believe it until you see it," she concluded, then caught herself — he would never be able to climb those stairs. And they hadn't even thought of it, she said to herself, in awe of how cruelly the young could act, once given the chance to act for themselves. He and David had been as close — and they had never given that a thought. Her hand went out to him, then, recollecting itself, dropped to his coffee cup.

"Oh, but I do believe it, I already do," he said. With care, this subject, so much dearer to her heart than his, could be pursued for some time. Indeed, face to face with what at first seemed paradox — that she, so imperfectly loved by her daughter, could not drop the question, while he, whose love for his son had ripened almost to its perfect end, had already done so — he was the one to be charmed. But it wasn't paradox of course, but utter reason, A to B. Holding it in his hand, another small crystal, he had his surprise — they kept on coming apparently, even *after* the goal was achieved. Absently, or not quite, he let her refill his cup, which made two forbidden ones plus the morning one he was allowed.

"Of course, it's to their credit, I suppose," she said, "to want to begin small."

"But it isn't that way at all," he said. "They're beginning big." With a sweep of his arm, much less constricted than he usually permitted himself, he cleared the room. "Big!"

"A clean sweep, you mean. Oh, I'm *sure* Elizabeth's responsible for most of it."

He returned her smile, not as sadly. Did she understand him, or herself? People more often did understand themselves — but couldn't help themselves. If *having* to help himself had until now been his pedestal, it had now been removed. And suddenly, with a movement almost swift, he got up from his hard, straight chair and plumped himself into the low, overstuffed one opposite, the kind he was always envying others sprawled in with their chests lower than their knees. His bones had never got used to what his aorta required. Nestled there, he took up the thread again. "Well, after all, it's a woman's preoccupation, isn't it? Externals?" His eyes were bright, teasing. Probably she wouldn't yet admit her child a woman, certainly not with the eagerness with which he had even reassured David that the allowance would be increased in case of children, pushing him on to that provisional manhood which, happily, his own death could now only accelerate. That was by the way — he no more wished to talk of it than she, apparently, was willing to call him by his first name, Nicholas. But if there was anything that women would listen to for hours on end, it was generalizations about themselves — that is, other women. "Externals are very important to a woman," he added.

"Externals?" she said blankly. He looked flushed and lively, not, after all, a man to be so pitied, perhaps not so ill. "Externals?" She let him see that she was even proud of it. "I guess so. But that's it — *they* haven't got any. Scarcely the common decencies. And no matter what she says — for a girl brought up as she was —" She flushed. "Not that I mean — that David —" She didn't much know how he'd been brought up, had wondered. But a man who had done the job alone, and under his circumstance — was that what had kept him alone? — might well be sensitive.

"Oh, David and I, we've more or less muddled through, of course." His tone was generous. In the tinted, hesitant face held up to his, there showed all the confusions that had kept it simple, of the kind of femininity she was either too unaware of to take pride in, or else had been shamed out of by that tight little bundle of certitudes, her daughter — of an old-fashioned need to be directed, to ameliorate, to serve. Pity from some types made him impatient, but from that perturbed face might be dealt with, much as one accepted the impulsive trinket of a child, as just what one needed — for he had lied. On the matter of externals, the life of Pagani father and son had been anything but disorganized; their house, down to the very inclines in place of steps, was one of the most clear-sighted houses to be found anywhere. As for the muddle beneath the surface for us all, or the devious current that made it seem so — she must all her life have been chivied into denying it. "You know — it's really not such a bad way of doing it."

He meant this, and had tried to teach David so — the only direction he would ever give him. No matter how tidy things were kept at the top, some current moving inscrutably beneath was bound to deflect them. Perhaps *it* had a single purpose, but since it moved in arcs imperceptibly slow or cursorily swift, never describable by compass beforehand — one called it a muddle. But there were ways that were not quite compromise, of gracefully giving in, to the point of riding arcs that would complete themselves in any case. He himself had no sure bills of particulars for this — no man did. He was like any traveler tracking what he had been led to believe was a subcontinent, whose daily rounding of its humps slowly hinted him the true enormity, on whom it was finally borne, as he climbed its scaly rocks and mapped the fixed hairs of its forests, that what he stood on was Leviathan. Down there, somewhere, it moved, but like that terra firma which one could never catch in the act of moving. He was that much enlightened beyond the norm, but no more. He knew only that it was there.

He nestled deeper in the chair. She was still studying him, in a pause that must be nudged, if the evening was to last long.

"Men really ask less of externals, you know. Often secretly, of course," he said. But this was only to get her back to the real lure. The idea that men as a sex had collective secrets always amused women — that sort of treasury belonged to them. "Women, on the other hand, have to be conventional. I mean — whether they know it or not, they always are. Even the most gypsy-seeming — or whatever the flouters are calling themselves nowadays." It was said with dash, but he shifted in the chair. Too common a crystal to please, no doubt, but his breath was worrying him. And the chair was overrated. Better get out of it, which would take effort — and in time to catch that night-clerk.

Whatever had made him look so suddenly disappointed — surely not at this date some vibration from the long-lost wife? She was more inclined to think it the shadow of a recent reversal with a woman, for charm like his, knowledge like his, came from living life at the fullest, no matter what. He was the unconventional one; no one had ever before paid her the compliment of talking to her in such simple profundities as she had always known were possible, even for her. For all her limits, she was woman enough to feel that he *knew*, and if she could keep him here long enough, might even tell her.

"Not gypsies," she said. "I was in a gypsy place once,

over in Brooklyn. They're coppersmiths, you know, and we had a chafing dish we — anyway, it was a store. That's the way they do here, settle in a store. And they've got heaps of things. Huge mattresses they make themselves, and quilts in circus colors. Piles of them. And the women have dozens of those skirts they wear to hide things in." She offered this with pride, as not on the subject. "They just hide what they have, that's all. But Elizabeth!" She leaned forward. "You know, I offered her her grandmother's linen, after all it's flax-spun and she says she likes things *basic* — and she just laughed. Oh, I know what they want. They want the kind of stuff they can pretend isn't there. And it isn't just Elizabeth. They belong to a whole crowd of kids live like that. Not from poor families either, and not just for a starter, some even with babies. They mean to *stay* that way!" She heard for herself, how she did seem unable to converse without harping on "things." "Oh, I sound like the typical mother-of-the-bride. Which I am. And I know perfectly well how —" she spread her hands to the room, the very chair he sat in — "how I had to have 'over-stuffed.' Because my mother had 'mission.' But this!" She clasped her hands in her lap, unclasped them. "Do you think — do you think it's because they're artists?"

He found it quite touching, the humble way she said that word, had accepted it. "No. Oh, no."

"I wasn't sure. But I am sure, when they say they want nothing — that's what they all say — they mean it. All of them!"

Because of an oppression in his chest that made his eyes water — the chair was simply not for him — he had to lean forward. He took her fingertips in his, looking at them as impersonally as a piano teacher. "Yes. Just as I said. *All* of them."

Would she get it? Was she capable of it?

She was trying, head cocked to one side, fingers in his in the unembarrassed way of the blind seeking direction. Her mouth made a silent O, her whole face rosied. "You mean — it's their convention — it's just that it's *theirs?*" She began to laugh, clapping her hands so suddenly, hunting a handkerchief, leaning back in such peals, that the vague, circular dazzle made him feel as if he had released a bird into the room. A continuing smile was all he had energy for; he sat there letting her laugh for him, a pleasant sensation, as if two might breathe as cheaply as one.

"You can't know what you've done for me." She dabbed her eyes. "I've never dared laugh at Elizabeth. They taught us not." She sat straight up. "And the wretches know it, don't they. That we aren't allowed."

He had to laugh. The pressure in his chest eased. "It's only a temporary tyranny." Actually, he had always carefully kept himself able to laugh at his son, to be seen doing so, for all their special circumstance, in the same way that he had been careful to send David away from him, to college.

"They'll come round, you mean."

"We've only to sit still." It will coil round them. Whether *we* sit in the wrong chair or the right one. He felt in his pocket for the pills that were always there — not that he cared to stay to see it come. "Do you? — I suppose you do."

"Do I what?"

"Sorry. Want to see them come round."

"Probably I do." She said it defiantly. "If what you say about women — but — tell me something else, would you?" In the same moment, she shook her head. "Never mind." The question would only jump them back to the first stages of politeness, make her seem so foolish — *Are* they artists, the two of them?

"Come on, you owe it to me." It would be another confidence from this funny little well of them, not to be plumbed perhaps in an evening.

"Well then —" She tempered it. "She's left some work here. I'd — like to hear what you think of it."

No! His protest seemed to him audible, did get him up from the chair. His antipathy — to giving these answers — had at least done that for him. People at home were always asking him for opinions like these, either because his own work was felt to be in alliance with the arts, or because, in spite of his good tailor and orderly silver hair, women especially saw something in his Italianate looks which they felt to be painterly — he was consulted in exactly the way that pharmacists were applied to with more ease than doctors, often indeed looking more professional. Few of his intimates knew that he had been a painter himself, for some years. He took a sip of water from a glass on the table. "I won't give you a bill of particulars, you know. Can't." That was the real nature of his protest. What he might know of life, of the way it moved, wasn't what people wanted. They wanted directions for tomorrow.

Going ahead of him down the long hall, she smiled at her fears that they might revert to mere politeness; motioning into Elizabeth's room that stiff back ahead of her, she remembered the card enclosed with his gift. His honesty was incapable of first stages, both this and its effect on others a tribute to his illness. The mortally sick often made one feel that they harbored some tremendous secret they despaired of imparting. But it wasn't about death that this man could tell her, if he would. As she watched him look about him, so pale and firm, she felt alive to the toes, almost in the expectancy of a verdict, not on Elizabeth, but on herself.

He was thinking that this room, young person's as it was, already had its layers, perhaps the least of which were the drawings of various sizes, one or two assertively large, the litter of small figures done in some medium he couldn't identify from here, grouped together on a bookcase, the line of life-size clay busts insistently before him, some wrapped in cloths but recently wet. It was of course the room of any of a thousand young persons, with its signs of successive projects laid by, of disorder alternated with strictures of that queer, self-imposed order which had nothing to do with neatness — a room, a picture which, if one knew it all now laid by, might be entitled "Situation Abandoned by a Young Girl." As such, it had more natural pathos than was ever felt in the presence of the girl herself. Several photos of her, taken by David, were scattered about, and the assertion each made was clear enough to him — a face that would take a situation hard, not a face to ride the arc — or be gracious with those who did. As for David, who ever knew a son's face for sure?

"Who knows?" he said. The number of objects in the room dizzied him, in so small a compass of time already so many strata, from the rows of fairy tales to the busts, on the bed a petticoat flung down like a tutu, forever.

"Oh, I know you can't say. I just brought you in to see — just as I hope to see David's. He's very talented, I hear."

"From Elizabeth, no doubt."

"She has great faith in —"

"In them both." He reexamined the face in the picture. No, it mightn't be gracious with his son on that matter — why should it? It wouldn't be so with itself.

She nodded, breathing carefully. He, flushed and almost garrulous, no longer seemed to be doing so. This was what she must have brought him here for — this exchange.

"Oh — he can draw. So could I. Doesn't necessarily —" He took up one of the camera studies. "He's got the makings of a first-class photographer though. Better than his father. Of course, I'm prejudiced."

"Well — as a father —"

"Oh no, that's not what I mean." He was speaking far too rapidly and must stop — he knew the signs. "I was a painter once." In surprise — not that it hurt him to say, but the nuisance way people always reacted to such revelations was why he never made them — he stopped.

"And you had to give it up." She said this very softly, quite as expected.

"Some things are — taken out of our hands." He was slow in answering, smiling at the very pomposity of it. But the platitudes, coiled in our sight as they were, were always the safest. First his wife's death, leaving a son, then his own illness. Sickness and need of money were among the most acceptable of single reasons for anything, though there were others. He might never have had the nerve to give up on his own. In retrospect, he would never be sure how much his own hand had assisted the taker, only how relieved he had been — to be forced. David knew the story, for any good it might do him if the time came. When.

"Yes, they are out of our hands." *Elizabeth,* she said to herself, the way she was, has been taken out of mine, but the expected sadness always to be rubbed from this amulet did not come. Instead, Elizabeth herself seemed to be standing here in the room she had left, nearer than ever before but relievedly far — too far to be helped — and already rubbing her own amulet. How sad! "That's why you said you couldn't — answer." Her voice was almost fierce, the voice one used to oneself, or fast over the depths, to a friend. "Because *they* can't say for themselves yet, which things will be, they don't know whether —"

"Some of it, they can. Not *all.*" But never to be known which.

To ease the cramp in his chest, he walked about the room, which sometimes helped.

"Surely —" she said. There must be some way to defend them, to deny. "They're just at the beginning."

"They've begun."

The group of small figures on the bookcase interested him, in the light at that end of the room just discernible as all done in the same dullish medium, related in attitude as one neared them, none more than eight inches high. He knelt in front of them; the bookcase was child-size. They were all female figures, young and old, together and alone, not as simple as Tanagras nor as calm, but with the same unity of gesture. In their half-lyric caricature, they had that still pure eccentric one sometimes saw in the work of *Wunderkinder* — or in the work of those still holding on to a power that could only be grasped with the smallest fist. No, there was never any surety, but for all his shrugs at the particular there was taste. If the girl could hold on like this — to a situation — then, perhaps? What was the dirtyish stuff she'd done them in? He picked up a figure, and stood up again to hold it under a lamp.

"Then —"

He turned. She was standing just behind him.

"Then — it's out of our hands. Then, we can give *them* up." She saw it clearly, like a door in a cloud. "Because we *have* to." She smiled.

In utter surprise at what she was capable of, above all at that smile, he dropped the figure, which broke. He stooped to pick it up. In the pieces that clung to the armature he saw what it was made of, still flesh-colored on the inner side, the outer thumbed to that dirty indefinable which comes of the heat of the hand — it was wax. In the same moment, as the heavy piston of pain drove upward, its rod stiffening him from groin to tongue until it retracted again and he with it, he knew that he could never straighten with that inside him, that the best he could do was to let his legs crumple to the floor, get his back against the nearest wall. Through the siege that invaded his chest, such an old image in which he himself was the image, his chest the world, a bladder swelling to burst while his brain in the voice of a pea cried out for it to do so, that when it burst would be the world, he heard her voice mingled with his own, felt her fingers in his pocket where the pills were.

"There are two," she was saying, "two sets of them. Can you manage to tell me —" and then, "never mind. I know what these are." The crushed ampoule was held to his nostrils. He breathed. A pill was held to his lips. "Open your eyes — if you need water." Eyes closed, he got it down. "Another?" Lips sealed, he refused it. Then he swung weightless, hung like an acorn from the point where she held his wrist. To fall from that point of life — or not. The pain-rod melted to pain-rhythm, to breath-pain — at last to that priceless rhythm which might almost be ignored. Ozone is the medium, his brain formed, informed. He opened his eyes. He was no longer the world. He was in it.

"I'll phone the doctor now."

He shook his head. "Fall — asleep now."

"Don't talk — just nod. Are you sure — ?"

He nodded. How to tell her? — how well he knew the image.

"You want to stay where you are?" She brought him pillows, banked them, slipped one, with a practiced move, under his knees. "If you want a urinal, I have one. This is no time to — okay. But let me know. Or anything else." She seated herself under the lamp. "I'll be reading."

On the edge of sleep, he found himself unable to drop off. She had a magazine, but wasn't reading it. "How did you know?" he said. "The pills."

"Shhh-h." She took up a book. "Don't talk."

"How?"

"My mother had them." She bent her head over the book.

Don't talk, he thought, when we have, we are, in the

code of people who have already had their greater conversation. The time from when he had crumpled until his return now seemed that — all before just prattle, and not on her side only. Her certainties rested better on the concrete, that was all, on the lore of copper pots, on the thousand-and-one scales that flexed a serpent she must never admit to be there; she knew how to slip a pillow under the knees of the dying. My mother had them. Had. He found himself unable to sleep without reassuring her. "I'm not going to die," he said. "Not this time. Yes, I'm sure." Having given her this extraordinary particular, he slept.

When he awoke, she was reading under the light of one lamp. His watch had stopped. He was able to observe her for some time before their eyes met. "What time is it?"

"One-thirty."

He took out a pill and swallowed it, feeling almost good, in the light, convalescent suspension after shock — arisen from that nadir of accident in which one says "This is it!" to the plateau of the only moment in life safe from providence, in which one is able to say "That *was* it."

"Water?"

"No thanks." Afterwards, it always left him tentative, unwilling to add by one minim to his body's economy, in the same way that people held themselves rigid after operations, waiting silently for their organs to renumber themselves, note what had been done to them and resume. Actually some movement was even good for him now — he always resisted.

"Can you — would you like to shift to the bed now?"

"Actually, if there's any way for me to get a cab now, it's quite safe for me to go. I know what to do from now on."

"Don't be silly. I'm sure you do. But you can't think I'll let you go back to that hotel tonight." If he still planned to fly back late tomorrow, there was really no need for him to go back at all. She might tell him so later, not now. The cozy air of convalescence in the room, lights alert in the stillness, reminded her too well of those hours after one had nursed a child or a husband, anyone loved, safely through an illness, but still short of the point where they could get up and leave — for the safe hours to come, yours was the loving tyranny.

"I won't sleep now, you know. You ought to." Lassitude held him. He mulled how to explain to her — since he clearly was staying — how a man able to go back to his hotel room preferred not to move from his corner.

"I won't either. I wouldn't have." She leaned forward. "You're doing me a favor, you know. This would have been — the first night in more than twenty years that I was truly alone — and going to have to be, from then on. The day after, that wouldn't be so bad. But tonight — tonight — I was prepared to be desolate." She shrank back. "I shouldn't trouble you, make you talk." She took up her book again. "I'm just here if you want anything. Stay as you are. You'd probably rather."

So that too was part of her lore. He stared at her bent head. "No, let's talk," he said. "Yes, trouble me."

Her chin came up with dispatch. "Oh no. We won't begin on *that* again."

Forgetting his economy, he laughed. To call women like her humorous was not quite accurate; rather, they helped one toward stations of wit or gaiety in oneself. But obviously it was up to him now, in the pause which always fell when anyone said, "Let's talk." "Tell me," he said, still laughing, "do you by any chance play gin?"

Before she could answer, he had embarked on the true story of their evening as first he had visualized it — of his vice. He told her of the room clerk, the garment buyer. It took him several lively minutes — this was how he entertained at home. "So you see," he said in conclusion, "how far I'll go if I have to."

She received this very seriously, in silence. Had he really gone too far? Talk, for most, meant that repartee of the personal which he had years ago discarded as too costly. He closed his eyes; let her think that it tired him now.

"The light's in your eyes, isn't it? And you have to raise your head to talk, if I sit here." She rose, turned out all lights except a blue night-light in an opposite corner, left the room, returned with an armful of pillows and had settled herself matter-of-factly beside him, back against the wall, feet stretched parallel with his, all before he had time to wonder what she was about. In the half-dark, he waited for some comment on what he had told her. She seemed not to be going to make any. Chin on hand, eyes possibly on him or not, she seemed to think that she had already answered him.

The moon came up in the window, or, at this time of night, dropped down. Yes, she was looking at him. She folded her hands in her lap. "You're very ill, aren't you, Nicholas." It was not a question.

No one had ever said it to him that simply. Not even the doctors liked to. None of his roster had ever done, never, of course, David. No one had wanted to dwell for the barest moment on what would have rested him where he dwelt with it alone. Her tact was beyond measure; she took him literally. All his self-amused explanation had meant to her was that he was in dire need of being talked through the night, and gathering her pillows, she had answered him. He drew a simpler breath than he had in a long time. "Very."

Words were awkward after that; so was silence. She chose to press his wrist at the same spot from which she had held him over the abyss, then release it.

Because the best sympathy was the kind that bred it, hers reminded him that she too had her situation. "And you?"

"What do you mean?"

"How long have you been alone?"

It took her a minute to see how he equated it. "Two years." She sat forward, hugging her knees. "That's — how it feels, then?"

"Oh, it's gone on so embarrassingly long," he said quickly. "Ten years. Actually — a lot of new medicines came in. There's a regimen. And I couldn't afford not to take it seriously, because of David. We had no relatives."

"How old were you? When it began."

"Thirty-eight."

"I'm forty-four." She contributed this as a child might. Indeed, the hour no longer seemed to hang in the suspension of convalescence, but, perhaps because the room was Elizabeth's, more like one of those in her girlhood, when one sat up for the confidences that came simply because the hour was late enough.

She stared at him intently, one hand pleating the big

petticoat on the bed above her. "What is the regimen?"

"Oh — it's not — anything transferable."

"Some of it must be. It can't all be — 'not boiled but fried.'"

She had made him laugh again.

Tentatively he moved, stretching an arm, a leg, while he enumerated the checks and balances that had kept him going, so far as he knew.

They seemed sparse, unheroic. David's name did not appear among the medicaments.

He leaned back in the abandonment of no longer having to think of his posture. The dial of his watch surprised him — nowhere near four. "No, you're right. That's not quite all." Why shouldn't he tell her? The later the hour, the less people lied to themselves or others. Few things sounded foolish by moonlight. By dawn, any man spoke the truth. "I've never told anyone. Every once in a while — well — I more or less put my name down for — one rash act. It's a way of imagining myself into living like everybody else — long-term. The first time, it was accident. I decided to build the house, and it turned out to be a fairly complicated house. The doctors hadn't given me more than a year or so. When the house was finished — I'd lived three."

For a space they were quiet, sailing on what last had been said. At some such hour, all rooms become barques. The outer light held the room for a brilliant second, then slipped down.

"And the next one?" Her face was hidden on her knees.

"I coasted — for about a year. Then a friend of mine wanted me to do an art book with him, one of those histories based on a fixed idea, probably wrong but interesting. It meant close collaboration, text, plates and so on. I figured, if he was willing to bet on me for a couple of years — that's about what it took."

"And then?"

He was a long time answering. "I made David — I sent him *away* to college."

She got up from their corner and stood at a window, pressing her face against the frame. "You gave him up."

"Oh no. I hung on for dear life. That was how."

The window was open at the top. She held her face to the air, to dry. No — it was not transferable.

He felt the gap at his side like a defection. She had moved so shadowily. "Whatever are you doing there?"

"Seeing where the moon went."

"You're such snails, here." Indoor people, for whom looking out a window was an excursion. The Coast had a great deal of illness, but like the gypsies, kept it hidden, often in apricot tints of health like his own. "I can tell you where it's gone. To California."

"You're not thinking of flying back tomorrow? Oughtn't you to rest, even in a hospital?"

"Just rest. That hotel's quiet enough. I'll stay on a few days."

She came and knelt down beside him. "Why don't you — you could stay here. You could send for your things."

He did not reply, or move.

"Yes, why don't you," she said. "At least there'd be someone — we could talk in the evenings."

His eyes, usually so quick, were as still as his face, not fathomable. She had wounded him then, by so clearly assuming — what must never be assumed. Women are conventional — he would know hers. She had wounded him by taking it for granted that he had no secrets, any more. "I just wanted to —" What could you give a man who had nothing, to whom you had just blurted that out? She stood up. "Would you — like an orange?" Let him laugh then. It would be something to have amused.

"Yes," he said. "I'll have an orange."

While she was gone, he put his head in his hands.

When she came back, she was carrying a short-legged bed-tray, on it a plate with two oranges and a fruit knife. He took up the knife, shaped like a scimitar for a baby Turk, and began scoring an orange. His hands were slow, deft, like a magician's. They intended her to watch them.

He presented her with the oranges, each rosetted in the center of its neatly laid-back skin.

"My grandfather used to do that!" she said.

"My father. Europeans."

The orange skins remained — acrid mignonette.

"What will the children say?" he said.

So it was settled, then. Her fingers were sticky. She spread them. "After all — they match, don't they?"

He considered. One to have. One to hold. Would that be David? Never sure which. But tender tidbits, both of them. "Oh, they match."

"After all — they don't want *us* to sit up with *them*."

"No," he said. "No."

Once an ambulance went by, trailing its sleigh-bell terror, then a homing plane, or so one thought of it, traveling steadily — fraternal signals from the never-quite-safe.

"What will the next one be?" she said.

"Next?"

"Your — rash act."

He had survived the plane East — of course, pressurized these days. Plus three cups of coffee. "I'd half meant — just to slide. Is that one?"

"But there is something else? That you could do?"

Down there, *it* moved, moving him with it. This, he could say, moving his hand an inch — this. He held on fast, to his economy.

"It's not up to me. I can't say."

So there was a woman, and at half-past three, their first awkwardness. She was remanded back to their subject.

After a while, she spoke. "We really have been — sitting up with them. Haven't we. Just for tonight, it can't be helped. It's barbarous, even the guests were. Following them in their minds, I mean. But it can't be helped, can it."

"Not tonight."

"I used to try and think that if she — that when she — went with a boy — that was her business. As long as I didn't know. But at weddings, I always found myself watching the bride's mother, wondering what she was thinking. Knowing. Because then — just for that once — it isn't only their business. Not then."

"Not the fathers," he said. "We watch the son."

"Do you think — ?" If she faltered, it wasn't because of any awkwardness with him. "It is their business now, of course. But I've thought for some time — do you think that they already —"

After some moments, he put his hand on hers and held it. "Think back," he said. "Think back."

When he looked at his watch again, it was four, and it was she who was asleep. He drew the coverlet from the bed over her. It was years since he had done such a thing even for David — all the gestures of solicitude had been pointed toward him, separating him. He got up, tiptoed to the bathroom, and came back. It was years too, since he had slept in anything but a chair. The one she had been sitting in pouted at him, its boudoir shape padded like a high, nubile bosom. He chose a straight one, from the desk. Wrapping himself in a thin blanket from the bed, he sat facing her, letting their conversation resume. The hard chair held him capably; it stood on terra firma. Even if she was awake, he did not have to say it to her. He did not have to. Saying it to himself, he fell into a sleep still vigil, where he said it to her. Prepare. Prepare, for a little while, not to be desolate.

3

For the young Paganis, the three and a half months they spent on Spring Street were a saga they knew themselves to be living. A dozen times a day, some small domestic act set a precedent, or would if not watched. Some they noted pridefully; more often they were too careless to watch. From home, Elizabeth had brought the wicker sewing chest given her by the grandmother who at the same time had put an embroidery hoop in her four-year-old hand and taught her the archaic lore of the French knot, the feather-stitch and how to hem invisibly, by picking up, with a needle so thin that it bent in the middle, a single thread of the cloth. Her grandmother's approval, usually so grudged to children — "See, Margot, better than you ever!" — had been the first hearkening of that praise she had always later on been able to win for herself by some skill of the hand. Inside the sewing chest, on plumply quilted lining the color of Christmas glow, a row of tin-gilt thimbles hung in assorted sizes of which she had used perhaps the two first, above buttons of all sorts — marcasite, bone, pearl — from the family button box, spools of the old mercerized colors, and a small tape measure of yellow cotton, inked in black, that at a touch still rewound itself on its reel. Opening the box to find a shirt button for David, the old spools, faded but lucent, had given her back the same unfocused eye that had taken in the *Blue Fairy Tale Book* and the *Green;* the buttons, staring from that last rainy playtime on which they had been shut away, were a collection of physiognomies too knowing to be deserted. David had been charmed, both by her cherishing of such an unlikely object and her ability to sew — was that why, deviously pushed from the lair of herself, she had brought it? Before shutting it away, she fingered the tape measure. Their life-to-be here resembled it, all linear and good, back of the first black-marked inch a firm, satisfying nothing. She ought to toss the whole box away, had a strong desire to do so. Finally, giving in to an opposite urge that seemed much weaker, negligible, she put it out of sight in a dark corner. After all, it served a purpose.

Water — basic hurdle for third sons and frog-princes, harbinger voice for the prettiest long-braided daughter — was what forced them from Spring Street. Broom won't sweep; water won't run. They already had their bed and table from the Salvation Army, their white dishes from the Japanese store — plus some tatami mats David had insisted on, and were admittedly handy. Whenever she could, in their sparse buying, she left such

59

choices for him; for whatever came into the household that way she was not to be blamed. They had already had their first mishap, as in all legends more gargantuan with each recital — the night the bookshelves fell down. David, in consultation with the crowd over molly screws and old plaster, had about decided to use bricks. The wall must be used, separated shelves being the same stigma that glass-enclosed ones had been to their parents. The crowd, dropping by, brought in only those presents that were proper to them — a bunch of flowers, a six-pack of beer — nothing to impede. From their own weekly dinner-evenings with Mrs. Jacobson they had brought back only enough of Liz's winter clothes to do until they built or bought a closet — it was now late October.

Going off to the first of these evenings, Elizabeth had sulked as before a chore; later she welcomed them. For once again over that threshold, she felt the tonic revival of all her antipathies; the house helped her to define what she was against; the doctrine of their own life in the loft — softened under the accidental rhythm of their days like a pure speech come to dwell among cockneys — once again became clear. This happened even though her mother's protests against it, once so frontal, were no longer dependable; tonight she had not even remarked on Elizabeth's dusty black leotard and lack of lipstick, and when they now dutifully suggested a return visit on her part, she smiled and said she would wait until they "got it all done." "Done?" said Elizabeth. "We aren't *doing* anything!" — and for a moment it was all as of old. Her mother was shortly off with friends who were driving to the Coast and Mexico, on a trip that might extend over the winter. She had several commissions, and thought she might turn these into a business; people were always asking her "where" and "how." And on the way, they would stop off and see Mr. Pagani, who from his letters to David was back in harness and well enough, at least the same.

"Get old Jacques to take you round San Francisco when you buy," said David, "don't just settle for Gump's. He's a real scavenger." And, oddly, it was not Mrs. Jacobson who asked, "Who is Jacques?" but Elizabeth, who had never heard of the old Frenchman, Mr. Pagani's partner, who for so many years had carried the main load. Mrs. Jacobson was most interested in how he and David's father had worked that out, but when that subject was over, fell back again, abstracted.

"What do you want to do about the wedding present?" she asked, when they were leaving.

"I wrote the thank-you notes," said Elizabeth. "*You* keep them."

"I've put them in your closet," said her mother, smiling equably. "You can always come and get them. There's some good flat silver, you know. And a steak set."

"Steak!" said David. He dashed off to the bedroom and came back with both articles. "I'm queer for knives and forks, somehow. Always was." He brandished them before Elizabeth. "She let me buy two sets in the dime store. We're forever washing them. When there's water, that is." Both his and Elizabeth's faces clouded over at this, but Mrs. Jacobson, smiling at him, did not take this up either.

Elizabeth went off to her old bedroom, which she hated to enter. Unlike her mother's domain, there were things here that made her feel small, unsure. Let David and her mother connive together. Unfair as that thought was, its anger was helpful. When she came out, she carried the little wax figures, laid in a carton. "You can throw out the busts," she said. "They're no good. Besides, I'm thinking of wood."

Throwing out anything had always been fighting words with Mrs. Jacobson; now she nodded absently. "That's nice. And where will you get it — I mean the wood?" She smiled pleasantly at David's account of the bookshelves; she did the same at her door when they were leaving. She smiled continuously.

In the subway, he set the carton on his knees. Since Liz had her house-face on, he reexamined the figures with interest. The grind and sway of the car made it hard to talk anyway. "So you're thinking of wood," he said, when they reached a station. "That's great."

"Great!" she flashed out at him, immediately. "What's great about it? You don't have to talk like that to me, butter me up. Great!"

"Well, it is."

"Oh, you don't have to encourage me. You haven't started doing anything yet either, remember?"

"So you told her."

She turned, aghast. It was incredible that he had taken the barb meant for her mother. "You know how I meant that — that we weren't getting tangled up in — we aren't, are we? It's just that we have to get certain things —"

He sighed. "Guess you two shouldn't see too much of each other. We always quarrel after."

Her mouth opened in horror. The car moved again before she could answer. To her mind, they had never.

That couples sooner or later did, she knew — but to a banging of doors, not come a-creep. Through the sinuous tunnel of sound, she heard again his light, accepting "always"; over the noise, his head, nodding with the car's movement, seemed to be ratifying it. Three months of living together, and they already had an always; an attitude, creeping upon them, had all but frozen itself in.

When the next station arrived, they did not speak until the doors were almost closed.

"But not with each other. Not really."

"No." The car lurched, and he carefully recradled her carton and his bundle. "No."

They got out at Spring Street. Going up these stairs last week, carrying her clothes, he had suggested the closet be done soon, and she, jealous of the order he had seen at her mother's and coveted, had scorned both it and him. "I don't want anything more!" Fearful that she might, she had added, "Nothing!"

Now, at the top, the air was colder, the night crammed with stars. They breathed in the dark, autumn elation. The pyre of the year was burning but they did not mind it; there was so much still to come. Because of his armful, they could not join hands. She touched her cheek against his shoulder. "When we get home, let's start on the closet."

He seemed to be smiling, but his glasses remained level. Recently he had discarded that gesture. "Of course. I just didn't know how much you really cared."

All the way to their door, she talked of the closet, but once inside, he dropped his bundles, they tossed their clothes after them and made love where they stood, stopping only to turn out the light. They were ashamed of making love in the dark, but the ten curtainless windows, even showing as few human lamps as spied here at this hour, were always too much for them. They always made love when they returned from her mother's.

It was not until morning that they found the water pressure had given out for good. By nightfall, they had agreed to move. It was easier by night; the sun, pouring into the room like courage, displayed its strange proportions like a confidence man. At night, under the weak light bulb, the scattered coziness of their belongings pasted like collage on the seamy shadows, it was more possible to believe that some nothing-can-be-done or other unnamable had all the time been living with them in a corner — an old circus lion, shabby but knowing, nudging them now and again with its paw.

"I'll never forget this place, never!" said Elizabeth, her throat arched Joan-of-Arc against the shadows, so that he could see its patch of down. David, not daring to tell her so, was glad they had been forced to leave. And now they could start again from the beginning.

For some months, it seemed to them that they had. In Mrs. Jacobson's apartment, an offer to caretake which — while they looked for other quarters — they could scarcely refuse, they were freed at one stroke from what they now saw to be the obsessions of nest-building. Looking at her crowded gallery, they congratulated one another on their small pile of salvage from their false start, on the wisdom of remaining as free. Meanwhile they basked in comforts conveniently not theirs, alternately savaging the house for several Grand Guignol days, then guiltily recleansing it; dining by borrowed candlelight, tumbling hotly in the parental bed, they were children left in command. Mornings, Elizabeth returned to class-work at the League; at off hours, in a corner of the photography studio where he worked, David sometimes painted. Evenings, like any wife to her businessman, she recounted anecdotes of the afternoon's house-hunting — strange encounters in which the telling all but took precedence over the goal — and when they went to the movies afterward, as she walked at his side, her hair newly cut short, she had the well-brushed, almost burnished neatness of a schoolgirl at her first courting. They were going to the movies continually now, to everything from swollen Hollywood epics to flickering art-kinos, for now that television had siphoned off the tired, the middle-aged and the stupid, the cult of the film could once again be seen as both the youngest art-form and the art-form of the young — taking the same place, in their bohemia of nearly-poets-and-painters, almost-actors, that the record player had had for their fathers — a secondary bowstring which anybody could twang. David and his employer-friend Barney were thinking of making a film.

One night, after a French film on upper Madison Avenue, encountering a couple, the girl of whom had attended Elizabeth's school, they were persuaded back under the marquee to the banquettes and potted vaudeville geraniums of the "Parisian" coffeehouse operated by the theater out front.

"It's not really like Paris at all, really," said Mitzi Halpern, too late remembered as a soft, stupid girl whose smugness had done her almost as well at school as brain. "Saul and I went there on our honeymoon." She slipped her plump trotter from its glove, on it a marquise sliver of ice. "*That's* from Paris, ooh no, the *glove*." Her glance went to Elizabeth's ringless hand. "Saul's father gave us the trip, they do business there, Paris." She tapped a crinkly tan boa worn around her neck like a dog collar, the exact color of her mocha eclair. "This too. He's in business with his father, Saul."

The heavy young man at her side smiled at them, as if lulled by the sound of his name, his collar lapped by his porterhouse jowl.

They were furnishing an apartment not far from here, said Mitzi. "Over near Carl Schurz Park where you know, those four-stories, you can still get three-and-a-half for one-sixty-five. That's where all the young marrieds." Her husband nodded at David, a boss approving his secretary's shorthand. Met like this, with the women to do it for them, it was not necessary to speak.

The waitress served them and left, filling the pause that should have been Elizabeth's turn.

"I adore those earrings," said Mitzi. "Different but not arty. Not arty — but different. You changed your style since you got —" Her glance strayed from Elizabeth's ring-finger. "You keeping on with your art work?"

"Mmm," said Elizabeth, squinting. A minute ago she had even felt glad of not having slouched out to the movies in jeans or tights, as she would have done six months ago. "David and I have a loft," she said suddenly, "on Spring Street."

The young man woke up. "Our factory, we got a factory that neighborhood, near Lafayette." He addressed himself to David. "Benjamin Novik and Sons. Feathers and Bugles."

"Bugles?"

"Beads. Dress beads. Imported only."

"On all the ballgowns at Dior this year," said Mitzi.

The young man made as if to speak, then took out a cigar. Everybody watched while he manipulated it, his wife most of all. They seemed already too substantial a couple to be supported by such airy fancies of bugle and feather, her skin as fat and white as nougat, his neck so prime — yet at the same time like an Aucassin and Nicolette playing roles into whose scope they had yet to grow. At last the cigar puffed. He removed it. "Don't forget Worth."

Mitzi stared with dreamy enmity at the blob of whipped cream on her spoon. "I shouldn't eat you." She ate. "But Saul and I we're dead, we went to all the rug houses, his father's giving us the wall-to-wall."

All this time, David had been watching Elizabeth. Now he took out a cigarette, tapped it, reversed it, rolled it for dryness. Finally he put it into his screwed-up eye and squinted at her down its length.

"Excuse me, cigar, Mr. Uh — David?"

"No thanks. Pagani."

"Novik. You doing art novelties down there, Spring Street?"

David lit the cigarette, looking over it at Elizabeth. He blew the smoke to one side. "No. We're not doing anything. What *are* we doing, Liz?"

Mitzi had turned bright red.

"It's a living-loft," said Elizabeth.

"Oh, artists." He nodded, like a cosmopolite over a word learned in Paris.

"No," said David, still eyeing Liz. "Matter of fact, I'm in films."

Mitzi leaned forward quickly. "Simply adorable," she murmured to Elizabeth's earrings. "Saul honey, I should get my ears pierced. I mean really. Shouldn't I?"

For answer, he removed her cake plate and set it in front of himself. The heavy intimacy of years together was already upon them. One could see them years hence, dressing to go out, he pausing absent-mindedly, cigar in teeth, at her bidding, looking out the window, not at her body, while he hooked her undergarment. "Have to watch her like a hawk." He nibbled comfortably. "No, I *don't* think. We running like mad to get the house ready for March the big event — she wants her ears pierced. Last week — a poodle." No older than anyone at the table, he already bore a mantle cast on him from behind, from behind even the flickering image of his munificent father.

"Oh Saul! It doesn't even *show* yet!" It was like an accent they had both agreed to adopt, which had as swiftly adopted them.

"Might as well get used to it." His neck shifted in his collar. "We're expecting, end of March," he said. "A baby. A child."

"In March."

They were truly in chorus now, even to the smiles half hangdog, half smug, in the end suffused with the honest radiance of those who have never had to choose.

"Might as well be modern about it," he said. Behind him, the generations, row upon row of Hasidim, nodded comfortably back.

Outside again, the four parted with a bright "Come *see!*" and a murmured "We'll *do* that!" The Pagani couple walked on without speaking. It was some blocks before either of them spoke.

"Brr-r," said Elizabeth. It was almost a question.

For half a block or so, he didn't answer. She had trouble matching his irregular pace to hers. Then he stopped short, put her hand through his arm, and answered her. "Brr-r."

Half another block on, she giggled. "She thought we weren't married."

"Mmm." He tightened the arm around hers.

She was encouraged. "A baby. A *child*. As if he wasn't quite sure himself what."

"I predict a marshmallow. Large, white — and beaded."

She simply exploded. "I kept thinking of what I'd do her in, but I couldn't quite — and that stuff around her neck?"

"Molasses coconut."

"On the nose."

Arms around each other's waists, they tramped on in an energy of closeness.

"David. Why'd you say that. That you were in films?"

He shrugged, looking up at the façade of her mother's apartment, just reached. "Let's scram soon, huh. Your mother likes the Coast that much, she'll stay on all winter, she and Jacques having such a ball." Mrs. Jacobson's letters were a steady inventory of their buying, though her going into business had not been further mentioned. His father had reported with amusement her conquest of the sour, lanky septuagenarian, who was teaching her how to "collect." She in turn reported dutifully that his father was well, that is, the same.

"Da-avid."

The elevator closed on them before he answered. "Why'd you say that, about Spring Street."

They rode up in silence, examining the brown dry-cereal grain of the cage. But when he urged her out with a mild cuff from behind, she recognized a familiar, faintly vying signal.

Under the light of the one lamp they had left burning, a heavy cloisonné vase with a silk shade like a pagoda, the long double room, cleaned that morning, received them aloofly, as established as a gallery. He parked the house keys on the pagoda, where they slid and hung, flipped on the "side-lights" that shed a tawny, not-quite-other-century glow, and fingertips to her waist, propelled her lightly, rhythmically down the room. "A — bmm. A-bmmm. A — bmmma, bmma, *Bmmm*-bmm —"

"Bmmm."

The small Oriental rugs with which the parquet was scattered at first tripped them, then collected around their ankles, finally islanded them. "Bounty. All this bounty," he said. Front to front, they wound themselves together, eyes closed. "Let's make tracks soon, hmm." He whispered it. "Out of here."

Eyes securely blind, she burrowed deeper. "Carl Schurz Park?"

Rocking idly, she heard his sigh through her flesh rather than her ear. "Let's not talk any more. At least not about them."

But in the bedroom, as he was helping her undress, with that gravely ritual interest, almost as if he were unveiling a statue, which often signaled that they were to make love, he was the one who spoke. Usually, he was quiet throughout this rite. Once she had said to him, mock-tough, "Never seen a woman before?" Coloring, shaking his head at her not to spoil it, he had finally replied mock-naïve, "Not till this moment, ma'am." She knew better now. If they were practiced lovers now, the woman, recognizing certain routines, must nevertheless keep silent; a man's finesse was to be remarked on only by enjoyment. Her responses, she felt sure, were less predictable, women being more aware of that repetition which was their enemy in life.

He touched the points of her breasts through the thin, Mexican gift-blouse. "Not too much candy. But enough."

She crossed her arms. "Never you mind. We have one — it'll at least be human."

"Oh, she wasn't so bad. He's the one bugged me. She was even kind of sweet, there at the end."

"Mitzi? Why, she's hard as nails, always was. She knows all the answers, you know — in that smug way? As if there aren't any questions. Him — he's a nothing."

"You want one — we could," he said. "Of course, not by the end of March."

"On the allowance? Mm-mm, thanks. I can wait."

"Can you?" He uncrossed her arms and drew her down.

In his embrace, she stirred reminiscently. "Fat, smug bitch."

"Oh, you girls, you always want to get even," he said. "He's the one bugged me."

In bed, they lay separately; they had talked too much. Neither wanted to admit that desire had lapsed, an occurrence too new to be without scare.

"You want the light out?" she said.

"No . . . but you know what? I think I'm getting tired of that audience." On Mrs. Jacobson's many, plump pillows, they lay in a direct line with her wedding picture on the bureau, flanked by both sets of grandparents, each in the formal dress of the period, each in its coupled frame. "I tell you what. Whyn't we go to your room?"

During their stay here, they had never done so. Although they had once made love there, in fact — on a weekend Mrs. Jacobson was away — the first time, the bed was of course a single. It had seemed natural to take over the other bedroom, in a latent way even revengeful. Now, going down the long corridor, each felt an obscure sadness. As they passed the bathroom, he inflected his head; she shook hers. It was the time just after her period, in the time they considered safe.

Her bedroom lay untouched in its blend of the frivolous and the intense, a museum air, less than a year away, into which she could almost step back if she tried. As in any unused place, old odors had returned to it, a babyish sweat from the books and games, some later sachet-stink of her early teen-age.

"Grow your hair again, hmm?" he said.

"You old roué."

"Still . . ." he said. "I wouldn't go back to that other time, would you?"

"No." Though this was true, for a minute she felt like crying for woes unknown but suspect, as if it were the day before her period, instead of after.

The narrower bed forced them together. Let's not talk, his hands said, let's not talk. Under this, the burden of their choices fell away. With the last flicker of thought, she felt that they were not repeating anything; this was

different. Both were smiling now, the fixed lip-stretch of
lust rising. Spontaneity was gone, but this hard joy was
as strong. If there was a revenge in it, its object had
changed. This time they were cuckolding each other —
their former selves. Afterwards, they lay purged, hands
locked. By next morning, they had forgotten. In the future of their life together, that night had no marker. If
they remembered it at all, it was as the night before
they found their place, the one that was really theirs,
where they began again — from the beginning.

4

Elizabeth, who found it, always thought of it afterwards as waiting for her, centered in its own day, one of a special oyster-chill, damp with port sounds and the decayed vegetable, salt port smell, of an air limned with the fewest, cleanly distractions to the eye. A sculptor's day, she said later to David. Later on, she came to be familiar with such days as indigenous to these old streets below bridges, in-between days as to season and light, predictable on any sunless one that was neither icy nor burning. With these, there came often the memory of the couple she had found in the place when she arrived. They clung to it like the small bootjack burr one pried from the cuff of an old hiking sock, discarding a past winter with it, only to find, further down, another of the same. Even when the loft had become so much hers and David's, so crammed with their goods and the history of its changes under their stewardship that they and it were an entity to their friends and themselves, the image of that other couple, ovaled in their stewardship, recurred to her without warning — a superscripture that her brain had encircled for her with a sweep of the pencil, noting underneath: "Retain!" David, of course, never saw them.

The ad had listed, "Living-lofts, various sizes, convertible, artists' or sculptors', some bridge views." Over the phone, the young man who answered seemed both eager and fumbling. "Yes, we're the ad. We're the ad, yes." When he tried to explain what he called "the setup," an amateur kindness broke through — this was no sharp owner or agent, yet he was partisan. "Oh, it's going to be a wonderful setup!" he said, when he heard that she and David were artists. "You'll see. You better come down." When he heard the part of town she was coming from, he gave her subway directions as if to a foreigner. Otherwise, he was scrappy and referential, as if to some private club whose nature on sight would be clear to her. She was to come up the stairs and yell for him — Maury. "Just yell 'Maury.' Or ring at Ivan's. Ivan's the one managing the place. He's the only one got a bell."

Usually, she ran like hell for bright chances which either came to nothing, or for which she arrived too late. The good ones were always gone by half-past yesterday. Today she dawdled, as if — as she marveled to David later — something in her consciousness, either forward or guardian-angel, already knew its destiny. Outside the subway, she turned east on a last, truck-rumbling big thoroughfare, then south. She passed a housing development made of that wrapping-paper-colored brick which always seemed to set a careful, welfare limit on what the people inside should aspire to, its walls angled for a sun it could not seem to catch. Within, Puerto Rican voices swooped like parakeets. After that, the streets were dead-beat, beat-down; walking between underfoot glass, worn soft and cloudy, and a sky like pavement, she looked into the green bottle-bottom eyes of empty stores. Down a vista more south than easterly, a viaduct cut off the street like an embankment, yet left it with that vague promise of exit which streets near water always have. Spring Street, dimly north and west, could not be far as city distances were reckoned, but its fussy jazz of small manufactures, that she had once taken for basic, was nothing like this — even in today's Saturday rest. "Here" wheeled off into the sky with a dockside energy, or slipped down toward the slow compulsion of the water itself, lapping old stairs in a beveled quiet that had not been made of a Saturday. This was the island's tip or edge, where the city had begun. Taking a turn, she lost herself centerwards again, even catching sight now and then of the high, bank-real Atlantis of Wall Street, but from low streets with names lifted from some old euphony, called Cliff, Pearl, Gold. The squared-off New York she had been brought up to was gone, into some foreign Amsterdam she would never recover after that day, along which she walked, flushed and dreaming, on her thin, uptown heels, through air that smelled of fish and other verities, in a brown dusk of closed coffee companies with a hint of Tudor to their roof lines. At last, treading the circle one expects of dreams, she found it, first inquiring of a lone truckman who shook his head, then a postman unloading from mailbox to sack, who nodded. "That's it, must be that big old building near the viaduct. The old piano factory. Some people living in it."

Like several other river ends she had passed, it was called a "slip," and under the viaduct, the cross street she had been hunting was still a cove. For one second, she saw the large, dust-gray structure for what it was, old but not old enough, not dark or queer or battered enough for any kind of grace — then never again. In the sun motes dancing against the flabby stone, sunny stone, something of what the building must have — footage and on its top floors a sight of water — united forever with what she had to have it be. The two sides she circled had no door, one old lading entrance, closed. Trucks hummed above, but below here, she could hear her own footsteps — how came this silence that she herself seemed to be making? Against a door in the third side, flat and stepless, she leaned almost drunken, hearing herself tell David: "The air is oyster down there. The moments file by like Indians." No — telling herself, in the same way she used to press her body, eyes closed, against her bedroom door, muttering softly to it what she yearned to say against the not-yet-met body of a man. Suddenly she was frightened at her own dallying, with almost the same girl-fright she had had back there. Others were up and doing, out after the pearl of price, while she murmured to a door. She pushed at the door, which gave to her hand. Inside, the light was as refulgent brown as an old stable, smelled of cracked wheat. A black iron stairway spiraled up into the shadows, ropes hanging in the shaft, dark.

"Maury." She was out of breath. Inhaling deeply, she called again. "Mau-aury." And again. Nothing answered her. But this must be the place. Looking up to where the Jacob's-ladder stair disappeared, she spoke inwardly, like an irritated child to its nurse, to that presence in which, when needing it, she still believed. I must have it, live here. No encouragement came, saying, "You will." But then she heard, from high up, "Co-oming!" and the rapid twiddle of feet on the stairs, down story after story, going round and round with the rising hop-two-three used by children or very young people. On the last few, she could see him, a very tall boy of about her own age with a high head of dark hair — a Modigliani head, its legs, in tight black pants, moving the way such a head's would, a marionette performing double-jointed variations around the norm. He settled in front of her with a final hop. She saw that he was not really so tall, just very narrow. But not the norm? Some of the homos at the League wore those pants, but some of the beards too and even a few boys in her crowd — none of whom were. The pants made them move like that; they had mostly discarded them. Not that they minded the others, or did not have friends among them, but they were never the crowd.

"You the one called?" His voice was normal, only shy, like his smile.

Her heart leaped at such innocence. Then no one else had. She nodded. "How many are there here? Lofts, I mean."

"Five, we put in, when Ivan started here, a year ago. He don't bother to change the ad. The landlord makes a dollar — maybe he'll put in some more."

"He's the landlord then, Ivan?" she said.

"Who, *Ivan?*" He was gravely amused, the way a

porter might be at a child, who when told that this is the Tsar's palace, asks who is the Tsar. "He should hear you. No, he's the one dreamed up this setup; he's on our side. Ivan Kostec. He's a sculptor." He pronounced it "skolp-teh," his inflection Bronx or Brooklyn, all reverence.

"Are you the agent, then?"

"I — been handling for Ivan, up to now. He don't have time for that."

The shape of his face reminded her of a pony or a burro — its long, planed nose, large-fringed eye. Or perhaps it was the expression.

"Excuse me, miss —" He had been eyeing her too. "You're not by any chance — from the Housing?"

"Housing? Me?"

"It's just that you don't look, you know. Like we talked."

"I'm dressed up. You know how it is. For *landlords*."

He laughed with her. "We got to watch it, you know — this izzen exactly a legal —"

"Oh, I know. We had a deal, over on Spring Street."

"Oh, yeah — Spring." He said it as if it were suburbia. She described it.

"Sounds like the greatest."

"Oh, it was, it was."

He eyed her sideways. It was in the expression, half between animal yielding, animal mildness, as if suspicion were a harness placed on him. "You'll excuse," he said. "Excuse, but — so why move?"

She explained.

"Water, for chrissake. How do you like that! You can't get around that; that's for sure. Jesus Christ, water, thank

God we got no trouble with that. Water everywhere, in the pipes, the view —" He swung an arm. "Everywhere!"

"Oh, it's a wonderful place," she said. "Wonderful. How'd you ever — ?"

"Isn't it! God, isn't it." A smile broke over his face. He touched her elbow. "You'll excuse I had to ask why. You sure don't *look* like you're broke, but sometimes, know how it is, because this place it's artists, we could get, you know — those floaters. Flop-artists. From one deal to the next, and no cash passes." He paused and she nodded, thinking of the boy before them on Spring Street.

"Oh, we're okay on that, we're *rich*," she said. "Oh, you know what I mean. We can take care of it." She explained.

"I'm sure," he said. "And you see, it's only because Ivan has the whole weight of this joint on his shoulders." He squared his own. "I don't subscribe anyway, people like us in the arts, they don't have to be responsible. Or to be physically dirty." His sweater was clean, his hands and nails also, the whole of what she saw now to be a gentle, rather clerkly person on whom the sharp pants were a uniform, in the meantime wondering what he did, imagining the small, neat home, mother he might have got such maxims from. "You agree?" he said suddenly.

She nodded. "Like leotards," she observed thoughtfully. "They always smell. In the crotch."

"Right!" he said, immersed in his argument. Then he blushed. "Anyway, some people, one faction here, just because Ivan has what to eat — He's a natural-born worker, that's all, if a sculptor has to do tombstones — so he does! Didn't he meet Kreisl, that's the landlord, through the cemetery connection, and sell him the whole idea? Kreisl don't take a hand, only to square the fire department and the garbage, the rest is up to Ivan. He don't make it a paying proposition for Kreisl, then —" he drew a finger across his throat. "Right?"

"Right," she said faintly.

"So — it's like Ivan says — it can't be helped. He's on a very thin margin. A ve-ry thin margin. And just one sour apple could make the whole barrel —" he cocked his head, frowning, "not *sour*."

"Rotten," she said.

"Right!" he said gloomily. "And it can't be helped, which one." He clapped his hands, whistling under his breath. "Well! Down to business. You'll excuse me for yacking. I got things on my mind."

"I think it's a miracle you're not all filled up," she said. "I usually never get to a place on time, not any place worthwhile. How many vacant ones do you have left?"

He took out a pencil. "Just one."

"Oh!" she said. "Am I lucky."

"Hey, you haven't even seen it. Could be one of these ratholes. Maybe *it* don't have water." But he was grinning at her.

"You're teasing. Because something told me. In the ad even. Even before I walked down this street."

"I also," he said, carefully grammatical with holiness. "I also. Whenever I walk down this street, something says it, it's a dream but Maury, you're walking. Even the first time inside, and believe me, Ivan and me worked like dogs, it wasn't what it is today. God, could this be a high-class setup, I said to Ivan, he wasn't only showing me the place, and meanwhile to myself, it's gonna be a high-class setup, Maury, and it isn't for you, you know his standards. I wasn't only ushering, maybe once in a while an electrical job on the QT. And what does *he* do but offer me to work it out in rent!" He put a solemn hand on her shoulder. "What's your name?"

"Liz. Liz Pagani."

He repeated it. "Say, that's nice. Make a good stage name, *Italiano, si?* — we're Hungarians. Well, Liz, you're right — it's a doozy. And something tells me you'll get it. Something tells me, you'll be the one."

She put her hand on his shoulder, like kids swearing an oath — he was such a one himself he made her feel about sixteen. "Okay then! What are we waiting for!"

"I'm in no hurry," he said. "Just Ivan. Okay, give me that dope again, will you?" He noted it all down on a pad, David's employer, Mrs. Jacobson, where they were living. "Now wait here. Don't make a move. Just wait right here." He made for the street door.

"Maury, wait."

"I'll take you up there in a minute. We just making coffee. But first I got to —"

"Just tell me one thing." She had to have some tidbit for expectancy to brood on. "Is it a big one?"

"Fifty by a hundred," he said, with pride. "The girl upstairs, Sonsie, she had twins they just put up a partition. Okay hon, I'll be right back."

He was gone quite a while, maybe to get the morning's rolls somewhere; she knew the routine. She stood very still, imagination brooding on one leg. David, off hunting locales with Barney, had no part in it. Inside, the building had a romantic darkness that smelled of good wood and stone, filled with overtones of what she had hunted for and now recognized, as if a voice had just echoed itself. "Beyond. We have come to it. Ond." Abovestairs, a whole context waited for her, people she would get to know, have coffee with. Except for Sonsie, the one leaving. Other people's *partitions* — she thought irritatedly; we shall probably have to remove it. Or — she could decamp, right now while he was gone, as she had sometimes done when left by a super in a place that was impossible — leaving behind her, she was quite sure, little surprise. People were so casual about these things, when where you lived, how, could change your whole life, the friends you met and loved, could mean almost everything. A lozenge of sunlight barred the door through which Maury had gone. She could step over it, annihilating at once a whole world she would never know. No one was keeping her here but herself, she thought proudly. But she would try to save in memory, to laugh over someday with one of the yet unknowns, this moment that still swung in the balance.

He was back, without rolls. "You don't mind, Ivan, he wants to see you." He led her into the street, around the side that she had not yet seen, where a line of ordinary windows was curtained in the harsh machine lace seen sometimes in the tenements near her mother's, sold by Yorkville drapery stores that still catered to the old, middle-European worker-taste, ugly but assertively clean. After there, a great, blind window went up for two stories.

"Old piano factory," said Maury. "Ivan made over the office his apartment, for the studio the delivery end. He saw the possibilities at a glance."

The door to the living quarters was opened to them

by a heavy young woman with the veal-colored skin of some Germanic blondes. Though Maury said nervously, "Helga, Mrs. Kostec, the young lady," she let them pass without a nod, down a long hall, past as many newly partitioned box-rooms as could be crowded into a space originally several fine ones, but even hurriedly passing, one could see that no starkly spatial drama was here intended, but its opposite. In the last one, a three-piece suite in eggplant mohair lay like boulders grouped around the television, on the wall above them a flight of wooden bluebirds. Only the kitchen was ample enough for all the happy leatherette and chrome needed to hold its special tide of gimcrackery. Its owner spent time in Woolworth's, with a sharp eye out for the inorganic and the double-functional — plastic whizamoroos which held clothespins, gingham dolls that were potholders, donkeys with china cactus in the saddle, plus a few showpieces of that streaked opaline or soapstone heavy in which "Under-a-dollar" hunted the art form.

Liz had seen such rooms before, but never among "artists," and never in lofts. Turning, she saw the woman looking at her with stolid satisfaction; this was what she scrubbed and bought for; her life was an open book. Short-necked, small-eyed, she looked indeed like the ruffled lady-porker in an old German morality tale, from Mrs. Jacobson's own childhood, that Liz had always hated having read to her. She was "the pig who was neat." Yet, behind the door at the kitchen's end, there came a steady sound Liz thought she knew — the knock of a mallet being used. Maury opened the door.

The high room, tawnied with dirt as the walls were, was impressive. Cables and winches hung from the ceiling, recalling what a large-scale craft had once been practiced here, one so lucidly near the good and ultimate — after all, pianos. Against that classic dirt, the tombstones which lined the floor in businesslike rows of dull granite, smartly polished moss-green or ham-colored marble, were ranged as they would be in any monument works on the outskirts of Queens, and it was like outdoors here, in this stone-harbored cold. Back of some unfamiliar machinery, several busts lay unpedestaled, one a copy of the Houdon Washington, and in a corner, a seven-foot saint in the style of Mestrovic bent ram-curls over smoothly flowing clasped hands. The man who regarded her, in his glove a power tool with a dangling cord, was covered with dust, from khaki cap and jacket to trousers stuffed in the tops of shoes — higher than the soft desert boots of the art students — ending in steel safety tips such as workmen wore. Even his beard, no silky, random bush of devotion but thick and squatly trimmed, was dusty and looked wool-warm. Despite this, it gave his face no majesty; she liked the man coolly staring at her no better than his Mestrovic. Nevertheless, if Maury introduced her as a sculptor, she would die of embarrassment. No one she knew worked directly in stone.

"Ivan, this is Liz." Maury pushed her a little ahead of him.

She smiled a weak hello. The man, Ivan, appraised her slowly from head to foot, until she could almost see herself in his calculation — hairdresser's bob, good coat and shoes, sweater and graduation pearls, in her ears the only sign that she might be not quite of these — Mr. Pagani's astute gift, dangling it was true, but gold. His eyes reminded her — of whose? Then it came to her — of the lady-porker's, his wife's. He nodded once, twice, not imperceptibly, over her head, at Maury. Then, without a word, he turned to his work. He had seen her possibilities — at a glance.

Maury was silent until they were again inside the other part of the building. "See, didn't I tell you? You want the place, you're the one." His puckering smile was jaunty, but his cheekbones had gone pink. "Come on up now, I'll show you."

She cast a look over her shoulder. "Not exactly wordy, is he."

"One must respect he's such a hard worker." It was said staunchly — a maxim that increased his own credit.

"They don't seem much like artists to me. Not the ones I know." As yet, she really knew none except the teachers at the League and her own crowd of would-bes. Yet that they existed — and according to the strict category of her own maxims — she never doubted. Somewhere they brooded, orbed above the bourgeois on some high Olympus toward which she must push her own orb. They were not the pigs who were neat.

"Now, don't you go sounding like the rest, like Sonsie."

"I hope the rest are more friendly." Following him up the dark spiral, she paused on the first rung, feeling for a side rail. There was none.

"Oh they are. To me and Footie, they been wonderful." He peered down to where she clung, stock still, just above the first spiral. "'Smatter, you dizzy?"

"Is this the only staircase? Isn't it against the build — I mean, isn't it dangerous?"

"What was Spring Street like, hah, Rockefeller Center?

Here, do like me, follow the ropes. You'll catch onto it."

She groped blindly after him. The ropes, lost in the black, hung apparently from the polestar, but they held. Spirals above her, he waited until she climbed to his perch. Once they left the stairs, the landing was broad enough for one door — only one loft then, to a floor. He knocked. Footsteps came, but the door did not open.

"You dressed yet?" he said. "The girl is here who called." The door opened a crack. He leaned down — the person behind it must be small. "Okay, okay, give me Sonsie's key, hmm. On a string by the towel. And put coffee, hmm." They waited until the key was handed him. "Put coffee, Fyush," he said softly to the crack. The door closed. He turned, gaily swinging the key in a pinwheel. "Sonsie's the same as ours. We all got *substantially* the same layout here. Course they got *regular* dough, they done everything." He led her up another flight. "She took off with the kids, upstate to her sister's. She and Joe split up for a while."

"Oh, too bad," she said, without sorrow. Enter the Paganis, smiling. Such is life.

"Oh he'll go after her, sooner later. He's one of these moody Irish." They stopped in front of a tangerine-painted door. It was lighter here. "Well, whaddya know!" he said. A large movie-theater poster was tacked on the door half sideways, as if flung there in haste. "Joe draws them, for a good living too, but he ain't proud of it, like her. Sonsie gets mad, she does this. Once she dressed the kids up in them." Inserting the key, he spelled out the glaring legend under the blown-up hero. " 'Flaming waterfront tale, watch the Man from Nowhere!' Hah, that girl!"

He opened the door, smiling with a proprietary air, then he disappeared from her consciousness. The loft was huge, huge and light — none in her crowd had any better, or as good. She even recognized it — one black wall, one white, one orange and one umber — the floating paper lamps, the drama of an emptiness freed from all but the prophylactic color — the orthodox void in which a soul, or perhaps two, might hang. The "Italian" café chairs were permissible, if one went in for chairs. Their owners might have been one of the crowd. It was a shame, of course, that what they had not done, their children had — a washer marring the somber umber, beautiful color they must have mixed themselves, a stroller and playpen stuck anywhere, a general fuzz-and-welter of the flannelly, plasticky world babies brought with them, the cute things one had to buy for them — melting this pure, stark order down to the coy. When her own time came — there was no excuse for allowing the candid shape of one's life to be so smeared. She walked the length of the place, tested the nursery partition with a knuckle, and passed on. Already she saw flaws in the way these people had managed the total space, and was annoyed at their possessions for still being in it, occupying what she yearned to be alone with, and already felt to be hers. On the far wall, bookshelves framed the window that took up almost all of it. A three-foot high, ebony reproduction of an African fertility goddess stood on one of them, the blind ellipse of her face pointed at a pile of Little Golden Books, her belly prolapsing toward the room. In the window, a central blue pulsed and changed like a flaw that would not be downed — the river. "Oh!" She stood there for quite a time.

"Seen enough?" Maury said softly. "Okey-doke. Now come on down to our place." At the door, he paused. "Funny. How all the way up the same layout, people did so different. But this is the one for me. We'd a had what to spend — this is the one."

"Do you all have the river?"

"Only from here on up. We get mostly the viaduct, but still high enough to be sunny. Of course, ours isn't so fancy — Kreisl gives only the stove. Less stairs to climb, cheaper. Otherwise substantially the same."

Going down the one spiral flight, she swung herself hand to hand along the ropes, with gusto.

"See you caught on."

She nodded, already hearing "Ropes! Only Liz would discover — !" and her modest "Wacky, isn't it. You'll catch on."

He knocked at the door again. "It's us, Few."

The opener of the door kept behind it. Urged past it by Maury, she was at first aware only of the room, the same indeed as above, but so bare that what it contained only niggled on its space, making it curiously smaller. When so little was owned as here, possessions could be left about in the true carelessness, in no hope of how they looked, what they were. Facing her was a small "center of activity" as the kitchen ads called it, containing a small stove (Kreisl gives it), a hodgepodge of tables, boxes, shelves that served variously and quite clearly for cooking, eating, dressing table (the one with a towel over it and a box of Kleenex). One could live here — there were probably all the necessities, a place to hang clothes in some corner, bed and bedding perhaps behind that screen; one was satisfied of this without interest to scan, render judgment as to just how clean it was or tangled, whether arrangements might be bettered. Once one got the hang of where things were, one could live here. That was all. In this small, decisive realm, there were no effects to abjure. This left the persons in it — its owners — pitilessly exposed, without possessions to speak for them. Although, in its way, of course, their realm spoke.

When she looked up, its owners were standing as if they knew this, their hands joined against her. The girl in the arch of Maury's arm stood revealed — that was her posture — as very short, reaching only to his armpit. This enlarged him.

"Footie, meet Liz," he said. "Liz Pagani, sculptor."

"Oh n-not really!" she said. The room extracted this from her, handing it back to her as if it were her own six-year-old shed tooth. "Not yet."

"Who's *yet*," said Maury. "And this is Footie, Fyush, Few — actress!" The girl nodded, with a set smile for the height he had given her, one hand spread on the chest of her jumper, a "gray sleeveless" much the same as Liz had worn to her own wedding. Her hair was long too, but its scanty, natural carrot had been slicked back to a knot at the crown, slanting cheekbones already broad, further widened by the way she had outlined her eyelids. She had the blunt muzzle of the plain redhead, the tiny, membraned, pink nose. When her lids were lowered, as now, two Japanese fish swam there, their tails curled at her temples. One was slightly smeared. Her free hand crept to it, then rested again on her chest. This thrust her hip out. "Pleased."

"I'm awfully sorry to bother you," said Liz.

"You nut buthering. We gut to show it." She spoke from pursed lips, in the voice of a person accustomed to comments on its lowness. Glancing at Maury, she gave a quick, gulping shrug. "We gut."

"Oy, good, you made coffee." Maury patted her shoulder. Her head went way back, to look up at him. Walking past her to the coffeepot, he strode.

Left behind, the girls nibbled glances at one another. Last year, sitting opposite in the subway, their eyes might have sistered each other. Footie wore the regulation sandal, thonged between second toe and long. Liz's feet squirmed in her shoes. Under those feather-fish eyes, more female prescient than Ivan's, she saw her fitted coat, bought in at a sale by a mother who carried her daughter's size in her head everywhere, put on her with a moaning "Not a copy of a Heim — a Heim. You could go anywhere." Anywhere but here.

Footie half-touched the smeared eye. Under it, above the cheekbone — yes, Hungarian — there was a puff of swollen pink. "We having coffee, miss. Wunt you sit down?"

"I shouldn't, really." She caught sight of the crate that served as larder. A protocol, thrust swiftly from nowhere, told her she must. It was all they had. Because it was what they had, she must. She felt proud of knowing how to act when confronted with the rock bottom, the true bareness. "All right — *thanks!*"

But as she walked behind the girl, an old-woman-of-the-sea sat on her own shoulders, making her see with her mother's eye, hear with her mother's ear. From Footie's topknot, one long lock dangled, Ondine. Hand to it as she swung her wide hips, despite her size she was not a dainty girl. She was walking as if she had heels on, and following the hard-apple curve of her calf, Liz saw her in high ones or in the sluttishly run-down French boudoir ones the tarty little bits from the public high schools wore, her hair not as now, in the style that meant "art," but in the huge air-bubble fringe, skewed over the forehead, that meant "films" — stunted little girls who thought of themselves as heart-faced, built for diminutives — Footie, Fyush, Few — who could be seen any day in the year along the Fordham Road bazaars, as perhaps last year she had been, prancing along on their slum-bowed legs, in twos or threes or alone, but always in self-drama, dime-a-dozen, any day in the year. Then, she would have met Maury. Who had been "offered to work" by Ivan.

She wondered whether they were married. Then blushed — for her mother.

"I take it black," she said holding up the mug they had given her.

"So do we, so do we," they said politely. They had to.

They sat close together now, like two birds in the nest, on one box, and they had seated her opposite, on the one chair. Now they fell silent, leaving it to her, after all, the seeker. Their eyes frozen, unable to leave hers, they sat close, while she felt herself grow altogether out of scale looking in at them, at their nest.

"I could've filled the place, easy," said Maury softly. "Sanitation Day, uptown the good neighborhoods, what they put out you wouldn't believe. Sofas, even. But —"

"I din want." It seemed the first time the girl had really spoken. Her mouth hung open. She spoke to her navel, some intense tattoo she saw there. "I din want."

"Start once wrong, she says, you don't go back on it."
If it was her maxim, his staunch arm was faithful to it.

"Nut you culnt, but you woont." Fyush spoke as softly.
"Like Helga's it would be. Like your mother's."

"I get a break, you'll *still* have," he said. "Or even a
margin."

The word brought cold into the room. Their dialogue
was not for her. But when she put down her cup, they
joined hands again, against her.

"Are you — are you in the theater too, Maury?" At the
party where the green drink had been served, she had
learned that this was how it was said, never ever "Are
you on the stage?" Two young women, who, from their
patented hair and figures like wax melted down a stick,
she had assumed to be, had asked it of her — they had
turned out to be models — and two young men had murmured it, "You in the theater, dear?" their eyes meanwhile, like almost everyone's, on a girl, dressed like herself then, like Futtie here — who was. That girl, her
round, boy-cherub head shaven "for that part, you
know," had hung on no one's words, not even those which
fell from her own prison-pale lips like rare gravel, but
had seemed to be staring into a little cup where all the
neuroses in the room were gathered to hers, all around
her watching where she held it, hypnotically centered in
her stubby, yellow-stained hand.

"In? You could say it. I monkey lights. Only trouble,
I'm not in the union."

"It's very hard," said Futtie. "The thitter." Chin raised,
she smiled suddenly, past Liz's shoulder, across the room.

Liz turned, thinking a new person had entered it. The
long rear wall held a solid line of posters like the one on

the door upstairs. If she hadn't been led straight in, she couldn't have missed them.

"Joe saves them for her. All her favorites." At that distance, not all the tags could be read, but the billboard code held. All the way down the line, heroes chinned life in the raw, blockbuster beauties offered it, each glimpsed from a heaven of word-bombs, a star on each megaphoned cloud.

"Even, he made one up for her special. Just brought it in one night, you could have knocked us over. 'Here's Fyush for someday,' he says. 'As drawn by someday Joe.' What a guy! Except that it's Futtie, you couldn't tell a difference, it's just exactly! Only with a redhead."

Futtie gave a slight shrug. She gazed again at her navel. "The one at the end," she said.

It seemed, indeed, exactly like.

"You must be going to miss them," said Liz.

"To us, they been — like a family." Maury's head declined as he said it. "They split up for so long this time, it's just bad luck for us."

The three of them sat looking into their laps, in that pause which comes when the sad circumstances of friends are emotionally spoken of — to a stranger. The pause lengthened into what Liz had come to think of as the house-hunting one. It was the one that came when all the closets had been looked into with proper shrieks of embarrassment and demur, the unmade beds had been passed by, the half-eaten meal apologized for, the babies smiled at — when all too much had been seen. Then the eye of both parties averted, and even when buyer had mentally turned on his heel at first glance, now for a moment he rocked on an ankle to save face for all concerned, maintaining a look on his own that said, "We-ell . . . " I'll let you know. But surely *they* all knew she was taking it; Maury had known from the first; the coffee had been meant to, well, ratify it — their coming relationship. Though she was not sure they had too much in common, they were going to be friends of a sort — she was going to live here. That was really the trouble, they were all too young for this sort of business. They'd all been impulsively friendly in the quick way one's elders always cautioned against, and now they didn't quite know how to exchange money — between friends. None of them had yet acquired the hard business shell that made one able. She liked them the better — they all had this in common.

But when they seemed to flinch as she fumbled with her bag, it was really too much — too much theater. And too unfair, just because she happened to be the one replacing their Joe and their Sonsie — let them take a straight look at those friends of theirs. Nevertheless, she felt a flush rising. It was the way they were staring at her checkbook.

"It's only a — deposit account, not a regular." She flushed deeper, in anger at her own position in life — at her mother. They must not know the difference. Too unfair. "We're really just — on a margin ourselves."

"Ivan will cash," said Maury. His hand was still locked in Few's but he spoke away from her, to the side of him still free. Few was staring at her, Liz. "Make it out to Ivan Kostec." He spelled it for her. "That way he'll cash, give me my half. You don't mind — did I explain that? So I can maneuver. Ordinary, I wouldn't take."

"I *know*," she said, soothing, rounding the c, inserting

the amount in numerals. "Sometimes it just *helps.*"

"This way you could move in any time, see? Tomorrow even."

Fyush got up and walked away from him.

"Oh, we don't have to rush." Liz waved the check dry. "We've got Mother's place, the way I told you. I mean, I'm *mad* to get in and *start* of course, but I wouldn't want to push anybod —" She held the check out to him, with a smile. " 'Ve you any idea though? When they expect to get their stuff out? Or are they going to sell off?"

"Stuff?" he said. "Whose?"

Behind her, she heard the girl make a movement.

"Why —" It was absurd to be made to refer to them as if she knew them intimately. "Why — Joe and Sonsie."

"Oh, they don't sell anything off ever," he said. "With those kids, they're always *getting.*" His mouth opened. "Oh hon. Oh hon, you got it all wrong, Joe'll be back here, go on upstate for her. They always get together in the end."

"But you said there was an empty." She saw nothing but her own wail. "You *said* it."

She opened her eyes at the touch of his hand.

"Why sure, hon, hey Liz, sure hon!" His long face nodded anxiously, large eyes consoled. "Sure there is, there is one." He stepped a little back from her with a side movement of his hand, just a turning up of his palm.

Then, at once, at last she got it. Perhaps it was the way his head was bent, ever so slightly, as to a yoke.

Oh. She didn't say it aloud, just made the shape. That was all she could do, once she saw it, Ivan and his margin, her money, that would help "maneuver" them out of here. Half.

"Oh —" she said, when she really saw it all. "Oh-h-oh." They had been made to dig their own grave.

"You don't worry, please," he said stiffly. "We'll make out."

"Oh, the *bastard*." The shit. If David were here, he could say all the flat, level words that at bottom only stuck to a man when they came from the mouth of another. She wished him here not to defend them, for that was useless, but to defend her to herself, for what she already knew she would do.

"Now — you got no call to say that," he said. "He can help himself?" He drew his narrow shoulders together. "He knows we not — flop-artists."

"Oh no," she said. "I guess you're right, I guess —" She was afraid she was going to cry — if she said any more. It wasn't fair, she could see that, to take *them* to task, simply because she saw their little ovaled lives with more theater than they themselves did. Surely, it was better that they never do, that standing on their pretensions, they never see themselves as they were, as she could see them. She looked everywhere but at them — for they had been asked to dig, and they had done.

"It's the same layout," he said. "You could have just the same like them." He nodded encouragement, on his face that muteness deeper than personal sweetness or repose. Burro, bird.

She nodded back, but her muteness was not the same as his. They are a different race from us. They know what their chances are; they have always known.

97

"Even you have a head start on them, with the window wall. See? I took it all down to the brick."

"It must have taken you forever." Would he never be angry, beat his head against that brick?

"Even a little piece the river," he said. "You don't have to lean too far."

"Oh, please —" I cannot bear it. They are different from us. They are the meek. "Oh, please *don't!*" she said. "You know I'm going to take it."

She stood up. It seemed awful to her now that she had gone on sitting there — like a friend.

"I wouldn't have like them," said the girl. Turning, Liz found her close behind, leaning against the dressing table, chest outflung. "Like their place? I wouldn't have! Maury likes, because he likes *them.*" She took a step forward, another, in church rhythm. "What *I* would have —" She raised one arm in a prima donna gesture. One could see now that because of her short legs, she was perhaps very slightly — a misfit. The torso was normal, the arms too long, and against any backdrop, what occurred was that slightest shade of comparison, double-take of the eye, which made it comic. On the Fordham Road or any other, last year or next-as-might-be with her market basket, she would be merely one of the commoner forms through which life-in-general was transacted.

"I would have . . . here — an ochway." She spoke softly, in that woodwind voice with which women project draperies on a bare window, children pretend a house. "And here —" In that voice, sweeping that arm, she waved into being the proscenium arch against which her story and Maury's could best be acted.

"All right now, Few," said Maury.

"Look!" said the girl, addressing Liz. Her circuit of the room had brought her back to the dressing table. She removed the Kleenex from it, took one from the box and began wiping the table's surface with altar devotion. "She's a girl likes nice things, Maury," she said, staring past Liz like a somnambulist. "She's a girl likes things nice. I want she should see one." With a last flick, she whipped aside the towel that had hung on the table, concealing its upper portion. Freed of it, the table was revealed as mirrored both on flat surface and three adjustable portrait panels. But this was not the best of it. In the center, the middle mirror reversed itself to her touch, to magnifying, to plain. In it a woman could see herself too near, pitted as a desert, or — oh relief — far. Finally, the side panels, as she bent them in, out, were rimmed with small light bulbs. In the center of all these, to be trapped by them, a vision waited. At her finger on a switch, the bulbs went on, off. "Maury — he made me." On, off. "From a magazine. Maury, he can do anything electrical. Anything." On.

"Oh-h." In echo, she heard how versatile an oh could be.

"You like?" The girl came closer. They were near enough, if of a height, to have seen the lights reflected in each other's eyes.

"It's — lovely. It's just right." It glowed in the room like a little fireplace of ego, and burning, it warmed.

"Even Sonsie, she don't even use make-up — she wanted."

And no wonder. — Until now, she had never known she wanted a dressing table. It wasn't just a miniature stage — of vanity. A woman didn't have to be an actress to crave it. She understood her mother's phrase, used on the most peculiar objects. It was a perfect thing of its kind.

"Sonsie, she was even going to offer Maury — to make."

The girl looked up at Liz. Was *she* offering — or did she only want to see what was hers, reflected?

Lowering her eyes, Liz saw the check, still in her hand. She felt the craving between her legs, almost sexual. For it — that thing — she would shame herself. She would exchange money for it. She would take advantage of her position in life.

"Whyn't you tell me?" said Maury. "All they did for us. I would have made for her."

"I —" said Liz. I would buy it. "If —" she said. If you want to leave it here. It was the other girl who saved her.

"I know." Even with Few's head held so high, it was hard to say where those fan-eyes were looking. Sauntering past Liz with a hip-thrust, she held the door open for her. What a help women were to one another! "I din want."

At the door, Liz stopped. Fyush was standing just under her own poster.

"Oh, so that's what it stands — your name, I mean. *Footie, Fyush* — I couldn't think what —"

The girl nodded. She looked over her shoulder at the twice-the-size-of-life head on the poster, her neck flung back in the same arc. "Fyutcher," she said. If it hadn't been for the legend blazoned above her, the word would have remained an enigma. "Future Foley. My stage name." Her face softened with the wonder of it. "Fyut-cher."

Maury stretched an arm behind her. Very delicately, as if not to offend, he slipped the check from Liz's hand. "Well, 'bye, Liz. See you in Schenectady, hmm? And good luck!"

" 'Bye, Maury, 'bye —" But she simply couldn't bear to — just leave like that. "Oh — I don't want —" she said. "I mean — we're all just starting out. We're all the same age. Isn't there something *I* could — I mean — what can *I* do!"

But they knew her meaning better than she did. They drew together, bird to bird. "Don't you feel bad about it," said Maury. "It can't be helped you was the one."

Outside, walking to the subway, she found the direction at once. She seemed to herself on the strait path marked off for her by whatever it was she couldn't bear to define. Now that the pair were out of sight, the terrible embarrassment to be felt in their presence was at least receding. It was too painful to be made to be audience to the stage set of another's fantasy, *in* it, like a god almost, all the time knowing what really waited for them in the wings. Especially with such as Futtie of course, could one see it, not even needing to watch her herself, or hear her dropping her poor little near-obscenity verbs, that name. One had only to think of that other girl — the one at the party. As for Maury, his meekness was as much to Futtie as to life. If Futtie was angrier, it was after all more *her* plan. At certain levels of life far enough beneath one's own, the muddle became clearer. For if she herself, of an age with them as she was, young as she was, was able to see ahead of them, it was only because of her position in life — and this was embarrassing. "It can't be helped," they said — of things-in-general — not of their vision of themselves. "It can't be helped," one said to oneself — about them.

She passed a beggar without putting anything in his cup, never able to decide in time. This time, she went back, and dropped a quarter in it. He didn't thank her, for which she was somehow relieved. Her own father, a man of no unusual kindness, had never passed a beggar without giving. She hadn't missed him to any degree; though he had so exactly shared her mother's standards, he had never made her so angry. "Such is life," he had been wont to say, "such is life in a great metropolis!", this in as lighthearted a refrain as the ditties he sometimes hummed, from the operettas of his father's day — *The Chocolate Soldier, The Merry Widow*, Balfe. Perhaps it had been some catchword of his own day. The harp that once through Ta-ha-hara's halls — such is life. But once, when out walking with her, he had done both together — dropped his quarter in the cup and then, passing on, had said it, almost hummed it — "in a great metropolis" — in that same mild tone. She had held it against him ever since. It had seemed to her indefinably callous of him — to have done both. Perhaps it was callous of her to remember him best by it.

That was what she held against the couple back there. Life-pity — they had made her feel it. In the great metropolis of life that stretched before her, there was a pity to be felt for people over and above their situation, inextricably tangled with themselves, yet not themselves. The two back there were the first of her own age whose life she could see before them, as not utterly clear perhaps, but surely not to be as they planned. Until she got far enough away from them and their bareness, deeper, ever deeper into the good thick weaves of her own life, this is what she would remember them for.

Seated in the subway, she began to gather those to her, around the loft. If it was not the one above all but the compromise one below, from which one had to lean for one's bit of the river, now that it was hers, she could weave rapidly round its flaw. A dozen plans for it occurred to her and she moved easily among them; she knew her tastes better now, and already saw herself trooping through the stores, tracking down her forevers. If she had a certain quality to her life, in it, she could compromise, still make the shape to suit her. If she made a certain shape of her life — she could live.

So, when David came home, he found her waiting there to tell him. She was not to be teased on her enchantment with the place, her sense of its fitness for them — which seemed to him exactly the same as she had had for the last one. At least, he saw no difference in her. By evening, she felt none. When he saw the place next morning, he agreed that she had had reason. It was swept very clean, beautiful in its bareness, nothing in it except the stove. To inquire who had lived there before did not occur to him; he was beginning to leave these things to her. So, she did not tell him. For the first time in their lives, she kept such a matter from him. It had been the first time, in any of the transactions of her life, that she herself was not the innocent.

5

After the crowd had gone, hallooing down those stairs, their hosts turned on the dark landing like parents at a christening, first to each other, then to look in at their prodigy. Such a pother it had been, and on their first night here. But now they were confirmed in possession, together with it now an image in the eyes of others. For weeks they had worked at the place while staying on at Mrs. Jacobson's, Liz resolved not to enter until all was perfected. To him, she had been obsessed, flying up from bed in the morning, working until past midnight, lips dry, hair hanging, until he shook her to a stop and then woke her again on the way home in the subway, never really at rest unless she was in the place, except perhaps in her furies of purchase in between. It was now as done as he cared about. He hadn't particularly cared about the party after all — he and Barney were so busy on the fringe of a wonderful idea. But now that people had seen the place, it looked different, even to him. It was in effect. The phone, installed that day, crouched like a cat in its corner. And now the two of them were here. Standing in the door, a light desire blooming along his arms, he waited for her. She remained on the landing, looking in. "They liked it, don't you think? They said they did."

"Why shouldn't they? You've done wonders."

The crowd, usually hailed to a place at once, often helping later, had not been allowed in here until tonight — Liz, with a sequestered passion that was new to him, had kept them off. But this was what they always said to each other, even if they were in a way congratulating themselves. It was the formal recognition of what spiritually joined them, and so it had been said, with the slightest change, tonight. You must have done wonders, they said.

"I?" She swung a rope from hand to hand.

Was he accused of not being too much present in spirit? "Well — it was you, really."

"I wanted it to be." She said this calmly enough, winding the thick hawser round her wrist like a bracelet. "I hated having to use — those people." They had discovered a race of nonunion plumbers, decayed carpenters, *sub rosa* jacks-of-trades, usually alcoholic, often subhuman, whose custom it was to work for "the lofters," as these people called people like them. "Having to direct them. Like having servants, almost. I know the kids thought so."

"Well, of all the artsy-craftsy," he said. "I don't see any of them spinning their own cloth. Just because they have more time than — or less money. Hell, not even that's true — aren't Dil and Beatty just back from the Grand

Cayman? All very 'on the road' of course — freighters! And rucksacks."

"Oh, David." He could still make her laugh.

"Hell, we had to get it done, so's we could get on with our real jobs. Now we're free of it, aren't you glad?"

"Mmmm." She regarded the rope on her wrist.

"Just because, to tell the truth, they've nothing else to do. Fringe-artists like Beatty and Dil."

"Oh, David." This was disloyal. The crowd was against too many things not to be very pro-themselves.

"Well, they are. They'll be leading the life of the artist when — when our grandchildren have gray hair."

She had twisted the rope on the other wrist. "Won't — won't we?"

"Oh, Liz," he said. "You've been as itchy, all this month. Listen, we're in huh, the way you wanted. And out of that china shop, your mother's." He skittered away from that. Though she hadn't replied to her mother's recent letters, she had been annoyed with him for mentioning it. The subject of her mother was still to be avoided — he kept forgetting. For he and his father wrote regularly, were as close as ever. "Listen, they loved it. Come on in."

"I know they did. They were even envious."

"Oh, why should you care so much what they think!" he said. "I don't."

She turned toward him then. "I don't *want* to. I wish — I wish I didn't care about the place at all. That's what I wish."

He reached her in a bound. Gently he rubbed a finger on the downy bit under her chin. No, she wasn't crying, not quite. But he would have to look in there as she was looking, try to see that fifty-by-a-hundred arena as she was seeing it — if he cherished any hopes, tonight, of getting her to look at him. And his hopes were of the highest; he was beginning to know how these matters went and even to enjoy it, suspecting that she did too — these variations of the original wooing, new positions halfway between drama and silence, between love and jiujitsu — that a married couple could practice without lechery. Marriage reportedly confused a man, making him glad enough to pedal forty miles a day between him and his home mystery, but this was the smoking-car version — it was not turning out so for him. His marriage was daily clarifying his life and his work, or leaving them free to be. During the party, for instance, he had taken movies of the crowd, mostly because he was always taking movies now, but meanwhile wishing that they would go home early, leaving him to make love to his wife. And now that he held her, waited for her, his mind dallied with the film he had shot this morning, would shoot tomorrow. Between the two, he had been powerfully elated all evening. Life ahead was to be had for the leaping — as she was. No doubt it had to do also with their at last being here. For, certainly, he had everything he wanted at the moment, and everything he had was in its place. Over her head, he looked in at it, taking it in as she must mean it to be, noting how she had set color against color, height (of partition) against darkness, breadth (of shelf) against light. The whole setup shone and receded, in a self-contained span that even nagged at him familiarly. "You've certainly got the knack," he said. From his chest, the word was spat back at him.

"I mean — I see what you mean by basic areas. You've certainly got — that feel to it. Basic." Her word, it should mollify.

From her twitch, it hadn't.

"You know," he said. "Food, Love, Music. Work — which is Art. And Sleep. Which is after all, back to Love."

She was not to be nudged. He withdrew his hand from any suspicion of it. When she wished to be taken seriously, nothing made her angrier than a suspicion that she was merely being taken.

"I mean that, seriously. It's really a wonder, how you've kept all the — issues — so simple. Why, you know — it looks like one of those seventeenth-century masques, like a program for one. You know. 'Enter Music left — with Lyre.' Or a twenty-buck piano." She had painted the old upright gray, gilded the scrolled stand. " 'Enter Food, back to audience.' " The food counter was reversed. "And now . . . let me see. I'd hate to think that sofa represents Love, even to old ladies. I think it represents Us, to Them." They had finally spent the gift certificate from Mr. Pagani's old cousins, drawn on the most modern furnishing store on Long Island. "And finally —" He surveyed it carefully.

The toilet, screened with that Moorish-style cutout to be bought anywhere, made a nice hutch somewhere between modesty and sense, not unlike a sedan chair. All wall surfaces had been spray-gunned with a misty recipe borrowed from Barney's camouflage-unit days — his own sole contribution. All the rest, brooded over as if she were giving birth to her own fantasy, was hers. Its charms, rather changeling for a man to spend twenty-four hours in — but then, he would not be — were hers. Which was as it should be. The partition which reserved her studio space was spartan enough, the space itself still bare.

"Even Phantasy," he said. "You know. Spelled with a 'Phuh.' Why — it's a real fine little old-fashioned *grotto,* that's what it is!" He was delighted with himself; in the semi-dark, his glasses slid down. The place probably harbored all sorts of other little arrangements, privately pleasurable to her, sensed only in the ways she paused here, mulled there — which unless she pointed them out, he would not be able to see at all. But if a man's farsighted scope made it harder to see up close — he would not say trivially — the way a woman did, he must narrow his focus enough at least to honor that — what she saw, or thought she saw. He grimaced his glasses back, and permitted himself a delicate squeeze. A vibration answered them.

"Issues?" she said.

"Areas," he said. "Areas." His fingers had already told him the vibration was wrong.

She disengaged herself from his arms. "Keep looking. Not at me."

He obeyed.

"And keep talking."

Uh-uh. Nix. A warning recall came to him, by sheer physical context, from his wedding night, of a moment when standing just so, holding the glass palette, he had rambled on in one of the flights that often took him when he was happiest, and had displeased — having just wit enough not to ask how. His father had used to kid him about these flights — "there goes David" — but had certainly never held him responsible for what he chanced to say in them. But women had such an extrasensory talent for putting distance between them and a man, even when they were glued to him. Then, swooping in near, they pounced.

"What else do you see?" From behind, his glasses were adjusted for him. It gave him the deserted, cloudborne feeling one had in blindman's buff.

"Well — for instance — those Russian-doll things you have in the kitchen, where'd you get the idea for those?"

"I saw them in the Soviet bookshop — that kind of frozen place on Lower Fifth, and I had to have them. I think I had a set once, as a kid. I sort of — recognized them. They won't do for a spice set, really. You can't see through them." The voice took him a moment to place. It was the way she spoke to other women.

"I think they're just fine, just fine," he said. He shouldn't have said it twice. She saw so near — without glasses. She saw so much that she confused things. "Anyway, it doesn't look anything like an apartment. Was there a particular effect you were trying for?" Oh, Christ. "Can I turn around now?"

"No." Coolly, so that he couldn't tell which it was the answer to — and about three feet away. She confused him.

"Anyway — it doesn't look like your mother's." Oh — double Christ. "Oh Christ!" he said, turning. "Let's go to bed."

She was standing not three feet behind him. Of *course* she was standing — even in the brown semi-dark, he saw the gold slippers she wore. But she had looped the thick rope about her neck this time. Above it and her black sweater, her face seemed to be hanging, tilted forward, the way a face would be if its neck were permanently bent by a rope that disappeared upward, behind it.

"What the hell . . . do you think you're up to!" His voice came out a snarl; he had scared himself. He shook her hard, her and his fury; they were the same. The rope flapped. She went limp, self-careless in his grasp, her face so unchangingly sad, as if any change in it were beyond her. "Say — isn't it about time —" he said, and of course he had already stopped shaking her. He even heard his own suddenly conspiratorial tone, as he had been hearing himself ever since the guests had gone. This often happened to him, happened between the two of them, after a party or when they had each returned from being with other people — for a while they continued to see themselves as mirrored in others. Often, he could see that she was doing the same — hearing herself — after he had been away the long day with Barney, as if he might be seeing her with Barney's eyes now, and must be won back. Whatever happened to him, happened to her of course. "Say, I know. It's about time for your period, isn't it. You're just about due."

"Just — about." She spoke as if her throat were sore from the rope. "But it's not that, really not." As he well knew, she disliked having him think of her as an object swung helplessly on that oestral tide, nor was he ever to baby her for it, or so she always intimated — while she was being. While she was — she had no humor at all. Afterwards, she often discussed very learnedly her own irrationality of the week before, describing how it came upon her, corroborating this from the lore of other girls, and all in the highest intellectual interest, like a bluestocking informing him of the habits of chorines.

But this was not one of those times. For now she fell forward on him, opening his shirt to rub her face there. "I didn't want it to be done, isn't that awful. I want to go on doing it instead. I'm not glad like you, I'm sorry." She raised her face. The tears were sliding down it in utter gravity and quiet. She made no show of them. He'd never seen anybody cry like that, staring — maybe the blind did. He'd never seen her cry at all. "*Instead*, see?" Her sob was the only sign that hurt was working its way out; her face was almost thoughtful. A tear slid into her mouth, unlocking it. "And so I'm scared."

"Why Liz. Why Liz, I've never seen you cry."

A storm of quite ordinary tears burst from her. When it was over he still held her, and they were still outside the door.

"You were crying in the strangest way," he said. "As if you didn't know quite why."

"I — do and I don't," she said.

"You looked very beautiful though. I'd have liked to have —" Taken a picture. But it was scarcely the thing to say.

She nodded. Gravity crossed her face, then puzzlement, as if she too would have liked to have seen for herself just what had been in that face.

"Imagine, I never saw you cry before. What a woman. And we've been married almost a year."

Almost a year. She didn't say it aloud.

They stood regarding it, the tide that swung them both.

"You should've taken a picture," she said, but there was no malice in it. She waltzed away from him, only to show that things were sunny now. "And we'll hang bells on all the ropes, when it's a year. Liz Pagani, housewife *and* interior decorator, hung by her own rooftree."

"No more of that." He held the door. "*In!*" He patted her fanny. "Bed."

She straight-armed him, locking her fingers behind his neck. "I love you," she said, conversationally. The role had changed now, and he was to know that, if not quite to what. "You're the mo-ost under-*stand*-ing —"

When he leaned into the kiss, her hand came up behind them, but this time, extending the noose to include him, she looped the rope around them both. "Cliché, cliché," he murmured, but loved her for it. She had caught his very thought, and was giving it back to him. Whatever happened to her, happened to him.

In bed, though she was cozy, she still wanted to talk, and he would almost settle for that now. The moment, so tenuous, had passed, exchanged for one in which to hunger briefly for a time when, stronger than anything it depended on, it would not have passed. He punched the pillow and lay back. It would return. Marriage gave that certainty as it took away the other — the pillow in place of the bare floor. From where they lay, he could see the whole joint in the paleness shed from the large pleated-paper globe, on an iron chain, that she had hung from the ceiling. It gave a poor light, but its occasional motion interested him — a shiver from a truck three avenues away, or from an earthquake half across the world?

"I *was* trying for an effect," she said, "but for the life of me, I don't know what."

Honesty was the role then. "Oh I can tell you. You wanted to bedevil me, until I made you cry. Women

often do that. At the end of the month." He lit a cigarette, in the pleasure of this. Beyond an affair in college,
from which no insights had been got or asked, and in fact
had ended in less than a month, his sole knowledge of
women came from her.

"I didn't mean on you. And you know it. I meant —"
She waved an arm. "This!"

"Oh that. Well I can tell you that too." He blew smoke
luxuriantly. "Women can't stand a pure globe. They have
to — what is that thing! — hand-pleat it." It was an aph-
orism worthy of his father. He made note of it, for the
next letter. Women can't stand a pure globe.

She sat up. "You don't like the lamp?"

Honesty was now basic. Once they had cried. "Like
I said before. I don't really care."

She made no immediate answer, staring at the long
expanse. Then she nodded. "Imagine!" She said it lightly.
"Imagine *us* having a sofa."

He was so touched at this that he put out the cigarette. She was trying to imagine herself over on his side,
look as he was looking.

"Not a real sofa." His voice soothed. "What's a sofa you
can't sit on. Only surreal." A six-foot-long, molded thing,
it was covered in some slick black plastic on which a
human being couldn't keep traction; unless he wore as-
bestos perhaps, inexorably he found himself at the edge.
And especially the girls, in the thin, sliding stuffs they
wore. He'd taken some angle shots of the crowd, as, two
by two or in groups, the sofa's unease crept over them —
like people gradually aware that they were conversing
on a raft. "A lot of these plastic things, they aren't really
objects at all. Just ideas for objects."

He sat up. "Say, I'm going to be able to use those shots I took tonight, say, am I! I haven't told you yet, what Barney and I are up to, have I." He kept his voice low, a secret agent for a far power — and that was the way he felt. "Well, come over here."

Crossing his legs, he made his old place for her; it was harder to do this on a bed. Cradling her from behind, he spoke over her head, drumming up his unseen for her. The light was just right for it, conveniently bad. "It's hard to say in words, but mainly we want to do a picture about people, mainly . . . by means of the objects they live through. You'll never see the people themselves, that is. A man and woman to begin with maybe, later maybe more, as we can handle it. You'll hear their voices of course, be able to differentiate them that way . . . see through the camera what the voice is seeing. That's the only way you'll know them. Each will be a . . . vortex, centered in the objects he lives through. Bounded by them. That's how the viewer will come to know his identity — the character's. And no character will ever quite know the other one's vortex. That'll be the *continuity* of it, d'ya see? It'll be like a succession of stills only all the time moving, never really still. God, film is wonderful! The way it's always moving. Barney and I are agreed on that, we could never work in any other . . . That's what kills us both . . . the way it moves."

"Now that we —" she cleared her throat, "now that I . . . have this all set up . . . I mean to work in stone."

Above her head, he nodded. "Not that the technique . . . it's the old first-person one. Even TV uses it, all the time. But sooner or later, they always pan in to the person, or from him. We won't. But how you'll get to *know* him! Barney says, what we're really trying to photograph is meanwhile. He wants to call it that. *Meanwhile.*" He laughed deeply, squeezing her. "It's new. It's never been done before." The words came out as the holy ones they were. "Let Beatty and Dil put *that* in their —" This was what they all kept themselves ready for, in the van. "Of course . . . it'll be something of a tour de force. We wouldn't want to do more than one that way. . . ." His voice trailed off.

"Smell the spring," she said. "Today was that first day, you know, windy, but the air just *reminds* you? I left the window open, you don't mind? . . . No, you wouldn't want to repeat. That's what I . . . what *I'm* so . . ."

"You don't mind?" he said. "That I'm keeping the dark-room at Barney's? It leaves *you* more . . ."

"If you lean out the window —" she said. "There's a little triad of lights down there — two down low, one high." She said it in the voice for secrets. "I think it's a boat. They came just after dark. They came just to-night."

"Yes, you framed the window," he said. "Yes, I noticed that." He cradled her gently. Quiet as they sat, a motion beneath, from the bedspring it must be, made him feel as if they were rocking.

"No, I don't mind," she said. "I like mine all in one place though, the house and — the other . . . All my things."

"It feels so good to tell you," he said. "I've been mean-ing to let you in on it before this, but you were tempo-rarily so — It's wonderful always to be able to talk like this. Other men's wives — even some of the kids tonight,

116

did you notice? To be able to talk together like this. It's wonderful."

"Look at that shadow," she said. "It's like a palm tree. I'm glad I left that studio wall bare . . . Oh darling. If we couldn't talk like this I would die."

They were silent in tribute.

He chuckled suddenly. "'Come into the Drawing Room!' Remember?"

"Sh-hh," she said. "It *is* a palm tree. I wonder if it comes every night. I wonder if it's us . . . Drawing room?"

"You remember. You said we were talking as if we were in one. On our wedding night. In the old place. We were sitting just like this."

"Shhh, don't move," she said. "We're in Florida. We're going to be in Florida here every night! . . . Oh, *were* we? No, I don't."

"Well, I know damn well I didn't dream it. You don't remember your own wedding night?"

"Oh — you moved!" she said. "Oh, it *was* us. The palm tree . . . Oh, that night, the public one. No, what I remember is — the first one. In my bedroom, at home. The real one. I remember everything in the world about that."

So must he, of course. His forefinger traced again the patch of down. But the memory that came of itself, without prodding, was always of the one she called with such disdain the public one, his long night's vigil. What she remembered best was the drama of her virginity and its loss, the same as any girl who had worn a bridal veil, the same as any girl.

He turned her face up to his. If he'd grown up with a

mother, sisters, perhaps he would know for certain whether a woman's face always looked so plumped and renourished after tears. He turned hers from side to side. Perhaps he would take much more for granted. "You've lost your house-face. D'you know that?"

"Have I?" Above her parted lips, her eyes looked back at him; they could be innocent; they could be frightened; they could be knowing. He hadn't an idea on earth of what they saw. He kissed them. The mattress springs shifted queasily.

"I remember the subway," she said.

"So do I," he said, in the greatest relief. "So do I."

On the same impulse, they lay back. Up on elbow, he regarded her. "Imagine," he said. "Imagine *us*, having a bed."

He put his face down on her stomach. Outside, in this end-of-the-island cove, the diorama of the world crept past them, its furnishings endlessly attitudinized. Inside even the quietest room, by the hint in the lamp chain, from the port-sparkle at a window, in the coil of a mattress, something shifted ground. Only they two stood firm. "We don't move," said the calm rise and fall of her navel, and his hands answered, smoothing, "We don't change." Only they two stood still, eye to Gargantuan eye. When the phone rang, he was already inside her; they were joined.

They hung rigid, under the affront of it, her neck arched. Once before, interrupted so, they had answered it, spending the rest of the day sheepish and reduced; they could not get back. Don't answer. But that had been the middle of the afternoon.

"Don't answer." Against his chest, her hands closed to fists.

The phone rang and rang; it rang.

"I — can't —" It was the long-distance ring. "— My father." By no will of his own, he was already outside her. Shrunken and cold, he stumbled to the windowsill where the phone was.

"California calling. Hold on, New York."

He already knew the worst, then. His father disliked the telephone, never used it merely for company or sentiment. Mrs. Jacobson called thriftily on Sundays from wherever she might be, or at the coastal dinner hour, as she had last week from San Francisco. It would be Jacques, on that death-call by whose prospect all his own dorm years had been haunted, during which he could always be depended on to run for any insistent floor-call the others ignored — "There goes Pagani again — who's the girl?" With luck, his father had not been alone.

Across from him, hiked up naked in the bedclothes, she questioned him dumbly and he nodded back. It was the call that, since his marriage, had not so much haunted him. His father would not have had him feel guilty for that, and he did not — only older — in a sudden acknowledgment of the way we all have to live. With luck, a friend would have been with him. With luck, it would be Jacques.

It was Margot.

"Hello? Hello. Hello, David." Then there was a silence, through he had already said hello and yes. Usually she burbled.

"Yes, Margot?" She had been at the house for the

weekend, as she sometimes was. Jacques sometimes drove her down from San Francisco. As luck had it, they both had been with him.

"I — hope it's not too late —" she said. "I thought — the party'd still be going on."

"No, they've gone." Even as he said the dull words, a heavy joy stroked him. "You're in New York!" That's all it was. She'd flown home.

"No — I'm . . . still out here." She paused. "Matter of fact . . . I'm down at Big Sur. We are." And she stopped again.

"Oh," he said. "Yes, Margot. Yes." The road to the weekend cabin was high over the Pacific and hairpin. He or Jacques had always driven his father there. It was a male place. And she did not drive. But now, she would have thought it a duty, as family — "Margot, please let me talk to —"

"I will. I thought maybe I'd catch Liz, first. And then . . . *she* could — I really *ought* to talk to Liz first —"

"Put Jacques on, will you!" He shouted it.

"Jacques? Why — Jacques's not here, David. We . . . I'm alone here. We came down alone. Just — just a minute . . . I guess I'm no good at this, after all . . ." She seemed to have left the phone.

He cupped his head in his hand, wondering how best to deal with hysteria three thousand miles away, death that far. There were neighbors down the road there, whose lights were visible, would be. Somehow that image brought home to him how far death was.

"No, she isn't very good at it. Hello, Dave," said his father. "How are you?"

"Fa —" He was able to make the right answers, noises,

in time. A lifetime with that casual voice now served him well. He was even able to send a reassuring nod across the room to Liz, crouched there. "Fine, Dad." He cleared his throat. "How are you?"

"Still a night owl. Hope we haven't — Margot insisted a housewarming was just the time to call you."

"Sure not. She want to talk to Liz?"

"Actually, *not*," said his father. "She just thinks she ought to." His words brought him almost into the room — his manner of saying, without dash, what often reverberated later as daring; the contrary look of youth given him by his silver hair. Over the very clear connection, his father now made a sound so slight that even the telltale wire could not quite calibrate it as chuckle or sigh, but David could see him as he might be standing, in the way that he himself was unaware of, that perhaps only his son saw — a sturdy enough body, almost too compacted and very slightly alop, carried as a body would be if it were a shield. "I'm no good over the phone," said his father. "And you'll get my letter tomorrow. So I'll be brief."

He was brief.

Just before he rang off, David roused himself. "Who drove you?"

"What's that?"

"Who the hell drove you *up* there?"

"Margot." This time it was clearly a chuckle. "She learned."

When he had hung up, he went over and sat on the sofa that could not be sat on. It slid him forward, coolly as a pinball machine, and he let it deposit him on the floor, where he sat with his shanks stretched nakedly in

front of him. If he'd had the will, he'd have got up on it
again and let it dump him even harder; he needed somebody to douse his head or bang it, or turn him ass-upward,
as his father had once done, when he swallowed the par-
cheesi button in the middle of a game. He sat there.

"Then he's all right then? That was him?"

He'd forgotten her, over there wrapped in her tepee
blanket. He nodded. In a minute, he meant to laugh.

"What's the matter, then?" When he didn't answer,
she came over to him, dragging her blanket behind her.
"Here, put something on then. You crazy?" He shook his
head weakly. She dropped on all fours, trying to wrap
the cover around both of them. He rose on hands and
knees to help her, the twisted blanket between them, and
for a moment they regarded one another over it, two
quadrupeds, their limbs moony in the stone-age light,
the brow of one of them knitted. She was getting ready
to be hurt at not being let in on it, not asked to join with
him against that enemy which waited always to separate.
He started to tell her precisely how joined they were now,
how related — and then he began to laugh. "Your father —" he said. "My mother . . . No . . . I mean *your*
mother. And *my* father —"

He sometimes forgot how quick she was, under all
that female miasma — or maybe because of it. "They — ?"

He nodded.

"Holy God," she said, words she never used. Slowly
they collapsed together under the blanket, which un-
twisted suddenly, as if wanting to help them huddle
under it, doubly un-orphaned as they were now. "*Ho*-oly
God!"

When they got into bed, shivering from the cold of the

floor, he put on his pajamas and sat back. Having gone to bed bare, as usual, she reached for his discarded shirt and slid it on. They sat pillow to pillow, not quite touching.

"Why do you suppose she didn't want to talk to me?" she said.

"Oh, I don't know." It seemed strange that she should ask *him*. "Maybe she just didn't know how to — maybe she was embarrassed."

"Why?" said the girl. "I'm not *her* mother."

They were quiet awhile.

"What did *he* say?" she said then. "I mean — how."

"Oh — he just sort of — said it. You know how — concise he is." How concise men are. It was because she couldn't be expected to know his father's code of it — which his son understood without exactly ever having been told — that there was no point in telling her. Those words were between his father and him; he even thought now that this was why his father had said them, to deny that anything had changed between them, their closeness. Yet his father's voice had had its own wonder — his father's son was not to be fooled. "The surprises keep on coming, Dave." He had repeated it, slowly. "They keep on *coming*." To me, his father had meant. To me.

She was waiting.

"Oh you know," he said. "He just said that — they were."

"He's very reserved, isn't he," she said thoughtfully. "I think he's the most reserved human being I ever —"

"Restrained. He's had to be."

"But you're not," she said eagerly. "I mean reserved. I think it's kind of wonderful that he managed to bring

123

you up that way in spite of —" She gazed at him, big-eyed. "Are you?"

"No." He smiled at her. "No, I'm not the least bit reserved." He sank back on his pillow, easing down in a straight line. She did the same on hers.

"They haven't got a thing," she said after a while, "in common. Not a thing."

"I suppose."

"He's so — sort of above things," she said. "And she's always running around after them."

"Maybe — she'll change." She had already. Seen, not through Liz's eyes, seen as someone's wife, if not quite yet his father's, Margot showed up as a woman whom all along they had ignored, clearly still a candidate as a woman. It was quite possible now to see her sexually, or see that a man could. He did not pursue this.

"I hope she — won't run him ragged," she said.

"Shut up," he said at once. "Shut *up!*" He found himself shaking. It was the first time he had ever felt a tinge of dislike for her.

"Oh Dave, I didn't — I'm sor —"

"I'm sorry."

They said it at the same time. They both were. Lips caught in teeth, they reached for hands, across pillows. After a long enough pause, he released her hand. He brooded. He grinned suddenly. "There's something we forgot about, they do have in common."

She wasn't as quick this time. "What?"

"Us."

She shrugged. "Oh let's — I hate people who say let's face it, don't you — but let's. They weren't thinking about us."

"They were alone," he said slowly. "I guess that's it. Both of them."

She weighed this. "They were alone before. And I'll swear my mother never gave a thought to — Well, maybe we introduced them. Maybe they got together over — I hope it's not *all* they have in —" She shifted quickly. "Anyway, it's just as well they're across a continent. From us."

"They want us to pay them a visit," he said. He turned to punch up the pillow. "You want to?"

"No!" she said at once. "I mean — after all, we just got this place — I — But if you think — You go, if you — I mean really . . . Dave?"

"I think I ought," he said. "I'll call them tomorrow."

"You're so much nicer than I am." She whispered it. "You want the truth, I think I really feel —" When there was no response, she inched forward, from her pillow. "I want to know how you feel. Not because of them." She disposed of them. "I want to — I have to know how you . . . feel. It might be about anything. It just happens that it's them."

He pleated the sheet. "Well, I'm used to worrying about him. I feel — you should excuse the expression —" He looked up. "I hate people who say that, don't you? I guess you could say my feelings are still — paternal."

"Oh, you're so smart," she said, but not as if it gave her joy. "We both are." She leaned back. When she next addressed him, it was over her shoulder. "You ever notice . . . when people really feel, they have to use cliché?"

"Or say nothing at all," he said.

"Christ!" she said. "Well, *we* certainly have *them*."

There was a silence.

"Maybe we both feel sleepy," he said.

"I don't, do you?"

"No. I'll turn out the light, anyway."

When she next spoke, she sounded as if her eyes were closed hard. "Still, it would be awful, wouldn't it, to live side by side, hardly knowing anything about each other, scarcely able to remember anything together. Never being able to — walk around in each other's minds . . . Dave?" Her voice had a break in it. "We . . . aren't beginning, are we . . . not to remember the same things?"

He closed his own eyes. "No."

"Then can't we talk about it. This. *Oughtn't* we?"

His slight movement, an ankle kicking out, brought his cold thigh against her warm one. He shifted it, away. "You mean, anything we think we oughtn't to talk about, then we should. Well go ahead."

At once, like a child given permission to speak, she fell dumb.

"Well, what's on your mind?"

"The same as — as on yours."

He stole a glance at her. Her eyes were open. She gave a flat sort of laugh, almost a cough, utterly unlike her. Or at least he had never heard it. "I suppose — she takes care of him. Of his health. What else could they possibly — Strangers!"

"We were — strangers."

"But we're young!" Her voice went high. She lowered it. "Besides, we were never —" She raised herself to scrutinize him through the dark, flopped back again. Her voice came even lower. "That's the way it's supposed to be. We have all our lives — to get to know." She lay back, stretching her arms above her. Again there was a silence. She broke it.

"What do you know . . . best about me, for instance?"

"I don't think that way."

"Don't you want to know what I — ?"

"What."

"That —" she paused. "That you always fall right asleep, after love." The merest whisper, it reverberated for some time.

As the darkness lessened, they could see each other. Noses, knees, toes pointed up, limbs articulated under the graven sheet, she lay like a thin crusader at his side, he at hers.

"When you were a kid —" It was her natural voice. "I suppose your father kept mistresses, or something."

"No! Of course not."

"How do you know? For sure."

"I never gave it a thought."

"Then, how *do* you know."

"How do you know. About your mother."

Under the marble sheet, she crossed a leg, as careful not to touch him with it as if it were bandaged. "Do you suppose —" She was trying not to whisper. "Do you suppose that they *sleep* together?"

"That's — their business. It's — not our wedding night." He sat up, clasping his knees. The idea that another generation had an emotional life of its own was shocking to him, far below the level of distaste. It vied with his own supremacy on the stage. Easier to dispose of it as she did, by mocking any thought that it might be a profound one.

She sat up too. *"Can* he?"

In the moment that he understood her wholly, he felt himself redden, tighten from scrotum up — as if she had asked this of him. In pure, blind answer, he slapped her full in the face. "To me," his father had said. "Even to me."

Then they huddled each to each, in mutual repair. Now it was she who was monosyllabic, he who grievously wanted to talk. The night was still black at the window, but they could now see the place clearly from their vantage point the bed, sitting next to each other as if it and the night were a stage they were doomed to until dawn. Deep in a self-hate he could not help her shake, she had said that she had deserved it, that she had been gunning for it all evening, then had fallen mum. He had brought them some of the leftover drink from the party, the green bottle over which, only yesterday morning, when he had plucked it from the shelf in the liquor store, they had both smiled in their old clued way, without a word. Only a far morning ago — and they themselves, standing as still as the grass on a windless day, or as the flower opening in a slow-motion film, had not moved an inch, of themselves. If there were only some way to warn her, each other, of that slow, expanding — bloom. He couldn't go beyond that, how he saw them both as all these past hours, playing about, with something most serious and theirs and still unknown to them — like two on a field somewhere, perhaps Africa, kicking back and forth between them a rock which, if they could only bend to it in time, they would see to be the Kohinoor.

"What I know best about you —" he said. At least he had got her attention. "I used to think it was because you were so fearless. But it was only because you were so angry, wasn't it. At your mother, her house, even about money. Even at — your own work. And now you're — not so angry, any more."

One shoulder flexed, neither acknowledging nor denying.

"And that's what scared you, isn't it," he said in a sudden flash. "Because you aren't."

She looked up just enough to look down again, like a woman interrupted at her ritual grieving over the dead loss in her arms, lifting her head just enough to nod at the comfort offered, and plunge again to what she held. Her hair was growing again to her shoulders as he had bidden her; she looked the same. He had a glimpse even of how women might live remembering best their losses, feeding on the intangible ones, living their lives by private stations of those very losses — of youth, of infatuation — which men, out in the public world, managed to hold up as gains.

The room stared him down. All these attitudes — they hung about in it like furniture. "I just wanted you to know," he said. "That I feel what you feel. That I see . . . what you see."

She smiled.

When he touched her, but only to comfort, she put a hard, swift hand on him. An hour ago, under that doubled image from the West, to touch had been gross — in sight of what he must still think of as those dark, northern wastes of parenthood where that other couple lay. Marriage now assisted him, with its simple favors. At the height of his pleasure, importance was returned to him; here he and she, not they, were in the van. In its declining shallows, he relaxed, still respectful of it. Often, after

129

they had done well, as now, she clasped her legs tighter, saying with a quirk that she wished she could carry him with her like this always, that they could walk about always the way they were now. Other times, as this was to be, they sank into sleep without speaking. He slipped away from her. Behind him, she stirred. "Remember," he thought he heard her say, "Remember the palm tree." He thought he promised; he was not asleep.

When she was sure he was, she raised herself on the pillow, into this hour's familiar cave. It was fluent with echoes. There was something in it that was new, but not wholly. After a while she spoke into it, to the dark. "There's something we don't know," she said into the dark. "About us."

6

Far below them, the immense of the Pacific moved its colors or lay still thereunder — a cruel green either jagged or icy jade, a blue dizzying ozone where must lie the navel of the Good, and a purple which should have been the utter profound and was rock. Year after year, the dreadful seaside painters at Carmel caught the three colors infallibly. No good painter ever tried. She and he had several times, in earlier weekends here, made these observations. Now they sat at breakfast before the open window, exchanging them without speaking. The cabin, of redwood and glass, had been first a movie star's hideaway, then a restaurant, and lastly, until Mr. Pagani had bought it years back, a boarded-up plateau for whatever gulls arrived that high, or eagles that low. At first, the heights here had terrified her. She had learned to turn her back on the ocean, leaning out the window on the garden side to steady her gaze on the foundation, which disappeared into the ground like that of any other house. The garden, set between it and the magnificently higher scar of the coastal road, had been reassured against the sky by shrubs and trees that pressed away from all but one glimpse of the sea, making an inland niche where one might rest from nobility. He had never made her feel that she must rest from his. They lived a quiet life together, never a sacrificial one on either side. Sometimes, with the fractional inner gasp of those whose lives have been halved, she was thrust not back but out, barely able to believe in this half — its reality went so deep. But they were not given to naming their state, any more than he the common enough disease he suffered from. In it, she and he were equal invalids just emerged from the examining room, stammering out to themselves, "Ah. So that's what I've got, is it!" When they were at the window as now, however, she always fixed her eyes, with a steady, humming sense of ownership, on the blue.

"When he comes," she said, "I'll make myself scarce, eh."

"It's us he'll be wanting to see." As often, he was laughing at her. "Besides — where?"

Large as the room was, even sumptuous in plan because of the movie star, it had the atavistic hut-comfort of everything provided for in one. Having been a restaurant had been good for it, leaching it of the personal. Leftovers were its comforts, the richest from Jacques's travels, but even these had the no-nonsense, quiet, saddlery tones of male usage. The long-haired Anatolian blanket, hanging from the gallery where David would sleep, hung there to air; shorter-curled Greek rugs, also goat, warmed the tiles. Presumably the air cleaned the place, working like a good slavey night and day, or else perhaps, now and then in their absence, the place shook itself all over, honest creature in its stall, and lay down again. She never thought of it as a house.

There was all outdoors, of course.

"No," he said, anticipating her. "The way you look at grass, very respectful. 'This is grass.' And the way you look down there — sideways. And the way you look at the hills — I'm not yet sure what that is. But outdoors, you're still a visitor from the city. And visitors must always be accompanied. It's only polite."

She grinned. She was his company. In the long night ranges, he often slept now. "The hills? I'm thinking, like any city person, that they're only scenery, with the world behind them really — I have only to peel them back. That's what going to the country meant for us. Two weeks of deep breathing and hard staring — and something tangible to come home with — like shells, or a tan."

"Going to the country." Behind them, the hills advanced like golden bears whom only an ocean could stop, down to a water-edge that farmed torn cypress and pelicans — she thought of this as "countryside."

"Go on," he said. "Go on, about your childhood." What she went on about was secondary, though she could entertain him there also. But it was her constant domestication of the awesome that most often moved him, never failed to salve; he had perched for so long on the nether lip of awe. To do this was her lore, sifted from kitchen middens she often did not even know she was sifting — her mother's and her mother's mother's lore.

"I'm beginning to feel at home on that road," she said.

"Though they'd never have believed it. Nobody drove. One uncle, from Hollis. Easters, he used to drive in for the whole pack, dinner, the cemetery, and return us. Later on, Ernest drove, of course — and the school taught Elizabeth. But lots of the people in the city were like that. Then."

"If you can drive this road, you can drive any road in Europe," he said, "even the Grand Corniche. I don't know about Yugoslavia. But all the rest." He repeated it with savor. "All the rest."

"You want to go, we could," she said. He often talked to her about Europe, what she would see, could do there. "We could take a boat." Then, perhaps a cottage. From cottage to cottage, slowly. Travel was harder on him than he would admit.

"Someday," he said. "For you must see it." When he could spare her, she him. For she would not go without him. He was saving it for the time when she would have to spare him, in the way a clear-eyed old man might make what provision he could for his young darling, setting up the long Europe of time when he would be gone.

She kept her eyes from the purple, steadily on the blue. "To see us — together. That's what he's coming to see? So quick?"

"He's doing some film he's all excited about." He was peeling an orange. "Wants to tell me. But I suppose the main reason is — simply because I asked."

"Because you asked," she said, on a sigh. "So simple."

"I never allowed him to do much for me," he said. "I couldn't afford to. But now, because of you, it's no longer crucial. So I can."

"So now you do this for him too," she said, with a smile

that covered no jealousy. Rather, it kept her from dwelling, even for the most fleeting instant, on whatever he was planning to do for her.

He leaned forward in his chair. "It's so still, today. I prefer it angrier. When I can see it moving." The chair had been his mother's. It was the only thing here that was much his, and then only because he sat in it, since it was high-backed and straight. It had no other distinction. Even she had noticed it merely because it was so un-Californian, belonging to none of the many modes here. It had been looking at one ocean or another for over seventy-five years now, he had told her. That was why it had seemed natural to bring it down here. "Let's go into the garden, shall we? Where we can watch the road for him."

"I like this place though," she said, when they were settled again, their backs to the trees with that one crack of sea. "This house. It makes me feel like a Hindu."

"Explain!" he said at once, always glad to be pulled into the delightful maze of her processes, a game that never left one as depressed as gin. They had not yet played the latter.

Usually she humored him, but this time she was direct. "No possessions. Isn't that what they aim for? Nothing here belongs to me. Not a thing. It's very restful." She gave a little blurt of a laugh. "I'm absolved, you see. Washed clean."

"It's no sin to love the particular," he said. "That's your lore." It was the first time he had said the word so often in his mind. She paid no heed to it.

"You are hurt then," he said. "Because she isn't coming."

"A little. I'd like to see her. But I suppose it wouldn't be of much use, she still has her old image of me. She hasn't given *me* up, that's for sure."

"Maybe it's still of use to her," he said, wondering whether the girl still did those figures of exaggerated wax.

"To stick pins in? Maybe." Her smile was wan. "All things considered, maybe it's better just now to keep the four thousand miles between us."

"Three," he said, tongue in cheek. The orange lacked only the eighth petal now. "Anyway, her image of you certainly isn't mine."

"She wouldn't see it. Or that it's what helped me give her up." Hair in topknot, anxious eyes rounded, she regarded him, short-waisted as a Bouguereau in her starched "country" dress, one slippered foot stretched as plumply on its straw cushion.

"She'd see us together too." The orange was finished. "That might shock her."

"Are they shockable?" There was the ghost of satisfaction on her face. "Girls her age were brought up not to be. She was."

"Not by you. And that's what counts. The continuity." He set the rosetted orange before her.

"For good or ill." She smoothed the grainy, outer side of one thick petal with a suddenly intent finger. Once, tapping the lushly granulated gold skin, she had remarked that the Italian gardener's new Sunday shoes were certainly made of it. She was always finding these analogies, compiling these notes on the basic stuffs of things. And as a woman who could squeeze raw, dark beef and offer him the blood to drink, or swab — with gentian violet — the impetigo scabs on the gardener's child's bottom, her acquired blushes concealed a dry inability to be shocked. Women were like near-sighted children, in their knowledge of surface detail, near-artists in their love of it. "Exactly!" he had caught her murmuring to herself over the Greek rugs. It had been their first weekend here, and he had had to probe for it, already knowing that speech was what embarrassed her, not the actions of love, never the substance. "Well if you must know," she had said, running her hand first over the blond rug then on the dark, chin tilted, cheeks pink, the voice dryly at variance — "Pubic hair."

"Why she's really very much like you," he said. "I've only just realized it."

"Oh Lord, she couldn't bear that!" she said, but she was already radiant.

When the phone rang, she was just reaching again for the orange.

They stared at one another. The phone was almost never used locally. Their only call had been to David, two nights ago, his answering call, the next morning, the only time it had rung.

"But he should be here by now," he said. "If he borrowed Jacques's new car, as he said he would, and that plane — got in on time. That car drives like the wind."

"I know."

"Hurry," he said. "I can't." She was already gone.

And David drives like the wind, his heart told him. As he waited, he wondered whether anybody ever gave anybody up. He heard her voice calling then, saying that it was all right darling — that it was only Elizabeth.

He waited more tranquilly now, his breath tapering down in the rhythm of a dog lingering to crouch over a find, circling once or twice back to it, finally regaining its master's side. Maybe the girl was coming after all, and the alignment they all now found momentarily queer would have a chance to work itself out in some amiable barn dance, alternately paired-off and four-square. As yet, he couldn't see the two women pairing off into those confidences supposedly natural between parent and child. But neither did he see the allegiances between any of them as necessarily shifting to what might be dangerous, merely because, as in some old riddle, his son's wife was now his wife's daughter, her daughter's husband her husband's son — the two younger ones skimmed on ahead of them, traveling their own center, just as before. What it had done for him, perhaps, was to bring him in even closer, in the role of observer already given him years ago by the heart that had given him so much. As for David and himself, once he might have said that the time of parallel confidences was over, terminated on the night he had discovered how ill he was. Now he would set it farther back, to the farthest vanishing point of not yet really having begun.

He glanced over his shoulder at the Pacific, the one lucent line of it through the in-powering trees. Short as life was, surely the continuity was long enough, spiral and devious enough for even this to happen, in time? The surprise of Margot had taught him once and for all that in some happy behind-the-scenes, parallels might be forever meeting as well as parting. And the recognition of this was the joy of having sons and daughters, the forward joy. It could happen that they would turn, or arrive — to see what he saw. It could happen at any time.

He sipped his coffee, his dog trotting nicely at his side. Probably the girl wasn't coming after all, the two women were making such a thing of it on the phone, even working it all out perhaps over that disembodying wire others found so much more helpful than he. He much preferred to see the complete body of this our life, all the particulars in which it manifested itself over and over, all the tints and murmurs in which it repeated the obvious — and subtly deceived. Not that those who best guarded the repetition necessarily saw it — any more than a good midwife had to know why babies were born. Margot, so grounded in it, never gave a sign that she saw. By now, those two in there might even be quarreling, each from her parallel. Maybe the daughters, in the wide, abstract lens of youth, briefly saw a repetition they must guard against, but the mothers who guarded it never did. Might be, they couldn't afford to.

Picking up another orange, he rubbed its plump, cordovan gold and held it up to the break in the hedge where he could see the horizon, so clear in this air that the fruit, if dropped, would surely break a great hole in that flat plaque of sea. Men and women both, he too, were confused by their love of the particular, which all their ethic, East or West, taught was sinful. Once he too had thought of it as the surface frivol of existence. He saw it now with the hungry reverence of a man who had not too much time for it (and had had to keep this somewhat more steadily in mind than most) as what kept men from flying off the planet altogether, or a man from sinking into the saw-toothed fires at his own core.

Above him, the thin line of the coastal road was visible for some miles to that north from which David would be coming, then, as it approached, seemed to brim over its own escarpment in a great swing toward him and away, disappearing onward around the mountainside on its curving way south, the narrow quarter-mile track down from it to him only a windstroke in the brush. Cars passed now and then, at a breakneck pace dwarfed by the landscape; they could not match the silent speed of the road.

David hadn't said whether he was bringing any finished film; in any case, there was no equipment for showing it down here. He himself had lost interest in his camera after that first attack of angina — not because he was coddling himself, but in the way any dying man might give up a passion for acrostic, in the face of the puzzle he was shortly to solve. And in a way that he could smile at now — for the surprises — he'd been made to find what he thought of as "the particular," elsewhere. He'd been forced to. The flirt of pain at his center had kept him fresh for it, an observer no longer content with the eye — though no abler than anybody else to define what he saw. But at least he'd been made able to watch, with more benevolence than when young, those actions and objects of life which kept men so busy mincing down to the forgettable their terror at its shortness — under all of which an immanence remained. What this was, could never be phrased in metaphor — even though the same metaphor appeared to be in every breast, so that even at high noon on a desert day, standing in a white unbroken for miles by even a lizard's head, the sanest traveler would mutter to himself or companion, "I thought I saw something move."

Across from him, near the house wall, a piece of tapestry she had been working on lay on the garden seat, dew-damped but already bleaching dry again, in the poignant frivolity of all such work deserted, rather like a nineteenth-century pastel entitled, "The Dear One Absent" — yet even its lightness could stretch to the metaphor harbored for the human by all the inanimate — the absence of something, never far.

He began to worry again, but, straining, he could just barely hear her voice running on inside, not the words but the warm import — they were making it up. If he had a special allegiance even against Margot and himself, it was to the young. Once, when young enough himself to choose more freely, he'd thought he would be a gardener, until he'd found out that what so moved him, and still did, were the toddler trees in the nurseries — such good kindergartens of them marching up the inclines, or the intricately veiling bones — just before spring — of the younger, smaller woods. When the maple buds swelled, printing Japanese summer on the sky, it was already too late; it was a stage that could be defined, or one persuasive of such. And in the same way now, years later, he kept a life-pity for the young among people, who still believed in the summer and winter of things-as-now. The ambiguous in-between of seasons, if not the best, was the most truthful, for then, when the now was less defined, that other motion almost came through; he was almost persuaded — that he saw. He did not prefer these seasons. They had come.

She stood in the doorway, shielding her eyes against the light.

"Everything all right?" It was not his style of question. He had waited before saying it.

She nodded, with the faint smile she always gave when she first awakened, a smile for him, not for the world. When she sat down on the garden seat, he was about to laugh, without any hope of explaining why, for she had sat on the tapestry, squashing all his metaphor, and as usual, relieving him of it. He saw that she was reaching for her sunglasses, on the table several feet away, with that same, vague sleepiness. He got up and put them in her hand.

"Give me some coffee, would you? We must have talked for half an hour." She came over to the table and sat down where she had been, the sunglasses still in her hand.

He gave her some, scrutinizing her. She so seldom asked him to do anything. "And, so now you feel — " He let it drop. They seldom pressed each other as to how they felt, rarely had to.

She took a long swig. "God, I was dry!" The swingy phrase was unlike her. "Now?" She drained the cup and set it down with an awkward clink, mulling into it just as she did each drowsy morning. "She's pregnant."

"Well," he said finally. "Well." Involuntarily, he looked up at the road.

"Oh, David doesn't know."

"Doesn't — she hasn't told?" That masked young face, from whom its own mother caught slang — he began to smile.

"She didn't have a chance to — she only found out

yesterday morning, after he left. She can't be much more than a month gone. She's going to have that test. But the doctor said he was certain."

"So soon. Then, I gather they were — " He had always felt a distaste for this sort of probing, in the mouths of others. But the thought of his own provision to David, for just this, was so warming.

"Planning it?" She gazed like a sibyl at her own fingers. "No." The breath she drew in repeating it made it come like a chord. "No." She spread the fingers, regarding them. "She was as surprised — as if she'd just found out where they came from."

"Shocked," he said. "Ah, the poor dear."

They were silent for some minutes.

"Funny — " she said. "I found out that I was, almost the same way. Paint. They have the whole place done, she said, except for her studio, and the morning after David left — yesterday — she was painting it with that rubber paint. The smell made her so ill — I gather she almost fainted. She never has, you know. Luckily, the girl from upstairs was there, an older one, with children. *She* told her." She shook her head from side to side in the tiny, ebbing shake of reminiscence.

It occurred to him to wonder why people, when they made this remembering gesture, almost always did so negatively. "And how did you?" he said. "Find out."

"Well, it wasn't quite the same," she said. "I think I really knew a lot more than she does — about those things. There were so many more women around our house when I was a child, all my aunts and grandmother, and they were so old-fashioned. I used to be in the kitchen and listen, and the old wives' tales just dribbled down. 'So many months *gone*' — that's the way they used to say it. Once, my mother must have been having my sister, and they teased her for complaining about the fresh paint on the cupboards, and one of them whispered in German — as if I didn't know German! — 'Mind the child!'"

"Maybe they meant you to know," he said.

"Maybe. Anyway, after I was married, we were at Ernest's mother's for dinner, and *I* didn't know yet, only I happened to mention that all the smoking at the office where I worked was making me ill, since they'd just painted it — and she suddenly looked wise. 'Young wives always smell paint,' she said. I was furious. And it turned out later of course, that I couldn't smoke, the whole time. So it wasn't exactly the same. Smoke."

"I suppose *she* was furious," he said, "when you told her that story."

"How did you know!" she said. "Ah, you'd think I'd learn. All the very things that made me so — in my time . . . that I swore I'd never. Right from the beginning, ever since she was a child. Why can't I help it? . . . But suddenly, I wanted so much to be back there, in one of those old Yorkville kitchens, that was all. They were so sweet and airy and full of everything. Always so full. And the women, in those high gingham aprons with the tight waistbands — why, the women were an altogether different shape, in those days."

"They always are," he said. "That's the way they fool themselves. It doesn't deceive *us*."

"Ah, you!" she said. "Anyway. We made up."

"Yes," he said. "Yes. And it's nice she has the studio."

After a while, he glanced at his watch.

"*And* you," she said. "Ah, you're so much nicer than we are. I never even asked you what *you* — what time is it?"

"Little after eleven. Probably they stayed up all night, talking. He's almost like a son to him too, you know. Old Jacques's known him since he was born."

They were both watching the road now. Along the top of the long swag, two cars crept toward them.

"There!" she said. "The hind car. It's a red one."

His sight was keener. "Not a Karmann Ghia. It could be hours yet."

They were quiet again.

"Ever since he was born." She made an echo of it. "And you? How do you — how does a father — ?"

"How can one say, except concretely? It's such a mixture. The first thing I thought of — when you said it — was that I was glad I'd already provided for the extra allowance."

"You don't think — he'll think you're only trying to — buy him in?"

He considered. Was he? Even as the great sea-and-sky-scape around him told him how impossible this was, to buy anyone into the fixed establishment of things in general, even though the jerky episodes of his own life, in retrospect as random as the wooden beads a child might string on an old shoelace, told him that there was no such establishment — was he still trying? "If he has a son — then I'll ask him, David. Or no. I'll wait twenty years or so, and ask him then."

She got up and went to the break in the wall of shrubs, where the narrow slit of sea was, and stood with her back to him.

"Point Lobos," he said after a while. "Is that what

you — ?" On Point Lobos near the wild bird sanctuary, as near the primeval as a park might come, they'd seen a fat tourist mother, her back to the wilderness, posing to have her picture taken — bending down in her mother-hat to a begging squirrel — by one after the other of her five sons. Each one had had his picture taken with her — and the squirrel. An extreme case, Margot had told him, but if he took notice he would see that women who had sons only were always coarser-grained — breezier, more accustomed to a claque. Not softened, put off their confidence by the lash of daughters.

"Yes," she said, turning. "That's what I was thinking of, Point Lobos."

She might or might not be. He didn't need to know, blow-by-blow, what she was thinking — to know. "And which would you choose for her then, if you could . choose?"

"A girl!" she said at once, fiercely. "A girl — so then *she* would see — Ah, I told you. We're not as nice as you."

"Imagine," he said after a while. "Imagine. When he was eight, we took him with us one day to a vineyard up at Napa, you remember I told you. It was a summer after-noon, very dank and quiet in the winery but sunlit at the farther end, oh they had summer in those days, and he had such a time running down the aisles between the barrels — higher than a man they were, and the guide let him climb the ladder to one of them and look down. And later, we went inside and had some of the special wine to taste, him too, and the guide translated its name for him. And that night, when we came home, he refused his milk, oh so very politely. 'No thank you,' he said, 'I

think I'd like to try some more of that white foolishness.'
. . . Ah, but I told you that story."

"Yes," she said. ". . . Did I ever — ? . . . Yes."

"Tell me."

"Oh, you've heard it."

"Go on. Tell me. About the shrimp."

"Well — " She still had her back to him. "You know, she hadn't ever seen one. And one night, when we were having them for dinner, we put one on the tray of her high chair — she wasn't even two as yet. She picked it up and looked at it, put it down. Then she crooked her little forefinger beside the shrimp and stared and stared. And finally, she picked up the shrimp and said, in such a voice . . . 'Finger.' "

He nodded, saying nothing.

She left the hedge and came round to him, sitting on the arm of his chair, taking hold of his hand. "You raise me up." Her voice was low.

His was quiet. "You — ground me." These were old, near whispers, allusions to stories in no need of recounting.

"What is it we — ?" She had his hand in both of hers, marking time with it. "They have so much yet to — I feel so sorry for . . . Oh, what is it we feel for them . . . oh what is it we know, and can't say?"

He shook his head, not answering.

"It goes up, it goes down." She still had hold of his hand. "Sometimes it displaces us — with them. Sometimes them, with us."

So she saw it too. Another surprise.

"And in the end —" she said, "it —"

"Look!" he said. "There he is."

147

A mile away or more in that clear air, the red car sped toward them, crept. Now it hid, dropped beneath, emerged for the long, straight stretch.

"Funny," he said, "how a red car never fits into any kind of landscape. In L.A., with people maybe. Or in places like Miami, or Nice. But never, anywhere, just with the land."

She gave a small cry, scarcely an "Oh," pressing it back at once with his hand against her mouth, where the knuckles met teeth. "I want to go to Europe with you. With you."

He caught his breath. At once she felt it. Warily, she drew her own breath, moving only to rest her forehead against his palm, slip her other hand to his wrist, where she listened. Are you all right? She asked it mutely.

He nodded, always honest with her. If anything, what had just been said had brought them nearer. Only, for a moment the landscape had seemed to change color — no, it was they. The color of what they were together had changed, as the quiet, implicit colors do when placed beside one that is stark. She was honest too, making no regrets, only bending her head to his bent one. They remained that way, hands clasped over a mutual wound, a mortal one, until the car was heard to turn down the narrow quarter-mile.

"Are we to tell him?" he whispered.

"No, she said not. No — that's hers. We're only to tell him — to call her. At once."

They were still clasped that way when the driver of the car, brought up short by the gorse, stopped with a twist of the wheel, leaped out, slamming the door behind him and peeling off his goggles all in one movement, and walked toward them — gaily waving the goggles as he came. In the dazzle, the couple before him appeared to him in dark eclipse, as one figure, or as one bending over the other fallen. For a moment, the pang always in readiness in his own breast so interpreted it. Then, as he climbed, ran toward them over the stubble, they stood up together, arm in arm. As he neared them, their closeness to each other daunted him, but face to face, seemed merely a trick of the sunglasses they wore, a nearness that the blind might have — of a pair who were momentarily blind. When they took them off, he scarcely had time to say, in relief and amaze, how well they both looked, before they gathered him to them. As they fell back, hovered again, a parental tenderness smote him, for their childishness. For as they bore him toward the house, questing at him with their eyes, touching him with hesitant, timidly helping fingers, it seemed to him that they were bearing him along as if he were the one who was the invalid.

7

The child came when due, and though while it was in the womb they had planned to call a girl Electra or Alison, when it was born they named it Mary like almost anyone, soon shortened to Molly, and by the child herself to May. For though each stage of her growth, from breast to cup, from diaper to pot, seemed to last forever, at the same time each passed like the wind, and in no time at all she was speaking, then walking. Heavy at birth, more than nine pounds even in this day of scales on which no midwife weighed her own hand to the extra glorification of the family, her night-cries were strong, but ceased as soon as honored. At birth she had a mark like a red V or Y between nose and upper lip, which deepened when she howled, but was likely to disappear, the doctor said, in the way of most birthmarks along the median line. When it vanished, they were not able to say on which day it had gone. Now and then, the ghost of an allergy, to egg, to wheat, flitted over her pure, classic regime, but was said to be also of a kind that was outgrown. She spoke early, which girls were known to do, but did not walk until fourteen months, which seemed late, until they studied a book and found this to be exactly on line. Aside from the fact that she was beautiful and utterly theirs, she was all median. The child herself had the fat calm of a calyx that opened slowly; to hold her was to be reassured. Good as she was, if she sometimes exhausted them, it was only as the ownership of riches exhausts. For she was their thing, their greatest possession — and expression. She excused everything, from the condition of the house to those states of being which forbore examination. Hands in hers, they were drawn out upon the gentle plateau of the daily, into that great, blending chapter where no sharp events were. And for this, they now could not be blamed.

Even before birth the child had been helpful, as Liz proved to be one of the girls whom pregnancy turned bland and stilled, the hunger for achievement at rest between hands folded on bellies. "Even when I'm asleep now, I'm accomplishing!" she often said to David, laughing at a world in whose eyes anything she did now merited praise. And so now that she could turn to her work as if it were merely avocation, she returned to it. During the months before the studio area, luckily so fresh and bare, must become the nursery, and now that David was working night and day on the film with Barney, the loft became more and more her domain. For the time being, she embarked on a series of studies for the plaster, very large line-drawings of the figure, which both David and the crowd thought showable, plus one practice piece in wood, as yet shown to no one, in which she had tried to learn how to let the grain work for her — an oddly beveled torso posed for her by Sonsie, the girl upstairs.

As she came closer to "term," the word itself like a darker overtone of the "semester" of schooltime, and so exact a one for this peculiar tableland of pregnancy — at in fact the precise month which the smiling obstetrician called the "impatient" one — she grew bored with the heavy-limbed, loose drawings, ashamed of their lack of neurotic fire. Besides, it was hard to work at anything large across the obstacle of her belly. What was needed was an object no bigger than fancywork. The figurines she did then, either in wax or compounds with a cerous feel to them, surprised her with their expertness, tricks that flowed from her fingers as if in waiting there, directed by some armature within herself. Otherwise, they differed little from the earlier ones, and wander as she tried, the best were always female. Those in wax had also that aura which comes from natural substance only. Clean as she kept her palms, gradually what was pinched and pressed between them took on a color not pink, not amber or gray — until in time it came to seem to her that in both ways, both from within and without, she was working on flesh.

When she was eight months along, the smiling doctor, telling her that she was in every way normal, cautioned her against listening to old wives' tales on what was awaiting her. The caution came too late; had there ever been a time early enough? She had always despised womantalk, under which she had classed everything from recipes to that gothic joy with which women explored their insides. With her head, she still did, rejecting it all with the collegiate laugh given by her zoology class to the notion that carrying women frightened by mice would bear children resembling them. But all the time she must have been recording it — to despise. There must never have been a time, from childhood up, when she had not been listening. And now she could no more flounce away from this gossip than she could insert herself into the waistlines of six months ago, even though she knew this to be as temporary as her measurement — girls of today became Dianas again in six months. For the moment, she hung ashamedly on the edge of those communities the women at these times formed even with rivals or with the scorned — she would have done it with Mitzi, had they met.

The talk itself was as silly as ever, dignified in part when its great subject — the enormous thing that only they could do with their bodies — was confirmed by the great presence of some who were doing it, but immediately absurd in proportion to them; for such cockeyed celebrants there was alas no hope. For, though beneath all their cluckings, one got an impression that they all saw the same Minotaur at the heart of things, the next moment, young and old had fled from that monster bison-face, in a rush of bric-a-brac. It was no wonder the men laughed. Yet the older women had something they half wished to impart to her — never any definition of what they guarded, just *how*. It seemed sad to her that this should be the case with those who saw so much — for in her present state, the women seemed to her the only ones who saw. No wonder the men laughed; they had to; they had nothing like. For the first time she began to think of David not as *David*, her husband, a person, a lover, but — with a divisive line so shadowy that it could scarcely be said to separate — as "men." Here Sonsie, who had been so able to tell her the score the day she fainted — who always referred to her Joe, in a tone halfway between an awed Germanic "*der Vater*" and a shrugging Irish "himself," as *Bailey* — here, once again, Sonsie helped.

"When *I* was eight months gone, oh brother," said Sonsie now. Opposite the wooden torso of herself, for which she had posed kneeling, arms behind her like a bound Joan, she sat now for a twelve-inch doll of herself, knees spread comfortably in the kitchen chair she had brought from upstairs. A six-foot young Goliathess with the fine complexion of the chestnut-haired (on which she put no make-up except a perverse touch of violet eye-shadow worn as usual, above a housedress, as if in careless acknowledgment of some beauty others saw in her) — she was said to resemble old Clea, the famous model whom Liz had once seen at the League in the last days of that ancient nakedness, and once, jogging home on the bus afterwards: a blunted Venus in an apple-woman's hat, her neck a ruined column in illusion veiling, on her the shadowy, violet impression, not of Renoir himself, by whom she could never have been seen, but of countless imitation Renoirs.

Sonsie, out of Hell's Kitchen, an alcoholic mother of eight others and a short career at "artist's balls" — taken from them twelve years ago at eighteen, by the twenty-year-older Bailey, to whom she remained a grateful slave, with the rages of a slave — had another-era look to her also, but only in the imagination of the onlooker, never in her own. If one dressed her up, one saw her perhaps in the gaslight era, an uncertain Lillian Russell in a swooping hat and dog-collar too big for her in all but size, sitting naïve as a young lioness and as deadly, perhaps against the beef-red portieres of one of the tough-fancy restaurants where the politicos went to drink beer over white napery — one of them leaning toward her on a thick-knuckled hand with gold wedding ring, just one second before she gashed him with her paw. Sonsie herself never dressed up; as she herself was the first to say, she was a kitchen-wrapper girl at heart. Like many models, she had no personality for beauty, or at least not the right one. Inside her was a woman of no vanity and but one assurance Ninth Avenue had taught her, that physique was to fight with, fist, elbow and heel. Joe was perfect for her — they fought. She saw his hundred bucks a week at the drawing-board as entirely honorable, never allowing him to slip into the sour-Irish failure he craved. When he drank, they rioted. Otherwise they met seldom, at meals or in gigantic meetings-in-bed where only twins were fathered, two sets of them. In the ring of these, she now moved on the other side of things, a lady lion-tamer before whose whip, street-cubs since the age of two, they scattered and returned, to obey without psychic damage, scrub behind-the-ears without cringing, and cleanly adore. She had, naturally, the lightest hand for pastry. Barney, who'd known Joe before, said the two were types really, a pair to every tenement, but to Liz and somewhat less to David, their resounding saga was the real thing — by which they meant whatever least resembled themselves.

She made a wonderful friend, particularly just now,

though Liz never thought of it as anyway but forever. Sonsie's every remark was racy to her, her laughter straight from the navel; yet certain of Liz's most hand-me-down concepts from school or family life she handled as if these were some kind of precious jewelry from uptown. When she came down in her sports coat and a fresh smear of violet, gave a flying poke at Liz's belly and said, "Come on, baby, I'll help carry you, let's go uptown!" this was not because she was chafing; the domestic day never occurred to her as something to be fled or "filled." She toured the stores with the gusto of the once deprived, and never bought except from catalogue. And in the studio, she would sit professionally for hours, taking out her pay in the only way she would accept — company. "Just think! We might never have met!" Liz said to her more than once. What fated riches she would have missed, of swapped cups of this for casually keyed confidences of that, of mutually sustaining hoo-hoos up the stairs. "Just think, if I hadn't come to live here!" An echo always linked itself with this, of something else she was supposed to say, but could not remember. And at these times, Sonsie never answered anyway, except with a smile.

"When I was eight months gone the first twins —" said Sonsie, "I was already fifty pounds over, two-ten. Watch the pressure, the clinic said, but I never felt more fine. And Bailey his usual skinny one-sixty-five, nights we used to die laughing, he couldn't keep to his side of the bed, he just rolled. His mother was with us at the time, what a sweet, white-haired jealous little old bitch she was. 'Laugh,' she says to me one morning. 'From now on

I'm carrying closepins in me apron pocket for you, from now on.' "

"Whatever for?" said Liz. The little seated figurine she held was finished, but something else was needed.

"That's what I said, what the hell for. 'To stick between your teeth,' she says, 'you get the convulsions. So you won't bite your tongue.' " Sonsie lit a cigarette, her time-out signal, and the two girls relaxed, at ease like two workmen. Outside, through one of the white, fog-bound end-of-island days, they heard the organ tones of the harbor.

"Cup of tea?"

Sonsie nodded. "Ah well, she's dead and gone."

Liz leaned over the tea. A faint, dark zest came from the pot; they both liked it strong. Behind, on the stove, smoke lazed from the kettle. "Eight months *gone*. I never heard it said that way."

"My mother. Lord God knows she *was*, mostly. Not that she ever told me nothing, not even about falling off the roof — I just watched. And would you believe it, when my monthly come on, I was young for it, eleven, wasn't a thing I didn't know about babies — except that. Bird's-eye napkins was what she brought me, like the old-style diapers. You *washed* them and used them over, if you can imagine. My older sister — one in Watertown I take the children to, she slipped me two bits and told me what to ask for at the drugstore. 'I'm not going let you do what she made me,' she said, 'having it come through on you at school. Having to hide them stiff things in your briefcase, to bring home again.' "

Sonsie brought her tea to the sofa, where she stretched

full length, hooking on by one arm. Both of them observed the habits of each other's houses in silent freemasonry, having a care for the chair that buckled, flipping back the rug that slid. Liz followed her, pulling up one of the new straight chairs in which she sat best now, legs spread. They had bought the Italian ones. "God!" she said. On this subject at least, she felt as learned as any. "How do you suppose they ever managed!" She took an emancipated sip of tea, elbows heavy on the table.

"Everything else, I already knew." Sonsie blew smoke. "Or I learned." She chuckled. "One time, I was only eight, my seatmate, an older girl, when she didn't come back to school another kid whispered me why. 'Oh honey,' she said, 'she fell in.' And what do you think I said? 'Down the *toilet?*'"

Liz laughed cautiously.

"Ah-h, come on, you don't even know what it means yourself."

"What?"

"Got caught."

"Got c — oh of course," said Liz. "Of course." She poured them each more tea. "Convulsions," she said, in an off-hand tone. "Why would she ever think you'd have those!"

"You gain too much weight, there's a kidney condition could give you them. With me, it wasn't anything but the twins." She stubbed out her cigarette, shaking her head at it. A deep ground noise was coming from the harbor now, not foundering but steady, sounding in the floorboards as if something might rise there. "E-clampsia," she said into it, with a delicately special enunciation, her medical one. The word floated there like an offering.

She looked up. "Oh honey, you're all right, you didn't put that much on!"

"I was just wishing it was over."

"Oh — it isn't so bad. You'll forget it the next day."

"Oh, I don't mean *that*. I mean this." Liz lifted her arms at her sides, describing their barrel-curves.

"Year from now, you'll catch yourself wishing you could put it back where you always had it handy. When you really tied down with it."

Far in the distance, she saw a figure still single, ghost who had nothing in common with the two girls sitting here. The nagging memory now returned in full — of the girl looking up the staircase with its hanging ropes, wondering who would be her friend here, dallying with an impulse to run, resolving to save the memory of it to laugh over with the still unknown — the day she had come here, since buried by the days that were.

"You're the kind going to have lots of milk, you'll feed yours. That's what the nurse in maternity used to say to me, every time she put the breast pump on me. It's the little ones have it, not the big lunks like you."

Sonsie had been here, that was all; except for Ivan's wife, avoided by all, she was the only other woman here. The two other tenants were homosexual pairs known only in passing — two who tripped lyrically down the stairs, ignoring the ropes, and two quiet, sad ones who cocooned their windows as if in hiding and lived behind a barrage of music from which one peeped out looking for the other, like elves behind a waterfall. Meanwhile Sonsie had knocked at her door the very first day, bearing a plate of her pastry and a gift packet of tea. This was the context that had been waiting for her, here. And so Sonsie, with whom she had nothing else in common at all. Even David, at first surprised at their getting thick so quickly, had later been glad of it, now that he was out so much. She stared past her now at that other lone figure — it could not be — who had so little in common with herself. "You don't mean they actually — you don't mean it!"

"Don't I." The other girl stretched now, flaunting *herself* against that image in the hospital, her face angry, then suddenly laughed. "Bailey. He come in once before he should of, when they had the pump on the two of us, the woman in the next bed, her and me. He turned green, I swear it, then he backed out. I could hear him making a hullabaloo out in the hall. 'Whatsa matter with him?' I said to the nurse when she come to take me off it. 'He throwing up out there?' 'Not on your life!' she says. 'He's laughing. He's laughing his head off.' "

Sonsie got up and brought the cups to the sink, holding them one after the other under the spigot, musing. "Not that I needed him, to tell me. Not even on the delivery table, when they put your feet in those stirrups, I didn't feel that way. Nothing else in the whole business made me feel — that lowdown. Only that pump." She stood there for a moment, head back, shrugging off the thought, then moved past the long worktable where the wax figurine sat patiently in the welter of its own chips and dust of them, and shouldered the chair with her purse hanging on it. "I told the kids — be back at five."

"Sonsie."

"Ye — ep?"

"What's it like? You know. On the table."

It was the unasked question. They would tell one anything but that — in a complicity as deep, one was never supposed to ask it. "Oh, it's not so bad," they said, fore-stalling it, or "They gave me something, you know — I wasn't really there." Or leaning forward, stretching their lips in steel-edged matiness, "You'll find you can take it, just like the rest of us." She didn't give a rap for the pain, nor, she was sure, had they. Still, she leaned forward, with the steady, lucid gaze people fix on the impossible, just as she had leaned in the doctor's office, when he told her. There was always the chance that they might still tell her the truth — that she was not like the rest.

"Oh —" Sonsie shook her head, sighing. "It —" she said. Her glance fell on the figurine. She put down the chair. Usually she had a bracing lack of interest in what was done of her, never came up to it afterwards as the amateurs did, never touched. Now, her face screwed up, she put out a hand, just above it. The figure sat patiently, as if waiting for final dismissal. "Why hon," she said, "how did you ever —" Very gently, in spite of herself, she touched it. "How did you know. I had a hat once, just like that. How did you ever know."

Both girls regarded the small statue in silence.

"I can tell you this —" Sonsie spoke in a whisper. "They lie, when they say we don't remember it." She put out a hand, in another unwonted gesture. The hand was rescinded. "Why, honey — don't look at me like that!" said Sonsie. "As if I were your mother."

At the door, she shrugged, enemy or friend, hefting her chair again. "They say you won't remember it — they lie."

That night, undressing herself, Liz stood naked in

front of the mirror, a game she sometimes now played. Behind her, David, already lying in bed, must be made to look. She had not yet caught him flinching from it.

She herself could scarcely believe what she saw there; it would be over before she believed it, the brown, secret navel now exposed forward like a rising third nipple, or as if there were about to poke from it the pink organ of a small boy. Under the belly, the skin was gauzy as an old wrist, the veins distended, unearthly blue. Above its curve, still high, her breasts rested, no longer triangular, not yet full. In the mirror, her face, for months a peach-bloom oval, now showed still another alien — the peculiarly socketed "mask of pregnancy," fallen inward, toward birth, as the aged face falls toward death. She felt herself a confusion of sexes, ages, indeterminate in the many-limbed toils of something antecedent to any.

She turned sideways, examining the line where hip met buttock, testing the skin with her fingers. On each of Sonsie's hips there were ridges whose glistening snail-tracks were deep enough to follow with the fingertips, traced on that calm Maillol curve like the marks the sea makes, withdrawing from sand. Common enough on women who had carried too heavily, the doctor had told Sonsie, tossing this into Sonsie's ragbag of tips from seatmate and sister, where it remained as the marks had on her — nameless, commonplace and permanent.

"I'm not carrying — too heavily," Liz said now. "I should go back to — pretty much the same."

"Of course you will," said David.

Oh, he was trying to keep in step with her, but could he have any idea of how far he would have to reach to be where she stood — as she saw herself in the glass —

heels dug in, leaning back against the hard, amniotic weight of all that had been thrust upon her? From another orb she regarded him in the glass, lying there feckless behind her, in the simple one-track rhythm of his world, between them, true or false, all the dark, venous coil that now defined her away from him — as if she walked in a magnetic field on which secret facts flew to her, to which he was lead. If I'm late, they'll "induce" me — castor oil. If the water breaks, it's a dry birth, girl. Hubble-bubble. The Kaiser was a breech — he had a withered arm. Spring forever, O Republic, from the dust of my bosom. Of course, my hair may fall out afterwards. The look on my face, however, is medically documented. Quite common — but, luckily here — won't last. I am still Persephone. It's only a mask.

Oh, she must try to reach him, therefore her nightly game.

"You were absolutely right," she said, "about Sonsie. We really have almost nothing in common. I just realized it this afternoon."

"Oh, I wouldn't say that," he said. "I didn't. What I said was, living so close, maybe you shouldn't get so — spend so much ti—"

"Well, it's the same thing," she said. "It's going to be a drag, to break off."

"You girls have a fight, or something?"

"Of course not. I just realized." She stared in the mirror, chin lifted. He seemed no nearer. "A girl like her. What do you suppose we could keep on finding to talk about? What do you suppose we do talk about. We girls."

"Oh — house-stuff. Sex, maybe."

"Se—!" As with most women, what they did with

their men was never mentioned in those terms, between them. "Why, she never mentions it." Sex was Sonsie's modesty — theirs. "Nor do I." It was the one adage in the manual that had not been discussed — "Intercourse should not be engaged in after the seventh month." She gazed at him now with a remote, calculated pity.

"Us, then."

"You? Oh — men. Yes — we talk about you, some." Her smile was almost for Sonsie. The men, never appearing intimately in those conversations either, instead were slid along in their grooves like puppets, moving jerkily in scenes devoted to the habits, care and feeding of, et cetera — never really to *them*. "What do you talk about, with Barney?"

"Work."

"See!" she said.

"She's a good egg," he said severely. "She may not be in it for brain. But you knew that."

"Oh, I know," she said. "I know. And she's not such a dumb bunny. The way she had to grow up, *kicked* up. By that mother of hers. Why, in a peculiar way I really love her, you know? Not just like."

"She's something to look at," he said. "I wonder if I could catch it on film. Not sexy. She's like some big, clean — not Venus exactly. But not Diana either."

"You should see her in the nude," she said. "She has one of those, almost abstract bodies. Like a good statue. As if it had already been through — you feel a kind of peculiar sympathy —" One hand smoothed her own hip. Suddenly, she wheeled clumsily to face him. "Dave! You don't think . . ." Her mouth was open, eyes screwed tight, ready for horror, comically trusting as a young

164

bird's. The child had not dropped yet, according to Sonsie, yet its weight on her thighs was such that it toppled her forward, unless she kept her hands under it. She held them so, holding her belly like a great football. "Do you think — you think I could be a Lesbian, or something?"

He had just been taking off his glasses. Without any intent of cruelty — in the surprise with which one repeats a habitual gesture — he put them on again. But then he began to laugh. Probably there was a touch of hysterical release from this last month in it, but anyway he couldn't help it. He rolled over and over with it, pounding the pillow, from which he rose, pointing a weak finger — only to fall back in another paroxysm.

At the core of the eye, lies the retina. Once it is "detached" as they say, even partially, the vision can never be the same. With the inner eye, it is that way also. She saw him there. Oh, she had her humor about her too, somewhere. With her outer eye, she could see well enough how she looked to him, even smile. When she spoke, though, it was from that dark, venous underground, always fresh with milk or blood, that he could never penetrate to, from which she herself had been running intermittently ever since she was thirteen — and to which now, in the full light of day, she was returned.

"Go on, laugh," she said. "Go on, Pagani. Laugh."

(They lied of course, when they said she wouldn't remember it. What she remembered best was her great distance from others who could still suffer shades of feeling, their distance from her, who was all one shade. Later on, when they asked her about it, she lied, and said she didn't remember it. How speak in the particular, of what should be all — one statement? Still later, when she asked herself, she responded also that she had forgotten. It had been the great obligatory scene of her life — hers — but nothing could make it a unique one. So she lied there, also, and said she did not remember it. It was an old wives' tale.)

And now that the praeludium was over, with that expected chord which everybody had heard, the days offered themselves to the young Paganis — for what seemed a long time — in a mixed bag containing only many a minor good. Sometimes it was David, man of action, who appeared to be in the forefront of the family, holding aloft its banner, and Elizabeth who was the contemplative; sometimes it was she who set the tone of that psyche all families have — and now and again, walking with that lovely gait the world recognizes, they were one. In olden days, they would have had some actual ikon, household god to which or whom each would have had his and her duties, but here too their heritage, itself a mixture, left them free to — set their own course. Everything now conspired to help them believe they were doing so.

To Elizabeth with the child, crowned by it, life was ravished by circumstance. May, sweet nugget of the same, absorbed the unscheduled daylight hours, or corrected them to one; at night, sometimes carried to parties on her mother's hip, she often allowed herself to be slipped into a quiet corner with others of her kind. Slowly her possessions entrenched themselves, trusted by her to bear it in upon her hosts that she was not leaving; gradually they learned to let all this creeping *art nouveau* abide. Meanwhile May, in return, offered them each day her small fistful of events. David from time to time patched together a film of these and sent it off to California, where each installment was extensively reviewed by letter, under the title with which Mr. Pagani had at once dubbed the whole continuity: "May's *Meanwhile*."

As was natural, some portion of her parents' own almost always adhered to it. The field of dandelions where she was shown, a wandering topknot almost as bright-penny, lay just outside the wood where they went to hunt wood for Elizabeth, where they had found that large bole she would soon be working on. Here was May again, in the secondhand car her father had bought with his own earnings. For though the big opus was not yet done, indeed enlarged itself monthly, two smaller sections of it — one on certain architectural leftovers in the city, and one on its municipal sculpture — had been purchased by a university, share in the payment refused by the already well-heeled Barney, on the true grounds that these ideas had been David's. More of the same, if he could turn up some, was on order.

Elizabeth, writing the letters that accompanied these installments, found herself a more eager correspondent now. Two addressees were more neutral than one — and she had found her subject, on which all of them could dwell. Under a still of May in the car — for an album which her own mother had started — she inscribed date and anecdote:

"The old bus makes a racket going up hills, probably needs a carbon job. First time out, I made a crack about it. We didn't take it out again until last Sunday, more than a week later. What was our surprise to hear her say, clear as a bell, what I'd said. 'Will this thing *exploge?*' At two-and-a-half! Can you believe it!"

The senior Paganis could well believe it. Though they had their accounts too, of the sniffles and nap-fevers a child could breed in a wink and a gust of wind, even hearing, safely afterwards, of the midnight croup, when Liz and Sonsie took turns walking the floor with the child upright on a shoulder, or of the time May got into the studio and cut her wrist, on a tool called a riffler that Elizabeth herself had never used — a half-inch more and it would have been the artery — the child of the pictures was the one they most truly believed. To Margot's anxious query, not of course a suggestion, as to whether the studio could not be locked, she received an air-mail answer: *It was. She opened it. We've taken other precautions now. You really can't realize I'm a mother now too, can you.*

Both knew this equally. On May's first birthday, when Margot had flown East, ostensibly to re-rent the apartment she still kept on there, the good intentions of each had made for a prepared formality — under which repression one lance from an old attitude had instantly pierced. "I've tried," each said to herself — "she will not accept." "*She* will not forbear." For walk about as they might and did, under an obscurely tender knowledge they increasingly felt themselves to be sharing, in speech they were helpless — birds striking in midair. "May hasn't yet made her suffer," the elder thought, and the repetition made her sad. But from these encounters,

Elizabeth rose refreshed, a phoenix-girl. If Margot's presence would not let her be a mother, then she would be a girl again, rediscovering her need, in all this happy humdrum, to rebel and not forbear, even to shut off from May that new fount of knee-high wisdom which May herself had opened in her, and fling up the single hand again — to push against the weave. All this was fine for work — but lasted briefly. So it was not quite possible to say who had conquered whom.

As for David, he had gone to the Coast once since, on the excuse of showing his father sections of the new film, and of course there was never any trouble between those two, though each found the other more reserved. "It must be because he has *her* now," David told himself. "Is it because he is beginning to *see?*" Mr. Pagani asked himself — and trembled against what David might turn and tell him. Meanwhile, the time was approaching when all five must really meet, foolish to delay that pleasure. May was old enough now to see California. California must see May. Jacques (Margot wrote), whose grumbles over his liver all but convinced them that he had one and might make good his eternal threat to take it home to France forever, must see her — they must see him. Mr. Pagani was never the one to press for this — he was the same as always.

This was the real news from the older ones, and the best — that everything was the same. Each side knew the marvel of this, but differently. David no longer worried, or had to remind himself to do so. To the younger lovers, the older couple had been returned to that plateau where all keep their parents; distance made the latter even more safely constant, and they sent no pictures; like all letter-writers who remain faithful but unseen, they did not change.

And this was the sum.

Though the young couple never spoke it aloud, it seemed to both that they now had everything. They saw their way clear to seeing life clear, in just those antitheses they had often glimpsed in the lives of others, and no longer thought of as grooves: the country, the city; leisure, work. On Sunday afternoons, on the last lap of the fifty miles between them and the discovered woods they thought of mystically as theirs, while they mused in the line of traffic that stretched ahead of them to the George Washington Bridge and the city, May nodding in her sling between them or blanketed safe in the back, all fours clutched to her bottle, they often spoke of the logic of someday buying a cottage or camp — terms for what resided in the mind of each as a piece of habitation untethered by price or drains, as mystic a refuge as their forest. They enjoyed a forward sense of this as probable but not yet possible, in the way one savors a night's anchorage in a place where one would not want to stay forever, taking a double enjoyment in their sense of themselves as being on a temporary plateau but steadily climbing; the angle of incidence that their life was to take, though free and always to be spreading, was set. In time it occurred to them, laughing at themselves incontinently, that they really didn't have to make these trips on Sunday, like people who worked a week of nine-to-five; thereafter, drawing imperious breaths as they loaded the car, they made it a habit to go on weekdays. After this, whenever they came across similar examples of the freedom which kept them special, they were careful to observe any gestures that went with it, in order to mark the fact that though they lived within the terms of other people, they chose theirs. It was at these times, when people saw them walking with that gait, that they appeared most united — one. Having another child was never voiced even in thought, since their triumvirate was still so ideal — this was one of the terms. But the warmth of people who have everything often overflows into a charitable desire to add to it. So they got a dog. A small tan mongrel, short of leg, long in the tail and utter in faith, it understood them immediately.

The loft was their center; it was their *way*. As they approached the bridge, in this the third year, the city, hung there on the late blue in its stencils of sunlight, stepped forward to them like their own creation, weighted down at its farther end by that homestead, reached by its ropes, which they had long since come to call — in a gesture forgotten — either the Slip or the Cove. Elsewhere in the city, when they parted from friends or each other, on the steps of the Main Library perhaps, or inside the Modern, meanwhile looking like anybody else — for Elizabeth dressed "uptown" when she went there, and the child was kept a picture by its grandmother — nonchalance thrilled to pleasure as they murmured, "Back at the Slip at six" or "See you kids Thursday, at the Cove." The wealth of what she had down there often overcame her right in the middle of Lord & Taylor's; David still saw his own address with awe. Someone told them that it was mentioned in *Moby Dick*. Though they could not help anticipating the cachet of this at parties, David, always quicker at sensing pomp in himself, usually nullified it — once sending her into stitches by drawling, "Mm-hmmm. That's where *all* the young marrieds." In matter of fact, although, on streets nearby, they once or twice passed couples who resembled themselves enough to merit a second look, no one they knew or had heard of lived within a mile of them — any nearer than the new bohemia of the "East" Village. As they glided down the West Side Highway, under the "Heights" that now belonged to "the Germans" (refugees of thirty years ago, who had nothing to do with the Yorkville of Elizabeth's parents), past the tired ball-park area of the newest Harlem, they thought of the city, like all New Yorkers, as utterly theirs — Elizabeth for having been born here, and David for having its ichor all the more in the veins because he had come. As evidence of this was the fact that each part of it had for them a social meaning which it took years to know. Impossible for them to live elsewhere than in its context — fish who would die out of these haunts that fed them a unique alga. In its godmotherly waters, even if they personally faulted, the city, friendly old savager of artists, shark-mother, helped them to keep on knowing who they were. This they took for granted.

And impossible to live in it except where they did — now that they had found it. Like any pioneers, they wanted no one else too near them, though there were other areas which by social meaning were right for their friends. On lower Riverside Drive, where the high-windowed towers gave back the gold in blobs and flashes, and one front was caught to a lurid, entire bronze, they exchanged smiles of scorn as they sped by. Here two couples of the crowd had defected to the solid apartments now returning to borderline bourgeois favor — and to all that went with this — baby-carriage mornings for mother, home on the bus for papa, and a half-time maid. Local contexts could not be shrugged off; these molded. If they themselves had not recently become privy to a circle that now seemed home to them, the melting of that first, early crowd would have been more alarming — one pair to the suburbs, two changes of heart (and profession) toward graduate school, two couples last seen grappling with an interest in their commercial jobs. As it was, Elizabeth was often frightened at the thought of it — they had all been so close. David, used to dormitory living, took these severances more stolidly, but she was not sure he saw the real tenor of them — it was not so much that the crowd had melted as the way they had, out of their own intention, back into life at large. Of the originals, only three had remained stalwart, two bachelor painters and a girl doing rather well in off-Broadway theater. They themselves were the sole couple — outside of Beatty and Dil, of course, those two who had moved on to new fringes but still were sometimes to be met and avoided, their experienced hanger's-on eyes watching, ever more brightly purist, waiting for the Paganis, now that the latter were in the family way, to slide.

Luckily, they themselves could now return the look with some sophistication. The people they saw now, of whom one would never use that adolescent word "crowd" — though they gathered as self-protectively and excluded far more severely — had almost all taken that indefinable step, however small, past intention, into practice. Ah, what a difference, and oh the relief of it, now that they both had done — particularly for Elizabeth. For once David had given up (on which day?) any idea of being a painter, he had stepped forward with the lighthearted confidence of one who pursues his avocation, plus perhaps the confidence of the male — of whom vocation, whatever it may be, is expected. She hadn't given him a hard time about it, turning it rather more harshly upon herself. For, six months after May's birth, she still had not started to work again — she was afraid to begin. At times she blamed the school for abetting her too early in her misconception of herself — and saw them all back there, teachers and schoolmates both, expecting things of her, waiting for her to fulfill or fail. Some mornings she was sure she had risen in ardor to a workday that the baby had then eased away from her, piecemeal. Then, slowly it was borne in upon her, like a soundless clap of thunder of which she was not aware until it echoed, that no one (possibly not even David) was really awaiting anything else from her — at least not on the heights of what she demanded of herself. For this, she had no audience. Luckier than David (as some would see it), even in this day and age no other vocation was really expected of her. All her life long she could blame the baby, plead the house.

Strangely enough, once more it was Sonsie who helped her. Even while Sonsie shrank back a trifle, like an alert sponge, before a certain new dryness in Liz, as audience she insisted, she expected, and not for her own vanity. The afternoons went on, less intimate than they had been, teaching Liz something of the help to be drawn from the ignorant, when they admire. When Sonsie left to go "upstate for a time" after a bout with Joe, she brought down a substitute, one of the shy homosexuals who lived in the shrouded loft above the Baileys — who rose at four to cook breakfast for a partner who worked nights, and then was left to himself like a childless wife. A country boy from Georgia, who proved unable to pose but was content to watch her work at something else while he sipped coffee grayed with his tin of "condensed," he was both fond and deft with children, and liked to sit with May when they went out, exchanging jollities with her until she slept, grateful adjunct of family ways he was not quite loosed from, pleased with his role of senior child.

During this time, Liz worked on studies of the baby in mediums from ink to clay, but the sketches and figures she turned out always kept to a stubborn abstraction, concept babies, genus "infant" — she could never make an identifiable May. She began to tour the museums, their libraries, purchase her books of plates. For the first time, school appeared to her not as a wishing-well or a theater of approval, but as the fountain where the water was. Once a week, she now attended classes in the studio of an old sculptor of Bauhaus days, superannuated but still famous, where she rarely ever saw the master but was exposed to all that really lay before her. To any casual queries as to what she "did," she could no longer bring herself to say "I'm," but sometimes, as some half-accidental success quirked from her fingers, she felt an apprehension of joy — she was learning. She was learning of the power to be drawn from her own ignorance. Gathered up, it must be what might make her an artist. It was surely not a power to be wasted on the daily event.

And for closer kinship, they had the cherished company of the people they saw now — whom they were going to see at tonight's party — who numbered among them several painters who had been shown in groups, the scene-designer and cast of a play shortly to open in an old auditorium in Chelsea, a group of art photographers who were sponsoring a gallery on East Tenth Street, and one whose film short was to be shown next season, at Cannes. Though the entrée to this clique had been David's — whose combination of small works paid for and magnum opus promised had set just the right tone — Liz's new-found modesty quickly made her the pet of those who had only just acquired their own confidence — and they had no sculptor. And after a while, by a process not unlike the old crowd's, her familiar presence made her talent assumed. Anyone who was associated with them! — their voices and miens delivered verdicts, exchanged gossip all in the consciousness of who they were; they were the coming ones; they were "next." Singly none of them could have said how it was achieved. The group had its acknowledged stars; newcomers swiftly learned to live at the same altitude. The effect on a neophyte was just that: first the bloodstir of the sudden climb, then the calm of the view. And in no time, the network of influence, mention, notice — modest as it was — was set going for her. She was encouraged to send work into competition, instructed where.

On opening day of the large, indiscriminate group show where the torso of Sonsie had made its debut, David, escorting the girls to the jammed gallery — two joined storefronts on East Tenth Street — had been lost to them almost at once in the buzz of some confrères from the camera gallery down the line. Liz, fearful of dressing wrong, at the last moment seizing something from a surer time, had worn her wedding dress. Here and there she had seen someone she knew and was nodded to, but everybody had had his back to the work on display, as if by design. Faces were tilted to other faces or bowed deeply into a glass, and one had a constant sense of chins averting, eyes shifting, as if some notable had yet to fill the doorway — or as if the same message for all, from Ganymede the cup-bearer, was still to arrive. She saw all this freshly, now that it was hers. When she saw the torso, she felt her own nakedness. No one was looking at it; no one had ever noticed the lines on its hips except Sonsie, with whom, by this secret, she suddenly felt once more warmly allied. She whispered to her. "I feel as if it's me," she said. Sonsie giggled back at her, "Think of how I feel."

David, just passing, gave them a brotherly leer. " 'T's okay *keed*," he said side-of-the-mouth to Sonsie, "they'll never recognize you. Not in that hat." The subtlety of this almost overcame them. Stiffening their faces, they gazed devotedly at his back, like younger sisters. Later they saw him leading an unknown man up to that exhibit whose listing Liz for days had carried about with her like water in the ear: *Torso, Jacobson, 124*. She made Sonsie duck out with her. From the window of an espresso house opposite, they watched the crowd thin while they gorged themselves on *cannoli* — safe as two housewives conning the passing show from the tearoom at Gimbel's, delaying their return to the sitter and their collective children. A vengeful delight overtook Liz as she watched people of whom she could have been one now emerging, exposed in the momentary caricatures of leave-taking. At the same time she tasted a present rich as the custard, the rich mixture of the chapter now. "Phonies!" she had said proudly. "What crap!"

Now, outside the building in the Cove — it could have been any day in the week but was Sunday, any day of the last year — they parked the car, went through certain other routine motions, with the silence of sleep-walkers, doomed but serene. She, the child and all the paraphernalia of their day, bottles and baskets and the finds of pinewood or maple to be mused over afterwards, were set down at their door, the child sometimes awake with a cry sent up like a skein of mourning, or on her feet toddling half-forward into sleep again, clutching a drained bunch of flowers. Then David ran to garage the car, which could not be left where it was because of vandals, and was therefore kept, at half the rental of the loft, in the basement of the "development" from which some of the vandals undoubtedly came.

This was a flaw, but like others in the scheme, was no longer regarded. When the loft was entered, if it no longer quite resembled either its exact first self or even their present memory of it when away from it, it now was pliant enough, old enough — as they were — to give way a little, and still stand. In it they no longer felt the presence of that network of intangibles which once had plagued. Its flaws were not to be held against it or even up to the light, any more than the nubbins in cloth of natural fiber were — any more than her own monthly intensities were held against her, or David was held to account for his solitary afternoon walks, on one of which he had now departed. Lightly suspended in the mind of each, what the one did not ask, the other did not notice, no longer was counted against him — it served to keep him separate. Lightly, scarcely yet coddled into being, there was the need for it.

Meanwhile, there were such beauties. As she went about preparing the evening meal, the dog fed, the child beating its spoon on its tray, the word revolved in her mind on a spit of gold and dark manufactured from the autumn effulgence at the windows and the room's inner shadows, until she had to laugh for it, a riddle to tell him or not to tell him — how is the word "beauty" like a capon basting? In this quiet goodness, for days on end her thoughts gave up their lances, pattering down in a gentle rain of detail. She made toast points, grated cheese, set out capers in a design, a rosette of pimiento, all her senses transliterating; food was affection. The light was cider, as in an old stable, autumn in a bottle, with a dust in it as clean as country ordure, a stone air that filtered up from the marble being filed in the studio below; who would mind this mica air, glitter in corners, dusty pollen of old pianos. It was the fine, hard blue day of the first shiver in the shoulders, the day of the first blanket. The child, fine loin-fruit, was so good; it fed itself, crooning. By the time its father returned, it would be asleep again. She gave it the button-box to play with and sat down, with a shiver of the loins, to brood for him among her happenings, her weave.

On his walk, David as usual went cross-island, on streets narrow enough for the short-girthed carriages of Dutchmen, even, in a forked alley or two, for the long, saturnine ghosts of Indians. A certain habit of thought always accompanied his footsteps, in a way descended, as a man of the present might still flatter himself, from those silent figures whose long, aquiline feet took their intelligences from the ground. As was his habit, he ended up at Trinity churchyard, where he sat on a certain bench against the south wall, from which he could see, over the worn script of the earliest stones, the towering shaft of the Irving Trust.

On weekdays, the place was his seaside, under wave after wave of people. Rarely, he was here on a Sunday. In this deserted, dune air, one could almost hear the centuries architecturally colliding. On the other side of the church, behind the garlanded buttresses at his back, the first quarter of his own had crept for burial, brought up short in one large cenotaph, good as new, that he ignored as he would his own grandparents. On the façade of the Irving Trust, between window and concavity, dirt had washed a secondary streamlining that made the whole building flow upward, in a movement beyond what the builders had planned. At its base, the nubbins of the gravestones were not downed, but seemingly flowed into the ground and up again. Before the small thumb-push of these, the tower flattened and fell back, eternally falling away. Facing this optic, he often thought of his work as the documentation of what was always in the air in every century — of the movement that was not planned.

He thought of his work now with the gratitude of a man who had *found* it, his narrow escape up into that vital air which both encompassed and played above the dead flat of canvas and book. These days, he and Barney talked of air as if they were technicians of it — as indeed they hoped to be. Many were already talking of the art that way, some doing it — this filming of the images "*in the air*" — but they usually attached it, if tenuously, to persons, plots. Though he couldn't always get his intent clear in his own mind as yet, he meant to do this — somehow collectively. He wasn't sure that his partner saw that. Stretching on his bench, eyeing those stones, he was fairly sure not. Barney, who had been analyzed, wanted to film the conceptions that floated in *his* air. He had an idea for two sequences on the identity sickness of the age, one on a man who knew who he was but couldn't get the world to believe it, and one, even more familiarly, of the man who didn't know who — et cetera.

Well, that was Barney's air, and who was to say whether another man's was ever passé? But if Barney ever stopped being a rake, long enough to live with one woman for instance, he might come up against such an intenseness of identity as might give him pause, enough to wonder whether even this age, unless it lost its woman altogether — et cetera. Women had so much of it, this collective identity, that it was a constant trouble to them to get outside it, a question to him whether they ever could. Liz's best work came from inside it, from what she saw in her own navel — all women's as much as hers. Women saw with difficulty any movement outside it. When one came up against this intensity of theirs, it was wise to duck out for a bit, else a man would fall back, diminished. It was given only to men, perhaps, to stare at the navel of all the world.

Someday, he would want to duck out from Barney, though such was the debt, neither financial nor tangible, he owed him, that he didn't see how this was ever to come about. For what he wanted to do was not just to film the maggots in the brain of the age, but to record its floating healths as well — even if he had to document the obvious. Maybe even and only to do so. He'd even thought of doing this historically, for other ages — think of a film *The Fifteenth-Century Air*. And here Barney, for whom only the present was chic, who was as much a man of it as a robot was, would be altogether out of it. He himself would have to learn so much, would have to brood. He brooded. And now — it was time — he wanted to go home.

Stretching himself, he rose and left without risking a backward glance, always reluctant to leave this seminal place, wondering whether it would be so next time. For if the rumen he chewed there was only graveyard thought of a kind men had been having for hundreds of years, he rather liked fitting into that groove. Far back in the mind, it was a comfort to have some assignation with permanence, at least an attempted one. He had no idea why he did not go home for this sensation, as he would have done in the early days of his marriage, when all the romantic thrust and blaze of things-to-come lay behind his own door. Now the daily, once outside it, lay behind. He was in no sense out of sorts with the warm, tender certainties guarded by that door, but opening it now meant coming *out* of the heat of things into the cool, into the place where all he loved and would defend was still gathered — but where he no longer possessed his own singleness. Back there, in that still eddy in the streets, was a strangeness in the midst of which he could brood. Sitting on that bench, he saw himself pictorially, an ocean swimmer out beyond the breakers, steady, not lost, his back to the beach that was home, treading water in the regular, pointed rises of the sea. So he had taken to going there now and then, either straight from home or on the way toward it, never telling anyone, always returning to his own door refreshed — as by a swim in that singleness.

When he came home, the bliss of ordinary evening had settled in there also. They ate in quiet. It was not necessary to say aloud that they were not going to the party. It existed tonight so that he and she might draw together against it; this was what friends were finally for. When he took her in his arms, the child, not quite asleep yet, lay looking at them, its eyelids blinking down and opening wide again, like a great doll they had bought themselves. A time would come, they were forward-minded enough to know, when they could no longer reveal themselves so before her, but now they stood there naked, their backs to her. Elizabeth's hair was long again on her shoulders. In the mirrors of themselves, they saw themselves the same as always. It seemed to them that they had everything. They had not moved an inch.

8

The click — if they had not been up and awake, hungry from lovemaking, prowling to the icebox for the party they owed themselves, they might not have heard it, a noise no more than a . . . click — as if the child, rolling over with one of those long, angelic breaths children exhale in sleep, had shifted a toy against the crib-railing — but the child was never put to bed with a hard toy. In the mother-pouch of her mind, so small a part then, so soon to swell, this fact was at once alerted. The dog's nails on the bare floor made almost such a sound. Although the dog was just yawning awake, still in its padded bed, they half thought it this. Sooner or later, they would have looked in on the crib in passing. They paused drowsily at its side.

A child in a crib has a certain shape — rounded. This shape was no longer there. She saw that before he did.

The thing that lay there, belly arched, was not hers — a long, stringy puppet, its legs still working in terrible ricochet from the kick that had flung it there. As she screamed, the clamped chin tilted; in the head, scooped up by her to an inner mutter that it was round, still round, the eyes had retreated but were there, pupil-less, white.

Later, they could not have said which of them bent to pick it up, which cried "Let it stay!", which said to get Sonsie, answered yes get her. The mother had guessed what it was — from an old tale. That she knew. The father, already outside, knew that he was the one who had gone. No, Sonsie said on the stairs, her old gown flying behind her, no. I never saw one, none of my kids ever.

By the time Sonsie stood over the crib, the stopped breath had begun again, the pupils were slowly returning to the eyes. The parents dared to raise theirs. Sonsie leaned across the crib, her mouth a wry, Greek gape; when the lips of that mask folded in, and two drops appeared on its cheekbones, the girl beside her made one retching, pulled sound and dropped toward the crib on her knees, her arms outflung. I thought it was dead then — she said later, over and over — then I thought it was dead.

"No," said Sonsie. "— Ah!" and then, in the softest yearn, but not a moan, "Ah, ahhh." By some grace, they understood her. No, it's alive. Ah — it breathes. They could hear the rasping. And for the last — gently cupping its head, she held it barely lifted. It was a child again, the mouth softening to human, the eyes dull as if from a journey but wide; it was May. Sonsie's forefinger touched the mouth and came away. She held the fingertip out to them. "Bit its tongue," she said. "Bit her tongue."

It was David who went to the phone, went through the pad for the number kept there by Elizabeth.

"Way up there on Park?" said Sonsie. "You want to try mine, Dr. Boda? He's nearer, he's in the development."

They tried him. Yes, she was breathing regularly now. Not hot to the touch. Cool.

If they wanted to bring her over to his office, he would meet them there. If they wanted to get her to a hospital, he could send an ambulance — "You feel safer, you want to."

Everyone was so careful to ask what they wanted, to put to them what was theirs.

"I think you could bring her over," he said. "Meet you there in ten minutes. Sure, bring her over."

They brought her over.

But first — when Sonsie bent to pick up the child, its mother came alive then, warmed out of her crouch of shock — and took May from her. *Ahhh*, this was what she wanted, said deeper in her throat than any of them, forcibly keeping herself from squeezing the body until it was one with her own again — if she could but have it once more inside her! Only the feel of that body could help her body's need to suffer in its stead — and could not allay it. The night when a child is sick is a simple agony, once learned. This was its lesson. What suffers in the center of such a night cannot be suffered for by the most willing substitute — is now a thing apart. Yet each time, with the same gesture, she tried.

On this first night, hurrying through the dark byways, she had time to think of her own childhood, safe on lighted avenues, family ones. Whenever any of them had been sick, particularly when she was, they had had the doctor. He came. Often, he might have come when it wasn't necessary, when — (never dreamt of) — they might have brought her over. But when it was needed, when her father roused them to his last attack, he had been there. It had been he, old and retired now, who had sent her to the joint office on Park Avenue, first to the obstetrician with whom she was as briefly and falsely chummy as a show-dog to its hired handler, who after their joint success had passed her on to his colleague in pediatrics, Dr. Dowlin: a healthy baby, scales, formula, scales, new formula, one rash, one allergy — just give her this in place of the cod-liver oil, a healthy baby, no wind of such a night ever, just give her this in drops. Dowlin might live on Park or in some suburb fifty misty miles away for all she knew; if met on the street she would not know his every-other-month face. No matter. House calls were no longer the practice anywhere.

"Shall I take her?" David said. His face was white, abject. She refused him.

They entered the development, its sweat-colored halls. If one lived here perhaps, and there was a doctor in the building?

They found the door with 1C on it ajar, as was the practice anywhere. Just before they went in, the thought came, and guilt with it. Maybe house calls were still made, in some places — perhaps on Riverside Drive. Then the door opened for them into a small entry tight with chairs; Dowlin-Boda-AnyFace nodded at her, and she held out to them her child.

On that first night, they learned that convulsions were

not uncommon in very young, otherwise healthy children. He examined very carefully. All was now almost normal, temperature lowered. He was not surprised. For this, not even seeing him, they loved him blindly. To check, they must bring her round at eleven the next morning. After sitting over the quiet crib almost until dawn, they were awakened at ten by a May vigorously shaking her railings. In the happy sunlight, they saw that Dr. Boda was young, wore a brown suit too old for him, and had a mild face — to which Elizabeth, though she hoped never to see it again, held up proudly, almost with scorn, this baby so round with health, this daytime child.

Until the second night, neither of them remembered the click. It was recalled to them precisely six weeks later, again on a Sunday but much earlier, around nine in the evening. On this occasion, Dr. Boda came to them. Met by David at the bottom of the stairs, he strode up after him, looking neither left nor right, as if he had been in a hundred such places, and went directly to the child, tossing back the blankets in which they had cuddled it, its spasm over. "No, don't bundle it — let it have air!" In the absence of other — conditions, a convulsion *could* be the body's own device against high fever. Humbly they submitted their own virtue — in having noted a snuffle, felt a forehead, kept it all this brilliant day at home. He listened, unresponsive, leaning his body over the child's like a thick, dependable log across which they could surely tread into sun again, bending to draw down its eyelid, absently holding its hand, almost as they might, to admire the small, perfect nails. After a while — he stayed for an hour — he gave medication, one of the antibiotics which they were to repeat every four hours round the clock. They saw he had a way with children. "Dis make me *fee* better," May even repeated after him. It made them feel — but once again, she was May. When they thanked him for staying so long, he glanced at his watch and said, "Just happened to be my poker night, I'll still get there. Right on my way." From the underground of that fourth-hourly tunnel they were to come to know so well, they gazed up at him in wonder — this denizen of the norm.

After the third occurrence, it was confirmed by Dowlin that, in the absence of *other* (had he been the one to say pathology?), yes, such explosions could be — she already knew how common among the young high respiratory fevers were? Yes, she knew. "No — you keep on with your young man down there," said Dowlin. "Way down there. We'll run double harness. I'll talk to him, in case anything else comes up." He flipped a registry. "N.Y.U. Medical. Flower Hospital. Good enough. Quite young, I see."

"Yes," she said without thinking. "He always wears the same brown suit."

"Ah, I won't tell him!" said Dowlin, with his jolly, terminating laugh. In the same way that she had noticed Boda's suit, without noting she had, she observed dully that Dowlin too admired, even to scrutiny, May's small, formally extended hand.

Nothing else came up. Nothing but that, but nothing else — nothing but that, that — at intervals of anywhere from a month to six weeks. That. Though Boda didn't come to them again, they grew to be old phone correspondents. She came to hate the mild sight of him in his suit, the flat voice now the symbol of the opening phase of that delirium which, once begun, evolved in exact sequence, like a theorem or recurrent dream, with the obsessiveness of both. Dowlin was the man she loved; ah Dowlin, large, pink and euphoric, was her man. For May never saw him except in the intervals — Dowlin at the Cove was not to be imagined — and in the intervals, May bloomed. One could almost believe she bloomed for him, that others, in anticipation of his kingly touch, did also, his very success being that once in his sight, no child was an ill one. What had he ever said of this one any more alarming than that these strep-type germs had patterns of dormancy and recurrence — and *amazing* resistance — or that May, if later found to be an allergenic — such a comfortable threat — was young to be tested, and might meanwhile outgrow the business altogether! For in his office the child was always May; there she was always a healthy Dowlin child.

Boda was the dark one, consulted only at evening, from their underground. Children's fevers rise at evening, ordinary children. May was still ordinary. In this she was only like any other child. Even Boda would acknowledge this. How the mother hated him for her dependence on him! It was he, she was now sure, who had dropped the word "pathology," making her surmise brain tumors and epilepsies of which, in Dowlin's bright land, she was ashamed even to inquire. And it was he who had remarked casually that convulsions, though a scare, often had little further significance in children-under-three, often ceased thereafter. But May was now almost three. What if after three? What significance then?

And what about the father? — for these days they scarcely any longer seemed "David and Liz" to each other, and were almost surprised, the few times when, leaving all in Sonsie's care, they were persuaded to venture out together, to hear themselves so called. He too grew weary of the name Boda, but differently; he grew tired of hearing it on the mother's lips. Between her and the doctor and child, he was made to feel alternately smaller and larger, now swollen to giant responsibility, now shrunk to helplessness; until now he had never been a man to dwell on his size. It had been he, too, who had noted that the child's tolerance of fever apparently teed off — to the other . . . trouble — at a temperature of almost precisely 103.6. At that point, she almost always abruptly — dropped. For this observation he was praised — and never quite forgiven.

For now they knew what the click was. Now they had seen. It was the click of the teeth, as the underjaw snapped closed. Another small sound, like a snuffle, confused it to the ear. This was the cut-off breath. From the first dread rise of the thermometer, they sat up in turns now, hers in a concentration so dense that he sometimes wondered — never to be said — if all unconsciously, she were willing it to rise. For when it came, it was almost a relief, now. Now it had come, and if it were she sitting beside the crib watching that hot, sleeping face, she knew what to do now. She even knew the small twitchings that preceded it, hoping these were ordinary, knowing they would not be — though children in ordinary fevers often twitched.

But sometimes she could not sit there — it was the waiting. Then she stood yards from the crib, paralyzed by her need to suffer for what was in it — and watched him. Then he took over, and she was blessedly only his handmaiden. At these times, with her following after him, her hands knitted, her head stunned from side to side, he was truly the father-God. For he was not hysterical.

But this too could chill — in retrospect. For even in sleep, when she was fathoms under, if a blind tapped, the dog sighed, she found herself at the cribside not even knowing how she got there, as if blown there by a cloud. And he was such a heavy sleeper the click never woke him; though he sprang on the instant, he knew this to be a lack. Less learned than she on all the vulture hazards, he deplored her womanly habit of superstitiously trying to ward these off by prenumbering them. He loved May no less — but then, a father's love! That was what it came out to. Of what she most resented, though he felt it, he could never be justifiably accused. A time might come when she was alone with . . . that. For he was the one who had to be away from home.

Meanwhile, there was more than enough to be performed in unison. She found a way to write the grandparents of May's "little ups and downs" without alarming Mr. Pagani — and to keep from Margot what she could not bear to have her mother know, that her own child had a flaw. When Margot, less watchful than she might have been otherwise, said that Jacques's illness was giving concern, she managed to mislay the page without being sure that David had seen it. David learned to efface any anxiety in his letters to his father, finding this harder to do than in the old days when his father had been its subject, learning that when the subject was young — there was no equivalent. When May broke their hearts by saying hesitantly, as an innocent chocolate was handed her, "Dis make me fee *better?*" the anecdote was not reported. If an old image of an Eden as innocent often recurred, it was not mentioned between them. Of all that they had learned, that night's lesson had been the easiest.

And when the time *came*, with the telegram calling him to Jacques's deathbed, neither bothered to comment on the unforeseen terms of it — that it should be Jacques's and not his father's — they were so deep now in that unison. She was now to be alone with it. It seemed to both the natural progression of the dream.

Four days passed, in sweet uneventfulness. May, never left out of sight, was her dear good self, and in a new way, almost a companion. Though heretofore she had always dogged her mother's steps, never more than a pace behind them, now, falling into the background, she had more often to be looked for; it was eerie how she could find places in which to be lost but still near, and all without puckishness, so gravely, never seeming to hide. Now — when she was never spoken crossly to or refused a story, never put off by, "No more questions, no not one!" or by Liz's phrase in extremis, "No! Mummy is a person, too. And Mummy wants a *quiet* time" — why did she just now one day lean her clasped hands on Liz's knees and say, looking up so primly, "Do'n you want a qui-et time?" It was almost as if she were somewhere amassing a little hoard of her own that she wished unnoticed. Though never a demonstrative child, now and then, with a certain art, she was. What could May be learning? The mother put such thoughts out of her mind. It was the bright interval, one in which a scare or two had even been surmounted without brewing to anything, and it was the longest to date, eight weeks. If the two hadn't been alone, she would have felt almost light-hearted — and if that secret milestone she lived for (having told no one, not even David), the child's third birthday, were not so near.

On the first reassuring morning, they had seen Dowlin. Each of the successive ones — she worked. The owner of a small gallery, the very man whom David had taken up to see the torso months back at the opening, back in that safe chapter of undifferentiated days, would take her for a two-man show in the spring, if she could give him a little more to choose from, even for possible sale. He had passed over her efforts in wood to meditate for a time on the wax ones. Their sameness, all stylized toward the same anger, all women, had contrarily pleased him. She set herself to be professional, to amass him an army of them, but after this long interval of her own, her fingers were not up to it, nor her heart, and she managed but two, both slack. Nevertheless, it calmed. The child, by now schooled not to touch anything in the studio, was content to sit in a corner, well away from the pans of water in which the slabs were melted, of which she was given cooled pieces for her own vague lumps and pies. As she bent there, now and then, for a rest, her mother modeled her.

She had been doing this almost absently, for longer than realized, perhaps even two hours, on that fourth morning when she put the figure down, rose to stretch, and turning, saw what she had done. Her fingers must have done it without her. For it was almost — May. Though it was the best she had ever done of her, she would say that much, no further. Her fingers must have

done it without her. For the figure was not of the child
at this moment bent in her corner, but of a child found
out in one, caught on the run there, learning how to hide.

That afternoon, as on other fair ones, they went to the
zoo, where no heart could be heavy, and where May
had even found a small, blond-braided friend, who, like
herself, no longer napped afternoons. Children often lost
the habit of it along about this age, said the other's
mother — along about three.

They came home to the Cove just as it was dusking.
At this season, it was not unusual to see the stone-cutter's
wife, Mrs. Ivan as she was known, standing in her doorway — rather, it was a seasonal sign. Winters, the stolid
family retreated behind its curtains on the far side of the
warehouse where all their life was conducted, scarcely to
be seen again during the cold except for the children, a
girl and boy of eight and nine or so, glimpsed as they
went off early "to the nuns," mufflered to their narrow
Alpine eyes, or on returning when, at a movement from
a curtain, they were nipped inside. Summers they all left
for some business venture in the country. But toward
spring, for those few, short New York days, Mrs. Ivan,
urged by some village atavism, came from behind her
curtain to stand in the doorway, to lend the Slip,
in which she was so strangely harbored, a gossip-on-the-
stoop, village air. In the waning light, on this her first
appearance of the year, she looked even more morality-
tale than usual; kind witch, lady-porker, false neighbor
whose gossip did not run to a nod. Today, she seemed
even to be waiting. As they neared her, she scrutinized
the child. She had heard of its seizures, perhaps, and
wished to see for herself what manner of child — she

would be like that. A ball of rage formed in its mother's throat, draining to a complicated shame.

But, it was not like that. Because it wasn't, her address — in the servile style of hostility when it wants something — was almost palatable. Against the lonely prospect of the evening's fears, it seemed almost like one of the heartening domestic favors women are stirred to exchange at twilight, before dark. "The dress your little girl wears once — " She wanted to borrow it to copy the pattern, for her Gretel's first communion. "The green and red one. With the smockings here, and here, the color *so*." It was almost a tribute. From behind her curtain, she had observed well.

"Oh, yes of course! If you'll just wait, I'll go on up — "

Liz hesitated, glancing behind her for May, who was not there but at the unfamiliar doorway, a few yards down. How wise she looks, thought the mother — the way they look when one sees them like that, suddenly apart.

"I watch her," said Mrs. Ivan. "Or my Gretel. Gretel!"

A blond girl with braids nipped from behind the window.

"Pat-ty!" crowed May.

"Oh, that's not *Patty!*" said Liz, smiling indulgently. This girl was about twice the size and age — though there was more than that to the difference between two blond little girls with braids. This was a cold bit already, with the bad-china complexion of some South Germans — as if attempts at Meissen had been made. "She met a little girl named Patty at the zoo."

"Can I take her inside, show her my new room?" said

Gretel. "Can I?" She didn't smile, but her repetition was childish enough to be nodded to.

Coming downstairs with the dress — a gift from Margot — freshly laundered too, and so luckily not by her own indifferent hand — Liz felt salved. Under Mrs. Ivan's thumbing of a plaid cotton fine as silk, her nodded I-told-you-so to an invisible crony (over the Irish lace collar), her quick squint at the label, the corners of Liz's mouth lifted, in a hereditary twinge of Yorkville. She knew well enough what was venerated by the pigs-who-were-neat.

"You come inside now," said the woman. The owner of such an article must now be asked to review *her* possessions; this was required, and this was her thanks.

They passed through the remembered train of box-rooms budding on one another with a respectability as infallible as cancer. Mrs. Ivan righted a faulty pillow with a fake groan, tested a table's proud polish with a glum "T-t-t" and a sweep of the middle finger, and Liz, following, was able to murmur the proper responses — "Oh no, I don't see how you — it's all so immaculate!" But meanwhile, such a mournful start of yearning had gone over her at the three-years-back sight of all this, it was not credible — at the sight of those wooden bluebirds? So immaculately preserved — the context of the past, then, did not have to be beautiful? A valve opened for her, widening on all the bowknots, rosebud dreadfuls, knots in time that people bent over with sick smiles — heart-boxes. A first inkling came to her of what "the past" could mean to others and progressively to her, included in it a clanged sense that the moment itself was not revocable.

Gretel's room restored her — such a travesty on girl-hood, on pink-and-green. But the children were not in it, not in the kitchen.

"They in the studio," said Mrs. Ivan. "You so nervous, *ja*, you only got one."

They were not to be seen in the studio, that huge, scattered place. Confused by the cables, the machinery, she at first saw no one. Then she caught sight of Gretel in a far corner, too far across that floor still weighted with its crop of gravestones, a Tyrolean grotesque of a little girl rising knock-kneed, furtive, as if she had just done dirty on a grave.

"May!" Where was she — what had they —? "May!"

"She wannud play hide-seek." Gretel smiled wretchedly, head moving on neck, hands kneading her crotch. "But I don't spy her, nowhere."

She was found almost at once of course, almost as quickly as Liz's witch-glimpse of them, old bookplate terror, faded when she saw her, safe — stone-dust in her hair, dust clowned in a smear across her mouth, gazing up at them in droll gravity from the crawl-space, a tepee of up-ended marble, she had to be so carefully wooed from — but safe.

"*Schmutzig!*" Crack! Mrs. Ivan's apologies were transmitted via her daughter. She whispered them. "Why you let the baby shame herself?"

Gretel had her answer ready, shaken out of her by the slap from behind. "Because she's a funny, isn't she, Ma?" Head tilted at Liz, she smiled for real. She had been told. She knew. "She's a funny, isn't she?" Gretel said.

Cleanliness was not for the mean-spirited only. Upstairs in the loft, with the child bathed and fed, cleanly powdered with talc, she cuddled it on her lap, pressing the round, sweet-smelling crown to her breast in almost the early, flawless flesh-joy. *"Stille Nacht,"* she sang, as her mother had. Night was just settling in when she laid the child in its crib, slipping the rail half-down so that the child's form could be seen from her bed, lingered there curved over with love, touched its cool cheek with a light finger, and let it be. Tonight, David's usual call would not come, for today was the funeral, and out there, hours back, it was still day. He was with many unknown people now; the certainty of that made him seem farther.

Here now, all was the same. Centered in her objects, among which she scarcely any longer drew a line between chosen and accreted, she took reassurance from their special gloaming. Gold and dark mingled as awaited, only angled now toward spring. The dog lay at his post, couched like an animal out of heraldry. From the window, a last iridescence flashed his collar: gules. And tonight, might she count her blessings, she had nothing else for which to wait.

The sky gathered at the window, of all the colors of black. After a while, she wished for music, but dared not disturb the child, so softly respiring. She composed herself on the bed, stretching a leg across his place, then, superstitiously withdrawing it, leaving a space free for his return, she burrowed deep, into the nest-sense, her nestlings numbered, into that wholesome dark. Down there, in the way some count sheep, she lay on a field of old summers, on the gone-to-seed garden that to a child had been pasture, above her shoulder, almost a companion, the lone faucet no one knew of, that at a mysterious interval, never to be counted upon, against function and with it, fed a drop to the field. There, she was not waiting for anything. *Heilige Nacht.*

After a while, she flicked on the weakest lamp. Across that nest-sense, another had stolen, of how tenuously she was connected with the city. Today, she now recalled, had been Sunday, now that nadir of the week in which no one was likely to call. In recent months, their neglect of people, a gradually returning compass needle, had been pointed at them. Despite that, she watched the clock for some time: nine, then ten, ten-thirty — not now any more. Even in this building, above her, the Baileys, in a rare spell of amity, were away, all six together; above them, the pale boy, briefly a sitter, no longer lived here; of those others below, she would not let herself think. She could not help the waiting — it could not be unlearned. The silence in the room was like water rising. Under the lamp, stiffly sinking, she drowsed.

And awoke, thudding. To no click. To the quiet. A shelf of sleep still pressed her down. She lay there, listening to that which creeps subterranean, louder than noise. She heard the dog rise to its haunches, as if it too were listening. Pushing against the sleep that coffined her, she drew herself up on elbow. The dog sat, ears high, muzzle pointed. She saw what it saw. In a room alone, the sincere do not scream.

Opposite her, the child rose.

It rose like an object, moving without breath, eyes distorted, hands at the bedsheets, mouth open. In the moment before she flung herself upon it, it resembled an object trying to turn itself into creature, straining to create itself. She ran here, there, with it on her shoulder, in a panic maze-memory of the croup, and at last the eyes suffused, the choking came, and with it, on and on like a new but welcomed torture — the breath. On each breath, she writhed with it, until again the terrible stillness fell and again the rigid half-creature labored. Three times this happened. Then she got through, she never knew how, to Boda — not there — to the answering service, the doctor taking Boda's calls, and at last, to the city ambulance. And the city, after all, responded well.

It allowed her to sit the rest of the night on a bench in its hospital, not in just the general waiting room downstairs, but in the smaller, privileged one of the terror-struck, just outside the ward. Though it could not allow her to enter the ward, since this was the section for infectious diseases, it sent an intern to speak to her personally — by the next morning, no later than ten o'clock. He listened with tolerance to her dazed answer to his "Kid's an asthmatic, isn't she?" with only slight impatience to the history of 103.6, and though she felt that this was not a fever up to his standards, he nodded a courteous "Yeah, after we brought her in, she had two." He had come to inform her that the child, though now resting quietly, was reacting to tests for muscular response with what was known as a "meningismus," which was not always definite, but could be confirmed. And after he had told her that the spinal tap they wished to perform was the test for meningitis, she was allowed to take her free way three flights down, and wait her turn at the phone. Then she returned upstairs, to her bench.

It was noon now, and the waiting room was sociable with parents come to take their well children home. A special hospital gaiety lingered on it, light as the floss on candy jars. She sat in it like a stone. The happier parents studiously averted their eyes from whatever plague was hers. "Oh, he'll do fine, just fine!" said a woman just coming in, to a pair just leaving with a child in a wheel chair. "Mine's leaving tomorrow!" she called out richly, to their retreating backs. "Ah-hah. Yeah. So long." She came and sat down, on the bench. "Polio, that one had. Mine had the diphtheria." She was all smiles. "Imagine, this day and age. We figure our landlord, he don't fix the drains." She was one wreathing, inner smile, her head moving circularly upon it, toward tomorrow.

The girl sat there, eyes on the hands clasped in her lap, not seeing them, deep in a vampire greed to be this woman, to be inside the flesh of this woman who was taking her child home.

"Hon —" said the woman after a while. "You got anybody with you?"

After an interval, she was able to raise her coffin-lid, speak from there. "California. My husband." It came out, a croak. "I couldn't reach him. They're all at a funeral." She saw the funeral still going on out there, the hours unmoved, in celebration of all deaths everywhere.

"Your kid, he in there?"

After another interval, she was able to answer that also. "She."

A nurse passed, looked in.

"California —" the woman said to the nurse, low. "And she —"

The nurse came up to her. "What's your name, dear?"

"Pa-Pagani." It was extraordinary, how the buried could speak, to the above-ground. When she got back there herself, she would tell them.

"Oh yes, your child's just gone up. She'll be down

soon." The nurse bent to look in her eyes, put a sharp hand on her. "You're not going to keel over on me, now, are you? That's right." She paused, before leaving. "Bet you didn't know they have something for meningitis now, they catch it soon enough." She nodded brightly. "Sure, ever since Korea, the army camps. We got it then." Going out, she passed another nurse. "I'm going off, now. Mmm — spinal."

How well even the grass could be heard. Tap, tap.

"Menin —" said the woman. She crossed herself, then touched Liz with the same hand. "You hear her? In the war, hon. Lotta good things come out of the war."

Traffic bypassed them now, on its way to the visiting.

"You a Catholic?" said the woman.

"My — mother . . . used. Used to be." I would be anything they said to be. Up there with you — if I were still alive.

The woman was silent then, guarded. Did she perhaps feel it, the vampire breath upon her? "You pray," she said suddenly. "In the blood, it don't leave you." Her hand came out in resolve, so careless of whether it was the coveted, the smiling alive. "Pray, hon." It began to stroke, over and over. "You can always come back."

Within the stone, the stone began to create itself, sweating tears.

"That's right hon. Try to cry."

Within the trachea, swallowed arrowhead, breath begins.

A shadow crossed her lap — on the floor, two shoes.

"California," said the woman. "Alone, I guess. Her baby's up there, for meningitis. A spinal tap."

A cry. She was raised, bodily lifted. Back from the

dead, he stared at her, David. They fed upon each other's ravaged eyes.

"I flew all night," he said. "I couldn't get you. I flew all night." She saw him — between the great wings, webbed and jointed, his peaked face, low-flying. You too. She could not say it.

"I know everything. They told me the ambulance. I had a time finding —" Though he surround her with his body, his flesh could not help her, being like hers. "They'll soon have it. I talked to them. She's already down."

When the intern poked his head in, they were alone on the bench, crouched together.

"Pagani?" This one was a Chinese, with a perfect face snubbed to the universal one, the eye-folds lifted, as if wisdom reined them from behind. When he smiled, he was — "Your child doesn't have meningitis," he said. "She has bronchial pneumonia."

"Pneu —" The word, repeated, peeled from her, a long rill of it — she was the spool. She turned to tell the woman. "Pneumonia, she only has pneumonia! Did you hear?" She turned to David — "She only has pneumonia" — to the other. "They cured penicillin with that . . . didn't they. Long before the war."

"Give her something to eat," said the other. "She's been here since they came in. Then you can see your baby. They've shifted her." He smiled. "Yes, long before."

She turned to the woman who was no longer there. "I only wanted to tell her —" The woman would want to know it — that the Jesus is a Chinese. She would want to know that. But she herself was already fading upward, above-ground. She looked down at her arms, melted again to flesh, vulnerable.

Left alone together, they recognized each other, in a long stare. He was back from the dead.

"I'm all right," she said at last. I am Persephone. How did one say it? "I'm back."

The pair sat, heads bent, near the bed in the ward where the child lay in the priceless, after-fever slumber, its lips wetted with rose, like the mouth of a vessel where essential oil had been burning. Down the long aisle between the uncurtained niches where the cribs lay, other couples, here and there a lone figure, hung over the bars and chortled, or stood, or sat like themselves, brooding on what they still had.

During the funeral days out there, he had carried his own livingness about with him like a tickle of the sexual — he knew his own size. Here, in this soiled, old municipal hospice of mottled gray zinc corridors vast as Edwardian sinks, castor-bean-smelling linoleum, he was not so sure. He had traveled thousands of air-miles, only to find himself yet in those orphic spaces between life and death; now in the way of the airsick, he needed to fasten his dizziness on some steady, oriented object. The cribbars, under their tan paint, were steel, set very close. The mattresses were raised extra-high — for easier nursing care, he supposed — but on the smooth metal legs, about a foot and a half from the floor, there was a contraption of plates and blocks whose use he could not decide, beyond the unlikely image of a creeping child. A nurse, carrying past her medicine tray, appeared not to have heard his comment. Two beds down, across an empty one, an old woman turned to him a clean, chimp face, the eyes in it as faded a calico as her sack-shape, its mouth crossed with a finger. "Rat-guards, boy dear. And that needed." With which she turned her back on them, to the still form she guarded.

At his side, he saw that his wife, awake a minute ago, her face fallen in now, was asleep in her chair. He was sentinel. Through a window, past a dockside tangle of viaducts and alleys, he could see a corner of a building crony to this one and of the same pallor, the school where a child must go down here, would go if — when she grew. From the bland, palmland air, fruit colors, to this place, his passage had been too short — he knew how he had shrunk. Yet he knew better how to repair this than his wife would, his instincts being surer. For all that he saw the image of his child at six, swinging her book-bag through the dockside, home to her dark rope-climb, and saw it as a negative, an impossible one — it was not a matter of place only. Or if it was, it was not so in the secondary sense that his wife, for all her quickness, might still see it. It was a matter of a place in life.

He bent over the child. Opposed to its mother's hoard of adages on the physical, which if queened over were her right and due, he had kept to himself one delicate secret, a small fatherhood that he had never told. In fever, the child had a certain smell to it, whether others had, he could not know — to him it meant her, only this one. He was the only one who knew. At first, he thought the odor lost to him under the sallow, city carbolic, and fought off an urge to steal out with the child's body close under his arm, toward that coastal radiance, the candid palms. Then, bending even closer, almost touching, he stayed there, taking in that warm, toxic chypre from this bud in such sick flower — his.

Raising his head, he saw that his wife, awake, looked young again. Ahead of him, his thoughts leaped like salmon, and though he knew the legend of that immolation as well as anyone, rushed on. In their center, one hoarse rage spoke. "I want —" he said to her. "I want another one."

Let her not understand — or not answer. It was his answer. Let her think he asked it for relief — from the terrible strain of having only one hostage. Yet, silent as she was, he saw or thought that she understood him. An answer flickered on her face, neither joyful nor sad, but complicitous. Life had not imposed this on them. He imposed it on her, his male answer to the agonies life imposed. It was what they were meant for; it was their excuse. They held each other eye-to-eye, in the sacred falsity of a moment they would remember — a crossing of the current, one that they themselves had made.

9

When Dr. Boda paid the Slip an unsolicited house call about a month later — a fortnight after the Pagani child had been discharged from Dr. Dowlin's splendid hospital, as *Bronchitis: recovered* — the one o'clock sun was running like hilarity along the Cove, dragging foot-traffic, even vendors into this coign. For two brilliantly hot weeks without a blow of wind, spring had burnt deep into its corners, stilling the greenish harbor voices, turning the dust to brine. The air squeaked with freshness, like pulled, newly washed hair. Distanced, the vendors' cackle turned Portygee; gulls dropped to the garbage scows from Caribbean skies. Above the viaduct, a marine dazzle whitened to sail. Two young boys went by, bound for it with string, hooks and tin cans. A young couple strolling hand in hand — he in full beard, she with a waterfall of hair down her back, both black-trousered, both sandaled — lingered to glance up at the old factory, even to ring several long, unanswered peals at the side door, then walked on, casting back wistful, house-hunting glances. Upstairs, the three young Paganis were laughing over lunch.

These last weeks, the two elder had discovered how joy can haunt a life (for they now thought of theirs as one) — in what willful corners it makes itself found. Up there in the new yellow-and-blue ward, safe as a teddy bear, the child was mildly recovering, a solitary happily stunned by the numbers of children in whose midst, alert as a tadpole to its own species, she watched and even swam. When her parents visited, she received them well, but with a certain absence of mind, as if they were not the sole resource now — the pond was the thing. The loft, when they went home to it, suddenly bid for their attention like a garden once imaged, planted and left, and now re-risen — with the season. The dog greeted them like a pet ignored, enough to remind them of that other yoke of love, now temporarily lifted. Downstairs, below them, all was sealed for summer, deserted. They rose at random, went out for buns, stayed in for love. There, that other agreement remained, unspoken, but they were not indiscriminate. There were seasons; that was the thing. But ever so often they greeted one another newly, like people immured together in a cave, who turn to each other upon rescue, to congratulate themselves on having been shut up there with the right one.

Meanwhile, the cost of all this was to be covered very handily, and not by Mr. Pagani. It was disclosed that Jacques had left David a small cash bequest, plus his half-interest in the business. To David's disclaimer of the latter, sent off at once, his father at once replied, in his own way gently disclaiming, not pressing David with any of the burdens of half-ownership now, entirely omitting mention of those which might someday arrive in full. He would hire a young man who might later buy in, half or all, as David might wish it; business of late, with two old fogies at the helm, had somewhat lagged. In any case, David's allowance would now arrive, with some increase, as his own income — which his father knew would please. He was now truly on his own, his father the same. When last seen, at the funeral, Mr. Pagani, to be sure, had seemed smaller, but so he had seemed also at the wedding — it was merely the way, his son now knew, in which one generation invariably shrank, under the ceremonials of another. Best of all, now that they were three again, the child, home from that sunny, pastel place, seemed to have brought some of its spirit with her, to the Slip and to them. They had all had their shock and it had nulled; whatever might be repeated, some vibration — of waiting for it — had forever gone. At times it even seemed to them that the child consciously acquiesced in some buried statement that they were all now party to — which made their triumvirate the stronger. This could not be, of course. They no longer, of course, made love in front of her. Though still their object, more often now, she was sometimes May.

At this moment, she and her father were engaged in an old game she still found riotous — in which, slowly, with compressed smiles and scary eyes, they brought their foreheads closer across her table, until, darting forward, she brought hers against his with a huge

"A-boo!" He never failed her; she always got there first.

"Watch your glasses," said Liz. Clearing the table, turning on her heel, she sighed with abstract pleasure. "I think I'll take her uptown. Too bad you have to go back to Barney. What a day!"

He removed the glasses just in time. "Golly. Her head is hard." He shook his, with pride.

Below, in the depths of the old building, they heard the Ivans' bell peal faintly, for the second time within the hour. As usual, they did not answer — they themselves had never had a bell. After a few minutes, there was a hallooing, repeated nearer.

"Meter man came yesterday," she said. "Sounds like a telegram."

They listened for the name. It was their own.

David went downstairs quickly. The man was standing just inside their open doorway, as if hypnotized by the shaft of midday sun, looking interestedly at his own shoe. As David approached, he stirred some dust with it, and watched the dust hang, floating like goldleaf, in the lovely, citric light.

"Why — it's Dr. Boda — isn't it!" Even in this improbable context, Boda's tanned face, in the focus of the stairwell's rich brown shadow, seemed such a usual one — usual as a face in Vermeer, and as limned. "Yes it is, how are you, Doctor? How nice of you to —" To what?

They shook hands.

"Sorry I was out of town when —" said Boda.

"Oh, that's all right, after all you couldn't —" David's tone struck his own ear as much too large. "We heard you were at a medical conference."

"Out of the country, yes. Rio. My wife and I. She needed —" He looked up at the stairs. His nonchalance was weak, that was it — he was after all not much older than David. A matter-of-fact young man really, yet by profession so far ahead in the daily shadow, always finding himself in such unordinary places, no wonder if he seemed — not yet accustomed. "Otherwise, I'd have come before. I —"

"You got a tan, I see. You're looking very well."

Both men smiled briefly — it was always such an absurd thing to say to a doctor.

"Well . . . why don't you come upstairs and see your patient. She's in wonderful shape, you know; it all turned out fine. A bronchitis." He was rather proud of the turn of phrase, the "a," at the same time ashamed of it, the sort of lingo with which amateurs of the camera tried to chum up with him. "Seems to have broken the spell. Of that recurrent infection." He knew he was talking too much and too fast, and could not stop himself. "You know?"

Boda nodded, his head depressed. Perhaps his vanity was hurt, at the ease with which, in his absence — Raising his head, he gave David a square look.

"Good stable weather," said Boda. "Dry."

They were an uncanny set, the medical, able to chill with the slightest — remark. The weather. Probably it was as much of a bore to them, to have their every cliché — examined. It must be what made them the more stolid, like the man here.

To his relief, Liz called from upstairs, asking who. "It's Dr. Boda, dear." His voice wavered up, artificial — when in his life, public or private, had he ever called her "dear"? "He just —" he flicked a side-glance — "stopped by."

There was no answer from above, or at his side. "My wife will be delighted to see you," he said. From Boda's lack of reply, he was sure, yes, now quite sure, that Boda knew how Liz disliked him, even how she put him up against Dowlin — relief washed over him. Of course, of course. They were as petty as any other set of men. Of course — Dowlin.

"I did stop by, partly, to see this place," Boda said. "Partly. I've often passed it. Tell me about it. Old wood-working factory, isn't it? And what's in there?" He pointed toward the Ivans' quarters.

"Oh, there're not many like this. We love it. We built our place more or less from scratch — my wife did. She's a sculptor. It suits us down to the ground." He recalled suddenly how Boda, on his visit before, had strode up without a glance, eager to get to his patient. Too late — he himself had already warmed to his subject, in words so well-worn by now, so facile, that they might have been prepared for him by someone else.

"Yes," said Boda to everything, "yes, yes." It took quite a time to tell him all he asked. He queried and answered himself, turning here, there, like a technician. "Grave-stones. Power tools, hmm, and probably carborundum. Away these past few weeks, eh. No thanks, I won't bother to see the place." He turned thoughtfully on his heel. "Yes."

On the way upstairs, this time at a pilgrim's pace, he touched the ropes one after the other and when he arrived at the landing shook the final one, leaned forward to follow the path by which he had ascended, examined his palm, and said it again — "Yes."

When Liz opened the door, she looked angry, which meant that she too was afraid. The child stood at her side, dressed in its outdoor clothes — smart gray coatee and leggings, miniature riding-hat and red strap-sandals, all sent by her grandmother — dressed by Liz at top speed, to whisk her past them. She stood there like a testimonial pushed forward by her mother, not a child to be examined, an outdoor child. Behind them, the loft shone, meal cleared, all in fast order for leaving, except the peeping vacuum cleaner for which there had not been time — the room too stood prepared. Even the dog quivered in tableau — we're just going out. At the sight of them, pride — it must be — choked him, and after all the talk, he could only gesture to Boda — my home, my brood.

"We're just —" said Liz.

"Going out," said Dr. Boda. "Yes. I won't take but a minute." He was unreal; he couldn't possibly be here. His face was stern, sad with its own unreality, but with the ease of a man who wasn't really there, he slipped inside.

Liz stepped back; the dog sniffed and circled. Only the child stood her ground.

"Well, here you are, eh. Little May." He dropped on his knees before her. Didn't he know how children were scared by that, the close confrontation of adult eyes, how they hated it — the pure nostril shrinking back from the cleanest adult, his skin, his breath? "Going out for a pony-ride, hmm?" He dared to tip the doubtful, tremoring chin on his long forefinger. "Long time no see, eh?" He was willing to make himself insufferable to convince them that he was flesh-and-blood. "You remember me, eh May, old Dr. Boda?"

"Bo-da," said the child.

He cocked his head to one side. "Ah, I'm luckily named, my old man changed it, short for Svoboda — Czech. My German patients think it's Boder — bee oh dee ee are; my Jewish ones know better — think I'm trying to pass; the Spanish call me Bodair . . . and the kids . . ." He rattled on, to the parents, and never took his eyes from the child, even drew down her eyelids as he singsonged "Pretty eyes," and then stood up. "And the kids —" He smiled down at her, courtly. "Can say Boda. Those are pretty mittens," he said. "My — little girl, has some like them. Could I see for sure? I'll give it right back." She allowed him to draw it off, even to hold the magnetized, not quite brave hand. It was not the mitten that interested him. "No nail-polish yet, I see." The nails, their color — at some length, he admired them. "Thanks." He patted them, drew the mitten on, gave the hand back. "Thanks" was all he said, in the gentlest way, and it was then that the child, clenching her face like an anguished clairvoyant, began to wail.

He turned red at that, almost as if he had been slapped, and oddly enough, this made him seem, for all his patter, for the first time false to himself — to be stolid was his role. And to listen to the breathing of a crying child, not its sorrow, to listen unmoved, unmoving. When she had quieted, he told them.

He was most thorough. "You must keep in mind," he said, summing up, "asthma isn't so much one disease — as a whole set of conditions that vary from patient to patient. That's why it's often not spotted right away — espe-

215

cially in a very young one. I did have it in the back of my mind, of course. So did Dowlin. But until she came to the hospital, she'd never been seen in attack."

"But he let us leave there, thinking —" said David. "Bronchitis."

The doctor stared at his own knee. "That's what she did — end up with more or less. Names aren't as accurate medically as people think — and often cause trouble prematurely, unless the family understands. Anyway — I happened to get back just then, and remember, I live in the neighborhood, I'd already had a vague idea, about this building. So, when Dowlin called me —"

"Why didn't he call us, tell us himself?" said Liz, staring. He, Boda, was not to get off free either. But if she could only divide the blame into words, hand it piece by piece around —

"Oh, he would have, I'm sure, if — but we'd already agreed, on the man you ought to see." He tapped the paper he had given them. "And as for the — we-ell, I was the referring doctor —" He looked at his knee, his shoe, his watch. He stood up. "And I was interested," he said, low. "It was kind of my bailiwick."

Oh. They thought they understood him. Dowlin was on the bright side. And May — May was no longer a Dowlin child.

"It was very good of *you*," said David.

"Oh . . . all in the day's . . ." Boda bustled in his pocket and brought out an envelope. "And while I'm at it —" Glancing about, he spied the vacuum cleaner. Very carefully, shielding it, he opened the dust-bag, transferred a sample of its contents to the envelope, and pocketed it. "Might I — ?" Standing again, he was holding his hands in front of him with a certain fastidious gesture that went through Liz with a great pang. That was how they had done in the old days, and her mother had always been ready with the towel for them, with her quick nod, as from a colleague — in there, Doctor, to wash your hands.

When he had finished, he was genial in the way of doctors at end of interview, as if they basked in some jollity the patient himself had been kind enough to lend them. He was himself again, or rather, all of them. "When you go see him, take a sample if you like, but I'll be getting a lab report on it. Meanwhile follow whatever regimen — he does wonders that way, even with severe cases. I'd say it's a foregone conclusion though — what I told you. She's been lucky in the weather lately, the machines being idle below, and so forth. But you really ought move as soon as possible. You're just courting trouble, otherwise. She shouldn't go on living here. Or in any place where there's that much stone and wood dust."

Perhaps he misunderstood their faces.

"It's not the worst disease a child might have," he said. "We've drugs now, more coming. On the psychological side, we don't have too much — we know it's there, of course. I won't say she's a light case. But sometimes even those outgrow it, depending. If she were my child, I'd get her out of New York altogether. Hell on respiratories."

They sat close together, not stirring, as birds do, in a nest crept up upon. When they breathed the question, together, it came faintly, barely stirred them, in the tone of questions which already know the answer. "Where?"

"Oh, you'll have to ask him, he's the expert. I don't

know too much on it. Generally drier, warmer perhaps. But relatively low fluctuation would be the main — I shouldn't think it would have to be Arizona. It's this so-called temperate zone that's such hell on —" He coughed. "I really must go now." After all, he had been so thorough. Carefully, not to frighten again, he stepped around the little respiratory in her corner.

It was Liz who barred the way, eyes narrow, arms dragging like wings. "Do you!" she said, between her teeth. Each word fell heavy, a missile too blunt to wound. "So you have children too, Dr. Boda!"

"Oh, Liz," said David. "Don't, Liz." He bled for her. She had no place to put her hate. For how could one wound them, these stolid men who gave forth, from dugs more impartial than Tiresias's, such a general milk? They knew and saw too much — as of yesterday. How get round such as Boda, mild man-in-a-brown-suit going on to his next appointment, who perhaps dared not get round himself? But he was answering.

"One," said Boda. "That is —" Hand out, he leaned forward to her, as if debating whether or not to give her something he held. "We lost him — Christmas."

She put her hand to her mouth, but the raw sound escaped. "Not —"

"No." His eyes keen on her, he hesitated, weighed. And finally, for what use it might be to her, he offered it — gave — the name of the disease which was the worst.

When he left, he was — for the moment their own misery could allow him — quite real.

In it, their child came up to them, looking into each face. She knew nothing, or everything. A memory perhaps struck her, of another day also mixed in its colors, but also begun well. "The zoo," she said, almost piteously. "I want to go to the zoo."

They sat looking into the room's center, entwined. Once the mother muttered to a child somewhere behind her to unbutton its coat, they would go soon. The child began painfully to do so; she had just recently learned how and the coat had a great many, in a double line. After she had come to the end of them, she began, in concentration, to rebutton them. From behind, her figure, seated in the tight corolla of its own clothes, seemed that of a doll learning its own mechanism, but they did not notice her. They were looking at their concern for her. She was their whole concern now. They had their eye on that.

When the mother asked the time, it was hard to believe that only an hour ago — but they were more accustomed now to the hairlines that bar one from Eden, to looking back. I was sorry though, to hurt him though, she said — Boda. But one never expects to, one never gets through to them, really. I know, he answered, it's because they can't get through to people, daren't, they know too much about them. Oh-h, I can't stand the breed though, she said in a long shuddering sigh, it's what I can't stand in them, and you, why do you have to be so understanding of *them*, so saintly — why do you always have to be such a saint?

He continued to hold her as gently as if he were, but after a while he said: Well, perhaps so, if compromises made you one — perhaps he was. Sometimes he felt he had compromised himself out of any existence on his own altogether, nothing but a grease-spot left of him, on his own. *You,* she said, and he answered *Yes me, why not me* — and then they left off, ashamed at this bitterness at such a time, for were they not talking, as people do, to mark time until what must be is taken in as being so? — and in all that low exchange of honesties, only this last had been heard.

And after a while, putting her head on his chest, not wishing to startle the child with wails of her own, she said his name over and over, Dave, Dave, oh Dave, and since he could not cry in any case, he rocked her, letting her say it for him. Behind them, the child murmured a song of her own; she thought they were singing. Then she was still.

Minutes passed. Then one spoke; it was only a matter of time, which. "The tenants in her apartment are giving up their lease soon. Next month, she wrote. We could live there." The voice paused. "You wouldn't hate it any more than I."

After a suitable interval, the second voice intervened. It began to describe the climate of a certain part of California, where the low-keyed days were so remarkably stable. Mornings, the sun arrived obliquely — out of a mist that fooled only foreigners — and always at the same hour. Evenings were as infallible — sunsets and subtropical sweaters. A land of health, where no one went pale, day after paragon day.

Then that voice paused also. It did not matter which had said which, or what would be made of it. The two voices were the same — the voice of the snake-swallower whose sibilance comes from his own mouth, but is not his own.

Luckily — for what mad refusals, failed jumps might occur, if people had time to stare at the depth of a crossing — the phone just then began to ring. "Oh Christ," he said. "Barney's been waiting an hour there, the Botanical Gardens, and our permit expires tomorrow. I'm afraid I won't get home to dinner." He was half out the door before he turned back to give her the look she knew so well — that pleaded not to blame him for having to leave her on the hook with it, not to hate him for always being the one to leave.

When he was gone, she stood in the center of the long room, her chest physically heavy with this new image of her life — the hook. It was no angler's thin wire, from which one hung suspended at lip or roof-of-mouth, but a heavy mass that pushed up from below and protruded like a deformed sternum, around which the body reshaped itself like a grasshopper's tailcoat, and was still able to walk. People hung in rows from them, yet like herself were still ambulatory. Glancing over at her worktable, she imagined rows of them there, even foresaw them replacing her wax women and babies in an exhibition whose theme was anyone's eternal, for which the medium must be plaster, then bronze, its title a phrase often said of older people, said, not too long ago in a letter, of Mr. Pagani, but a phrase that might be said of anyone: He Still Gets Around Very Well. Hung there on hers almost humbly, at the same time she felt the angry balm, the upsurge of her powers — what it might mean to be an artist. She stretched up her arms — ah, she was healthy enough! — and saw the room. Both lurid and deflated, it was watching her in the way of the room that is going to be left. But there was something more presently wrong with it. May was gone.

When a child is lost, all tenses become the present; everything is now. She was — is not there in that corner, under here, behind. She is all the corners where she is not. She is not. On the threshold lies the dog-leash, thin green leather from the dime-store, pick it up, follow. Befores are afters, dog is out and followed, pick it up and follow nowly. All imperatives are present, go. She is not on the stairs, never traveled alone, that now have been — are. The street is not filled with May, at its far end not dotted with her. The street is filled with not May. There is minute after minute, street after street, not present with May.

And May is now May forever, no longer or ever to be only "the child." She is more now than the mind-pictures ever have been, *are* — the spoon, the stories of her and to her, the small sounds at elbow, even the half-creature rising — to see even that would be — she is more. She is more than the empty hole left where the hook was, is. She is May in the moment, panted after, not yet here but present above any, when she is to be found. She is May — found.

On the viaduct, two blocks from home, a boy with a slew of fish in his grasp pointed down, and shouted. The girl walked toward the hidden place he pointed to, lifting and setting her shoes like hods, hearing her own raucous breath, feeling the raw blisters, the breeze on her wet temples — this is the hairline edge, this is the now.

May stood in the lonely untrafficked arch beneath the viaduct, all as she had been, the mittens dangling from their sleeve-string, beside her the dog. As her mother

advanced upon her, she remained as she was, only looking up, into the giant swell of her. She said nothing triv-
ial — that she had followed the dog, and had buttoned
her buttons, or had been bound for the zoo. She had,
above all, the wide look of a child who was learning. It
was the dog, sidling his culprit eyes, who whined.

"Don't you ever! Don't you *know*? Don't you *ever* —"
Choked, the girl was forced to spit to the ground what
she was surprised was not blood. In her hand, the leash
came up, doubled like a crop, and lashed twice, and
again, on the gray-plaid shoulder. In her dream — in-
cubus that sat on her at once and she knew would never
leave — it was only twice. Then she knelt, putting her
head on the child's breast, and circled the gray, silent
coat with her arms. Kneeling, she prayed with the intensity of the unbeliever, to that god who must be somewhere behind objects, or in persons might reside. It has
come upon me, she said, and I'm not old enough, I'm not
yet twenty-five. Oh God, she said, with the certainty of
a daughter, this is the way it will be, between us. And
still kneeling, felt, in soft, continuous answer, the wet
menstrual blood on her thighs.

At home, though her mother could not eat, May ate
heartily. Rosily cool, tonight she would neither cry nor
suffer, in order to let her mother make amends. Afterwards, she was taken into her mother's bed — for comfort — but though she submitted to being held hard
against that yearning, nursing body, she did not relent.
After a bit, she crawled out, toddled softly away and was
heard puttering in the studio, on the forbidden table.
At once, the mother sat up.

"You will break—" she said, when she saw what the child held in her hands, surely that was to be its revenge. Then she saw what the child was doing and thought to herself, shamed to the core, it is *my* idea — that she would break it. For the child, holding the wax baby before her with even hand, took a napkin from her own table, wrapped it round. Slowly she climbed the bed with it in her arms. Gravely she cradled it, with a sad, perfect tenderness, showing what might be done with a child. From the other side of the bed, her mother reached out — only to help — but was put off with the same grave look. "It's sick," said May. "It's mine."

Finally May lay down with it, but did not sleep. In her clear eyes, still so short of memory surely, it was not possible to see what she had learned. Opposite, her mother pondered in them. Once she saw them tremor, and thought: She is afraid of me, my own child. And finally, shrinking back in the bed, she separated herself. I am afraid of her, she thought. I am guilty of what I have made. But then, the other, falling back in sleep, stretched herself out against her, in open trust. Watching, the mother guarded it, in this room so full of love and poison. So they remained, gathered there, waiting for him to come home to them — and rescue them.

IO

Mrs. Pagani Senior was setting off for Europe. To her, as well as to the other passengers on the great liner still in dock, its dark stacks slanted across the sunset, toward another continent — or would that be the *other* way? — all this New York of pennant skies and gesticulating wharfside was taking part in their adventure. Offshore, two tugs were darting about, skirts gathered, flanking their charge in snub profile.

"Ah, the darlings!" she said, leaning over the railing. "Just like governesses. Exactly!" At her side and eye-level, her grandchild regarded her from its father's shoulder, dear, solemn little missy who wasn't likely to know what the word "governess" meant — and not likely to ask, either. She had a way of seeming to know the difference between what you might easily have explained and what you couldn't, and of choosing the latter, as if this somehow pressed to her advantage. She was far more likely to ask you to define "exactly" — if she asked at all. But then, they had only known each other — this second time — a week. And aside from her quaintnesses, plus, for the initiate, those tiny stigmata at the eyes and the elderly little hands — she was like any other child. Any other fair-cheeked child — these still so round and reassuring — whose limbs were a bit stretched for her age, her strength (as the old women in Yorkville would have put it) perhaps a little "outgrown."

So far, their relationship had been all one could anticipate. At first meeting, she had minutely examined her grandmother's person in all its fresh, coastal tints, all the winking delicacies at neck and wrist and shoe-buckle — lifting the veil like a peruke, laying out the pearl-clean contents of handbag, to pronounce finally, to what heartfelt merriment! — "You are like a shop." Across her head, the eyes of the two generations could meet in relief — in, yes, pride. And when, lying in her grandmother's lap, she leaned into her grandmother's ruffled collar to smell it, dawdling her Mary-Ann sandal, lying back just as Mrs. Pagani had pictured it — and Elizabeth said, "My! She never does that with me!" — her mother did not reply, "Nor you ever, then or now, with me." For, ever since learning of May's trouble, and that only at the last moment, when she herself was due East because of her own — what she had wished for Elizabeth, at Elizabeth's wedding, had rarely been out of her mind. That her girl should be made to *see* in this way was not to be borne, not to be thought of — if borne. It underlay all their conversations, and in this life would never be said.

For Elizabeth and David, both so worn, she bled and said nothing. How much she herself had been taught was only now clear to her, and they would never notice. More than merely their bedouin life of the last two months — first at Barney's, then at her place — was now visible in them. Still young in face they looked in some way exposed prematurely — as if, in whatever overnight experience had come upon them, only youth had kept their hair from white. It would have done her own heart good to see Elizabeth her old, savagely untidy self, slopping about in her old wolf-colors, instead of this thin, pinched non-slattern, so sallowly clean. And David, though so unlike his father in feature, now had a thin aura of him — of that nameless quality not resignation only, not just gentleness — drawn around him now with no more emphasis than the fuzzy lines-of-feeling around a figure in a cartoon, but enclosing him. Probably the likeness would have been lost in comparison, but now was strong, in remembrance.

And in time, perhaps her son-in-law could annul what she had unwittingly transmitted to her own daughter, by teaching Elizabeth (as just short of too late, his father had taught Margot) the alternative aspects of one's own selfishness, martyrdom and worth. For to her mind — and how Nicholas would have laughed to hear her! — the male was still the *only* corrective for the female. In any case, as a grandmother, she was prepared to be selfish; she could not stand the strain of watching all this in solitary, and was therefore as glad of her pilgrimage for this reason as for its other one. All his gifts to her had turned out gracious ones, and always would. She looked brightly at her blessings, down there in the water. When she came back from her tour, it was as well that they were to have the five thousand miles from coast to coast between them, though with the direction reversed. A corrective came to her. Three.

"When I get to *Lon*don," said the grandmother, taking the child's hands in hers, and emphasizing with them, "I shall write you *all* about the Round *Pond*." And May, in her way, did not ask what that was, instead patting her father a silent request to be set on her feet, from which posture she peered up. Hands against her little held-in chest, did she, whom did she resemble? The grandmother held her breath.

"Oh, Mother," said Elizabeth. "What a romantic you are."

"I'm a grandmother. I have my rights." She was able to say this lightly enough, expectedly enough, compelled as always, in Elizabeth's presence, to act out her daughter's image of her. Elizabeth, she was sure, was equally so compelled, in hers. There was a cure for it. She glanced at her grandchild, so gracefully compliant in the little Kate Greenaway summer smock which had been her own gift, and yet already, at just past three — so choosing. The cure was long.

And meanwhile, her own cure lay only partly behind her. There must be no more attempted revisiting, at least not with others — as just now. "Why that?" he had said with interest. "Why the Round Pond?" — Oh because, you know, she had said, that's where all the "tecs" go, the lovely educated English ones, to interview the nursemaid, or brood on clues. Or else, she had added, the guilty pair tryst there, and are put off sinning, in the sight of all that innocence — "Aren't they ever encouraged by it?" he said — and when he had got over laughing, "Yes, what could be more Britishly innocent than a round one, yes, I guess you must see it. Put it on the list." — There had never been any real list of course, just as there had been no discussion when, gradually, he had stopped saying "*We* must see."

"You must see." That had been her only directive, beyond the designated fund already in the bank under her name from the first, not to be willed. At her own request, nothing else was to be willed her, she having come to him already provided. All property was to be David's. It had come as a surprise, to find that she and he, plus Jacques's illness, had made such inroads on their capital. Aside from the "good will" of the business, still very good if made use of in time, there wasn't too much capital left for David — just about enough for that use. Plus the house, and the weekend cabin. It had been odd of him to let things slip through his fingers that way, just at the end — and the mentioned young man had never been hired. Could it be that he had *managed* to let things slip just so far? Or merely, that all his life he had been a man who knew just how much, how far, to give way? It was not hers to say which. As he had taught her: Surprises . . . still come.

And she had her clues — all her particulars, gathered now and ahead to be gathered, on her own. A French boat, but disembark at Plymouth. Downstairs, her cabin, a single if he was not to go with her, smelled of glacéed pineapple, just as predicted. Her trunk, empty, was in the hold. Who travels with a trunk, these days? You. She had Jacques's list of shops, but from him only one name, from the time when "we" was still the phrase — "Jacques's family will expect it of us. Bordeaux." He was no greedy old man trying to catch at her through all eternity — instead, he had given her most particular directions on how to leave him behind. When the boat left, she was to go straight down and arrange for her sitting — the second — choice of which would establish her, as the experienced traveler she already was. In her handbag was her international driver's license. Beyond that, she was on her own, the decisions all hers. She hadn't quite yet decided on Yugoslavia. But she was almost sure of enough courage for the Grand Corniche.

"Yes — they are just like," said Elizabeth. All three of them were looking down at the water, as people do at these ceremonials. "*Exactly.*"

"What are?" said the grandmother. She had forgotten. A small hand, playing at her waist, reached up to touch the Russian-enamel watch, the size of a robin's egg, that hung above. Smiling, she bent her lapel within reach. This child was not afraid of the attraction of objects; on the other hand, she liked them, she — good Lord. She bent further, to stare — was that the resemblance which for a moment back there had haunted? — dear Lord, was it only that?

"The tugboats. Like governesses. Mother, why is it — you certainly have an eye for it — why is it *you* never drew?"

"I?" said Margot. She was utterly surprised. It was such an intimate question — from Elizabeth, who never.

And such a confusing one. "Why — it wasn't — the right time for it, I guess. I . . . wasn't . . . the right generation. I mean —" She arched her neck high, meaning them to see that this was not a plaint. At the same time, she had to mask her mouth with her hand, covering the deep, rose-shock of pleasure at being so newly observed. "I mean . . . it was for *you*."

But Elizabeth had already turned away, monitoring the little girl, who was now a few yards down the deck, squatted over the pattern for shuffleboard. At her mother's approach, the child did not move away, but turned her back.

"She's forever tagging after her," said David. "It's no wonder May hides."

"Ah, but David, in such crowds," said the grandmother. "After all — *here*."

"At the table, anywhere. She can't take her eyes off her, in the same room with her. You saw. She knows it herself. 'I know,' she says, 'but it's as if I don't dare lose her, I can't stop.'"

"Ah, well. Maybe she'll get rid of it, out there." This was ambiguous.

He did not ask her to specify. "When you come back — you'll come out to us, won't you?"

She stared at the useful water.

"For at least six months of the year," he said.

"For a visit."

"Ah, I know your visits — a shower of presents, and away. But we mean to take care of you. You're not going to get away from us."

"Mmm," she said. "Such presents as I mean to bring

you! Why else do you think I have an empty trunk!"

"Oh, Margot." He gave her up, but with a headshake and a smile.

She sparkled up at him. They might have been flirting, she with a man years too young, but still a man. "And in Paris, I shall buy another, what is the name of that wonderful luggage, begins with a V, I've always wanted one." If she no longer believed quite as she had once in the efficacy of *things*, this was no time to begin living without them. One could live — one must — as if one still did believe. To be able to, even now — was what *he* had given her. It had been the spiritual experience of her life.

"Oh, Margot," he said again.

Yes, David had given her up, for Elizabeth's image of her — he wasn't as discerning as his father, nor did she intend him to be. Let him think she had no idea of the coil at the heart of things. This was her lore — as she had pretended not to hear his father say. "Your father said —"

At once, he was alert.

"Your father said — that like most women, I had no religion. Only a simple faith in the faith of others."

He seemed disappointed. She didn't blame him.

"Listen, Margot — I want to ask you something." He spoke as if in a hopeless cause. As he scratched his head, she remembered that he hadn't had a mother. "Would you — would you let me talk to you about him, sometime?" He amended this. "Sometimes. I find that I —"

She was silent, only thinking how to say it. "I promise you. You may always take care of *me*, like that."

"Oh —" he said. "What a beautiful way to —" Then he plunged on. "What I value most about him is that he never — even with his illness, through all of it — never tried to buy me in."

"Buy you —" Where had he ever picked up that phrase? Then she saw, of course. From Elizabeth. Who had got it from her. Who had got it, no, not from her own people, really. From Ernest. What a weave!

And how to answer it? If she answered, "No, he never did," if she let it rest there? Would *he* rest better? Or his son, here? Watching the two others coming back now, May's hand squirming in her mother's, she was about to do so.

"Oh — I don't know —" she heard herself say then. The answer came from behind or below, using her mouth, but surely not hers. A corrective. "I think he'd've said — that he wasn't quite sure himself, never was — whether or not he tried." An exhaustion came over her, like a medium's. "And that you oughtn't to be either — that sure." She was close to tears now, but at the same time profoundly lightened, as if someone had for years been offering her a medal which, only now good enough for it, she could allow herself to take. The flat voice was her own, now. "That's — what *I* value him for."

The tired, boyish face above hers looked thoughtful. She'd done her best, she told herself; she'd been as honest as his father would have wanted. Yet, when David had time to be disappointed, she was fairly certain that it would again be — in her.

"It's almost time for the whistle, May!" said Elizabeth. "Get ready for a big noise."

All four of them now stood together, Elizabeth taller by a head than her mother, David slightly taller than Elizabeth, by as many inches as he had exceeded his fa-

233

ther, at the base of the line, the still unpredictable dot of the child. The time had come for clichés; all over the deck similar groups were hunting them. "So tall!" said the grandmother. "Always so much taller, you young ones. Whatever's to become of the race!"

"Oh, there's some gene, they say," said David. "Keeps on dragging us back to the median. No danger of giants."

"I don't think May will be *too* —" said Elizabeth.

Each of the three in his own way smiled down at the child, looking to her to lift them up, yet be as they.

"Watch out for how things grow in California," the grandmother said gaily. A pall fell, but that was happening all about them. She clasped her hands together. "Oh, it's like any place. You'll have friends."

"Oh — friends — !" said Elizabeth.

"And the house, you'll find that —"

"I expect you've done wonders," said Elizabeth.

She refrained from answering that she'd done nothing to it — which would not be believed — or even from retorting that Elizabeth in time, in turn, would do them. These days it was her task to refrain. Little enough.

All over the deck, the same cold wind was blowing, though faces flashed warm. The grandmother dropped to her knees, hugging the warm child. "What shall I bring you, eh, mmm, mmm, sweetheart, what shall I bring you?" Encircled, May trifled with the tiny, dark-blue watch. "Ah, she has taste, this one. Shall I find you one just like this, hmm? Yes, that's what I'll do! For when you're grown-up!"

"Oh, Mother," said Elizabeth. "You've corrupted her enough, already."

The three turned to the child.

"Shall I?" said Margot, her eyes bright on May — who withdrew her hand.

"Mummy doesn't have such a pretty watch," said May.

The three brayed sudden laughter, quickly stifled, but that too was going on nearby, all around them.

"Whichever does she mean, do you suppose," murmured her father.

The two women exchanged looks, dared not.

"I'll tell you what she means," said Margot. She stood up, put out a hand, halfway, to her daughter. "She means for me to give it to *you*." The hand touched. A rueful smile crossed her face. "If I may."

"Oh-h, Mother . . . *please* —"

"You always loved it — you know you did. Oh, I know you don't like jewelry. For the color. And the shape." The pin was already detached, the watch in its owner's hand. "And I'd love to, I so want to . . . Elizabeth? . . . And I'll have all the fun of buying another, you know!"

"Mother . . . will you please —" Elizabeth spoke *sotto voce*, glaring about her as she had done as an adolescent. There had been a time when she had been ashamed of her mother's habit of carrying brown-paper parcels. Now she reddened sideways, disowning her mother's untidy bagful of sentiment, for the benefit of anyone who might be looking. Only those were who were doing the same.

"Elizabeth," said Margot, "will you for once in our lives — allow us grace on both sides. Will you, for once in your life, and mine — allow me to really give you something — of mine?" She held out the jewel. "It might be anything — a box — you know that. Won't you . . . just for once . . . *take*."

235

Hypnotized, the thin girl, the more worn of the two anyone would have said, stretched out her hand. She glanced away, but public leavetakings such as this one seemed to be made for just such conformities. Exchanges between the generations were being made without rancor on all sides of her. She turned back; was there even a greediness in her own eyes at last, for the thing itself, the helpful object? As she took the watch, the rueful smile passed to her face from her mother's, as if this too was exchanged. And now, around them all hands clasped others, arms grasped children to steady them, faces pantomimed consolation — "We can't speak now" — all firm, stand firm together now. The seismic blast came, enfolded them, exhausted itself above them. All knew where it really came from. It came from below.

In the silence, a child was heard crying. Not May. But May's face crumpled. "I want to go home," she whispered. The dents below her eyes began darkening.

"Oh darling, don't *cry* —" said her mother. "You know what it — oh darling, please don't." The father knelt down also.

No, said the grandmother, I cannot stand it, to watch their diminishment. "May," she said. "You're going, we all must now. And look at us, we're not crying." Never say it the other way, poor dears, never say *don't*. She tilted the child's face. "Aha, we are really laughing, aren't we? Because we know what a pretty we're going to get from London."

When a child succeeds in not crying, all hearts are rewarded.

"*Such* a pretty."

"Lon-don," said May. Her breath was even again, her color.

"How beautifully she says it. Oh, I know! — there's a place there — a dollhouse! One with real furniture. Shall it be that?"

The child stood mum.

"Hurry, darling, there's the all-off. Just say."

In their tender, lowering circle, the child stood its ground, yet withdrew. "What you said you would," she said. "Before."

Their mouths opened; eyes stole glances. "The — ?" Could it be? Of course it could. But they so wanted her to say it herself, to be able to cherish her for it. Their eyes and mouths prompted —

"The round thing," said May.

And in the general laughter, she joined them, just as if she knew what they most expected of her kind — even of her. She clapped her hands with them as if she knew. She had lifted them up.

At the rail of the turning ship, the grandmother scanned and scanned the crowd massed at the wharfside, but could not find the two with their burden on a shoulder, though they had said they would be there. They were there somewhere, only smaller, shrunken, as one generation must always find itself at the ceremonials of another. She herself felt herself the ship's figurehead — that large. She took out a handkerchief and held it to the breeze in their general direction, still unseeing. It was her ceremonial, after all. It could not be helped.

The child, grasping the white handkerchief given it, held it sturdily aloft.

Sooner or later, they would have had to do it anyway, to go back. So many personal things were still down there to be disposed of or packaged for the West — what better day than this glorious, still light, summer-saved one, along the path of which so much had already been dispatched? In their car, jammed in the throng of taxis bearing away from other ocean liners or toward them, the child strove from side to side and stamped with joy, shrieking answers to the deep proposals of the boats, giving away smiles at the window, a wild cherub flying, thriving. Under the streaming, effulgent light, pulses came and went on her, fed rainbow on the marvelous substance of which she was made; once again they saw that she was beautiful. And as they spoke, now and then, she tagged their speech; boat, *boat*, West, *West* — wherever their sentences ended on a note of departure, she echoed them.

"High, today, isn't she." He spoke from the side of his mouth; he was driving.

"Mmmmm." They were nearing the time when it would no longer be possible to speak freely, though the child, when they spoke of her, gave no sign of hearing. "But I don't think — *too*. It'll be okay today, I think, I'm getting so I can tell."

"You were always better with her, that way, always," he said.

They let this statement — lie.

"One thing for sure," he said, "Margot herself hasn't changed." She did not immediately answer him. "Your mother." He spoke as if over the checkerboard — your move. "She hasn't given in an inch."

Still she did not answer him.

"You were always right about her, from the beginning," he said. "We see clearer, then. And it isn't that she won't see the abstract — she can't. Of course it's what saves her, just now. In Paris, for Christ's sake, she's going to get a — some kind of trunk."

"Oh — do you think — ?" she said at last. "I thought — it seemed to me — that this time . . . she and I were —" She brought it out almost fearfully — "nearer."

"Oh, she can feel," he said at once. He glanced down. She wasn't wearing the watch, had put it in her hand-bag. "But only on her terms. It's part of her charm, of course. I suppose that's what *he* found so —" He laughed slightly. "On about the level of May. It's no wonder, the way the two of *them* —"

"Resemble." Her voice was almost inaudible.

He seemed surprised. "Get on well, was all I meant." Traffic was about to move. He risked a hand across May, now silent between them. "Don't worry yourself, keed. After all, her highness here has us too, you know." He clipped the wheel smartly. "I'm beginning to see that. And understand it. Very deeply." He spoke in the firm, brash voice he sometimes adapted at parties, or in gal-leries, the voice for the technique of things. "The way a child goes. We set the example. Some things are — be-yond our control. But *that,* my love — is up to us."

She sat with her hands clasped, eyes lowered, as if in some church where, having entered to admire the chan-cel, he had suddenly informed her, "This is the one. To which we shall convert."

"To get back to Margot," he said in his natural voice.

"I suppose that frivolous quality was a relief to him at first. My father. Until he found out it was also her strength."

"Of *course!*" she said, turning to him. Her voice was full of light. "His influence. That's what I saw in her. And I'd almost begun to think . . . if somebody'd changed . . . maybe it was I."

"Oh, she's caught — a certain patois, something like. The language of it — of his —" He broke off, as if there were no way to explain what his father had been like — or no need. "For a moment, even I thought — but she's quite a little adapter, isn't she. And if you live with a person like that, even for just a short time. One — like him."

"I'm sorry I didn't — get to know him better." This was her natural voice too.

"Just as well," he said. "Just as well we all didn't get out West."

She held her breath. None of them had ever said it that baldly: Just as well he didn't know about it, about May. Just as well.

"I saw it at Jacques's funeral, but it just didn't register," he said. "If I'd gone West at any time but the funeral, I'd have seen it." His throat felt sore with the effort of believing what he was saying. "The way — *she* changed *him.*"

There were now so many confused voices in the car that it was no wonder they both fell silent — and traffic was moving again. Only the child chose to speak. "West," she said softly, but no one noticed the clear articulation; it was only her little song. "West."

The Cove, when they came to it, received them with

the remote clarity of a place abandoned by the daily, not yet seated in memory. In this interim, its outlines were cruder, theirs fading, as in those way-stations, sat in for too many hours, where it is finally the traveler who blurs. Yet, down in the street, they were still able to persuade themselves that here was only such a station, against whose semipoisonous attractions they now had drugs.

Upstairs, they wandered in the wrack of their effects as if these were emitting a light gas, not dangerous, for which there was however no antidote. Only May, settling down to toys she might have dropped yesterday, seemed to know without question the distinction between herself and the inanimate. Above her head, her parents worked briskly, ever more silently. A dull, off-season ache possessed them, as if they saw the world not as people see it in a powerful season, but through many little neuralgias of the mind. Already the room haunted itself morbidly forward toward others in turn disintegrating, not yet conceived — a procession whose connected secret would be no use to them, no matter how many times learned. Packing the books, the records, old easels, unused tools, they moved finickily, always wary, tidying as best they could the irreparable confusion of things with events. Once in a while they spoke, but like people who have really given up language. And now and then, they looked at each other dumbly, as if they at last understood the substance of which they were made.

They had sold the loft *in toto*, all but their "personal" things. A couple had come by, just on the door-to-door chance of it. Excitedly, they declared that they had first rung the bell weeks ago — the street was so unique. When for weeks then, they had seen no lights, they had

tried again, and this time had had the luck to meet Mrs.
Bailey upstairs, who'd told them of the prospect — Sonsie. They stood in the space vacated by May's crib, other
impedimenta of hers that had been transferred uptown
— and marveled. Turning here, there, they congratulated each other on every arrangement. Many of these,
almost forgotten by the owners, now returned to them
newly. Between the four, like intelligences had quivered
too, or almost — from girl to long-haired girl, from
bearded young man to shaven — if the new pair had
been taking another loft above, the four, in the course
of things, would have been friends. Confronting the daz-
zling pair, the young Paganis, not quite so young, fell
back a little, as if before some flaw that had given way
in their own flesh, leaving them no more knowing, only
humiliated. No, the other pair said, they had no child.
Otherwise, everything else here was so much what they
themselves would have chosen, it was hard to believe.

"I think — I'll go for a walk," he said now, his voice
hushed. On his way to the door, he had to cross the rug
where May lay with her toys. He stood looking down at
her. She had fallen asleep, face upturned, in a bouquet
of them, one shape in her fist, one in the crook of her
arm, blocks scattered between her slack limbs, one tether-
ing her lengthening hair. By the silent covenant of parents, he thrust an arm behind him; a small blanket was
slipped in his hand. Before shutting the door, he knelt,
tucking it round.

And now, though the child was in the room, their
bodies no longer one, she felt herself to be as good as
alone; she had willed herself to the child. Now she had
time, as he did, to be separate.

Seconds later, when a knock came, she guessed at once who it would be. It was what David and she in their place would have done. Not due in here for two days, they would have found themselves unable to pass by without a sneaked sight of their forward joy. It would be the couple.

It was Sonsie, in company-gingham and fresh eye-violet, lips parted in readiness — the new packet of tea in her hand.

There was nothing to be said — good-byes had been said weeks ago, with the exchange of a box of those compressed washcloths for the train, a wax figure with a wide-brimmed hat. But there was something so — both their faces were burning. Then, so luckily, Liz thought of the sleeping child behind her. Finger to her lips, she stood aside to display it. And Sonsie, making her woman's soundless "Ah!" stretched her neck to admire; finger to her lips, Sonsie stole away.

And now, in her interim, the two sets of gestures, hers and his with the blanket, hers with Sonsie, kept returning to her mind. May woke with a cry, was trotted to the bathroom, fed, still in her drowse, from stores still on the shelves here, and put to sleep again — and still she walked again through those actions and others like them, all the covenanting gestures between people, the fingers to lips, the tucking in of blankets, the packet in the hand. Through all the weathers of the day, still others, in their small absolutes, passed her, from th time at toothbrush and stool to the evening setting of tables, with whichever dishes, to the turning on of lamps, of whatever lamps. If she spent all her days, she could not total them, or stop their tide. Either in fear of their benefice, or in its safety, she must conduct herself through them. Outside, in their own darkness, to a rippling unheeded, unending, they totaled themselves. Glancing in the cupboard, she saw what a snug harbor she was passing on, and warmed her hands at it. When he came back, if they had a mind to, they might still make a meal.

In Trinity churchyard, the centuries clashed in good stone, our side stretching toward that awesome gossip of the heavens which might still us all, the old side stumping itself crankily into the ground. He sat on his bench, watching their metaphor. It was of the good, visual kind he understood best, which while reserving his death, spoke to him meanwhile of his work and his life. All people thought of the end of the world, then and now; it was the supreme communal thought, as much of a dogma now as in medieval times. Once, he had wanted to do a documentary along that line: a series of old engravings, lithographs, not in chronology, but all of a kind that showed people, always people, either massed in crowds for their Red Sea Crossings, or in their provincial coveys, and all now re-edited — in each of the open-mouthed Doré faces dropped like doll-pennies on the page, a small bomb would be protruding; stuck in the great, bawling maws of the Rowlandsons, where once the tongue had been, would be the tongue-bomb. Final dissolve — for modernity — a line of subway posters bearing these same, simple graffiti, where once the moustache. And now, once again, he discarded it, as he had later on discarded his histories of the air — these were ideas that came to men in cities. Towers of the height of this one in front of him were that kind of temptation to the sight, their destruction so easily effected by the closing of an eye. Such ideas came to mind more easily under these towers than in the low, entrenched villages. But the truth was that no man could hold a communal thought in his mind for too long.

And now that he was making his good-byes here, he got up from his bench and began walking among the graves. A healthy man lives by constantly discarding the idea of his death; in a place like this it was much easier than supposed. The supreme graveyard thought — it walked with him now — was, most naturally, of one's life. By these low, brown nubbins, sad smooth dears, all personal, one was, for one's own moment, consoled.

For one thing, he was out from under Barney — and without reproach. Death and the little maiden, a sad tale also, but irreproachable. Despite this, he was giving Barney all rights to the opus. Done, it was not a success; the essential, overdocumented, had slipped the sieve. But many sequences were salable, and these, over Barney's protests, he was ceding. It was what his father would have done. And out there, living again in that house, he would begin, as he had not yet begun, to grieve for his father. By walking the path of his father's insights, in the way he was walking this green-mounded aisle, he would come to it, and he would not be surprised if it took him the rest of his life. He was to try to keep in mind — and after this year it seemed within his powers, that other surprises would still come.

And treading that wonted path between surprise and compromise, he would carry his family along — it was his role. A man's role was to see at least that he had one, to keep scanning it as honorably as he could; the women, meanwhile playing theirs to the hilt, never saw. Liz

245

would make other friends, the loss of these too in time to be accepted. For if one took too sharp a look at the lives of one's friends, one saw one's own. The crowd here had been at a certain same ripeness for dispersal, one to be found even in California. They had all been the same age.

Walking the clear maze of this garden, he stooped now and then to touch these stones that made one see. Out there, treading his path, it was just possible that he might do something — unwonted. Here in the city, it was so hard not to see oneself as part of the fated mass; even for Liz, a native, it was hard. For women like her, the hardest might be to have to see themselves, as she perhaps would have to come to do, not as an artist, but as life's model. If she thought he didn't see that, it was because he had to stand aside from it, unable to bear her suffering, as she was unable to bear the child's. While, for him — a man's nativity had its uses. Perhaps a man always saw the formal image of his life best in the place where he had been born and grown. Out there, on those common streets posed against the battering ocean-heart, he could see himself seeing it. He saw.

He saw. If one could imagine a loom, or looms innumerable, warp-and-woof radiating everywhere, perhaps not even from a center. The texture was so tight that one could never see, even over as much as four years of it, where any one part had begun. From such tips as were given the senses, the movement seemed centripetal. Then, almost as if one lived on the top of a secret machine, the centrifuge sucked in. But all this was only the metaphor. All that happened was that now and then, the serpentine shifts of the ordinary . . . suddenly . . .

added up. The real secret was, that all the time, *everybody knew*. By God. Everybody knew.

But how in God's name would one show it pictorially? Or any way. It would be such an illumination of the obvious, stretched thin as a skin that enclosed all the world. It was not original enough. It had no center. It had no uses — this was why no one as yet had tried. Still . . . it was his — for his uses. Bending down, for luck he touched a grave.

When he rose, he found himself near the gate, not far from Captain Lawrence's memorial. He risked no backward glance. Facing just as he was, he walked past the inscription, known by heart anyway, and through the gate. He himself was a man not dependent on friends, led or forced by no one, brave in the minor actions of life, a lonely householder scanning his skies. "In private life he was a Gentleman of the most generous and endearing qualities. The whole nation mourned his loss, and the Enemy contended with his Countrymen, who should most honor his remains."

The waves washed over one, and there was never any permanent crossing. Back there, at that seaside of graves, it was easier to see this clearly, with less dismay, since there was no dishonor, even for the most vigorous of men, in being made frustrate by the sea.

When he opened the door, the child was asleep on the rug, covered just as he had left it. She, on the other hand, was stretched on the bed, in the room's special light, the oblique honey-dark of this room at this hour. He turned on a lamp. Then he stretched himself beside her. They lay for a while in this privilege they had earned — of not speaking.

"She sleeps so," he said after a while.

"I fed her. Big day."

They lay there for a while, calm in effigy.

"Where did you walk?" she said. She could ask him, now.

Now he could tell her. "Trinity."

"Trinity," she said. "My, that far."

The room was dark enough now for the continuity of shadows.

"I thought we might — stay for a bit," she said. "I could make a meal."

Nodding, he rubbed a forefinger back and forth, back and forth on her wrist. Otherwise, they lay quiet, calm as effigies who still owned enough movement to see each other in profile. If they had certain secrets, this no longer frightened them. They had shared enough each to want a secret place of his own where nothing was shared. They rested so, hands locked under the covers, not further troubling each other's bodies. It was not uncomfortable here, in the safety of knowing at last what they were going to be. It was not the end of things, only no longer the beginning.

From his mound one turned and put his lips on the throat of the other. The down was gone from there, as he had known for a long time. He thought he cried it aloud, and as always, did not; it was the soundless cry that was woven into the very weave of life, that no one ever made.

Over the curve of his back, the one beneath him saw the shadow rising, not on the wall, not the palm tree of themselves, a thing apart from them. It had its identity now.

The child put one foot on each of her parents. Against the long room, her form, in all its weakness of outline, spoke to them of their own substance, for their forgiveness. Her great cheeks hung down heavy as she laughed down on them, as she bestrode them — this thing that was not of wax.